WISH UPON A STAR

A Collection of Holiday Romance Stories

Blair Hayse

ELITE PUBLISHING
HOUSE
YOUR LEGACY. YOUR BOOK.

First Edition

Copyright 2023 © Blair Hayse

All Rights Reserved

No part of this book may be reproduced or transmitted in any form or by any means, electronical or mechanical, including photocopying, recording or by an information storage and retrieval system – except by a reviewer who may quote brief passages in a review to be printed in a magazine, newspaper or on the Web – without permission in writing from the publisher.

Cover Graphics: Kathryn Denhof

To all those who need love and holiday cheer. May you find it in these pages and then within yourselves.

Table of Contents

A Very Darcy Christmas
By Athena Law 6

Sunshine and Snowflakes
By Rev. Libbii Armstrong 26

A Little Girl's Christmas Wish
By Beth Walker 48

Firenze, My Love
By Jen Taylor 56

A Typewritten Love
By Kerri-Ann Sheppard 65

Mr. Merry's Christmas
By Emily M. David 81

Fighting Spirits Relaxation
By Zachary Shiloh Watts 102

An Unforgettable Stop in St. Pocono: A Heart-Warming Tale
By Alicia Thorp 120

Christmas on the Cape: A Season for Second Chances
By Roberta A. Pellant 133

Diamond Haven
By Magnolia Tiberii 146

Christman with Blueberry Girl
By Lisa Stamey 167

Wonderful World of Riverville
By Paula Eberling 183

Wings of Love: From India to Iceland
By Pallavee Yovana Periapayen 197

Whispers of Sakura
By Mayuko Fukino 213

Happy Holiday Vibes
By M. LaRae, M.Sc. 237

Jingle Bali
By Kim Pierre 255

Père Noël
By Kathryn Denhof 266

Dear Universe
By Heidi Plumberg 295

Last Christmas Wish
By Blair Hayse 312

A Very Darcy Christmas

By Athena Law

It is a truth universally acknowledged that a librarian in possession of a mug of hot cocoa must be in want of a –

"Excuse me?" A small voice squeaked.

Maggie's train of thought skidded right off its icy tracks as the top of a tousled head appeared in front of the ornate circulation desk. She reluctantly uncurled her hands from the warm mug and stood up to better see the speaker, who she recognised immediately.

"Bailey! Are you here on your own?"

The small boy nodded in the affirmative. "Well, Daddy is out in the car, but he let me come in on my own," he said proudly. "Daddy said to remind you to bring dessert tonight, and to bring this back."

A book slid across the counter, a popular crime novel and one that Maggie knew was at least two weeks late.

"Hmm. Well, you tell your dad there's a late fee coming his way along with the apple pie. You stay warm, and I'll see you all tonight."

As her young neighbour pulled up the hood on his anorak and headed off through the mistletoe-draped archway to the exit, she smiled to herself. Trust Luke to use a Trojan horse of cuteness to cover up a minor misdemeanour, definitely one of his notable traits since high school.

The library was rapidly emptying, the patrons keen to get home and snuggled up, with the weather unseasonably inclement this early in December. Only thirty minutes until closing time, she mused, just enough time for another chapter, and then she'd make her final rounds.

Several chapters later, Maggie was startled by the antique foyer clock striking six p.m. Whoops! Firmly closing her worn copy of *Pride & Prejudice*, she glanced around to ensure the foyer was empty as she strode to the huge double doors and slid the bolt across, spotting the flyer advertising Santa's upcoming visit right next to the poster for the Christmas Eve Gala Ball.

"Santa," She boldly asked the cartoon man in red. "If you ever find it in your heart to bring gifts to adults, I would like to request a romantic hero just for myself, an iconic love for Christmas. Surely that's not a big ask?" She giggled to herself as she set off on her rounds, not noticing the new library janitor hovering in the shadows, with a twinkle in his eyes and a thoughtful look upon his face.

Maggie was almost done, but she always saved her most beloved room for last, the historic reading room with its timber panelled walls, deep leather chairs, and carved stone mantelpiece. The room was empty at this hour; however, across her favourite green leather armchair fell a strange shadow, which, in the half-gloom, began to take on the shape of a man. She hurriedly switched one of the lamps back on and squinched her eyes shut before opening them again. However, to her disbelief, there was indeed now a man sitting where there had been only air moments before.

He rose to his feet as she took a hurried step back.

"Forgive me," he said, bowing, "It is unforgiveable to sit when a lady is present; you have my sincere apologies."

Maggie could only gape, her usually mobile face frozen, eyes wide with shock. Standing before her, admittedly with extremely nice posture, was a tall gentleman dressed in Regency costume, crisp white shirt and cravat, tight breeches, high boots, the whole enchilada.

"I don't believe we have been introduced, Miss..." His crisp British accent echoed in the book-lined room.

"Maggie," she blurted out.

"Miss Maggie. May I enquire whose fine residence this may be? I apologise once more. However, I do not seem to remember arriving. And please, allow me to introduce myself; I am Fitzwilliam Darcy of Pemberley." He bowed once more.

She couldn't help but laugh out loud in a most unladylike manner.

"Of course you are, and I am Miss Claus of the North Pole." Still smiling at the prank, she gestured towards the exit. "Let me show you the way out."

As Maggie unbolted the front door, she turned to see the stranger making his way slowly across the grand foyer, staring all around, especially fixated on the strings of electric lights glowing on the towering Christmas tree. Eventually, he gathered himself and stepped briskly across the threshold, bowing to her a final time and vanishing into the snowy night.

Moments later, as Maggie steered her car carefully out of the parking lot, she braked suddenly, tires slipping on the slick ground, to avoid hitting the same man standing in the middle of the road. She'd never seen the proverbial deer-in-headlights, but it would look much like this – feet firmly planted, body tense and still, utterly transfixed, staring into the bright beams.

Pulling on her beanie over her auburn curls, she jumped out of the car, landing ankle-deep in slushy ice.

"Hey!" She shouted. "You can't stand out here like that; it's freezing! Can I give you a lift somewhere?"

After a few more entreaties, he acquiesced, settling himself uncomfortably into her passenger seat, staring around wildly.

"Miss Claus, this horseless carriage and the front lanterns of unnatural luminescence. How can this be? What is this place?"

Maggie shook her head pityingly and reached over to pat his knee reassuringly, which resulted in a scandalised look.

"You're either a brilliant actor or having problems with the old grasp on reality tonight. Either way, I'm taking you with me to dinner, and my friend Luke can take a look at you; he's a special kind of doctor."

When Maggie arrived at his door, Luke's face was a kaleidoscope of expressions: delight at seeing both her and the pie box she was holding, then dismay and confusion when he noted the tall, dark (and yes, handsome) stranger hovering behind her.

"I'll explain in a moment," she muttered, ushering 'Darcy' inside, who first solemnly stamped the snow off his boots and brushed his top hat clean before shaking Luke's hand and introducing himself formally.

"Mr. Darcy," Maggie said brightly, "Let's pop you on the sofa here, and young Bailey here will introduce you to a new thing called television." She winked at Bailey before whisking Luke into the kitchen.

A few minutes later, with a Simpsons Christmas episode blaring in the background, Luke was sitting at the kitchen counter, getting his thoughts in order. His tawny blonde hair was sticking up due to his habit of running his hand frantically across the back of his head when he was concerned or confused.

"Let me get this straight, Mags. You want me, tonight, to give this guy a psychological assessment to see if he is having delusions or is actually a time-travelling English lord?" He was shaking his head in disbelief.

"Yes. But also, no. Mr. Darcy isn't actually a lord; he doesn't have a title-"

"Maggie."

"Right. Okay, so I'm going to finish getting dinner ready while you two have a lovely chat, that's if you can tear him away from the 'box with small people and music inside'," she said jovially, although a small part of her was aching to believe that Christmas magic truly was real.

Dinner turned into a strange affair indeed, from Bailey shamelessly copying the flawless table manners of their guest to Luke's assessment that they were dealing with a harmless man who was simply having a 'holiday from himself' (not the actual doctorly terms he'd used) along with the man in question who conscientiously conversed with Maggie through both courses, much to Luke's bemusement.

Maggie offered her spare room to Darcy, who was horrified to hear that a young lady was living on her own without the protection of either her husband or parents and at the idea of accompanying said young lady without adequate chaperonage. Fortunately, Luke stepped in with an invitation for him to stay overnight, although he muttered to Maggie that she sure owed him a huge favour in return.

"Of course," she murmured to him, "How about I start with decorating your house a little more festively?" Said while shooting a pointed glance at the lone Christmas card sitting atop the bare mantelpiece.

"No thank you," Luke hissed back. "There's no point when it's just the two of us here, and you know well enough it's not a time of year I celebrate."

Maggie knew Luke well enough not to push a point when she heard a certain tone in his voice, but she'd seen the wistfulness in his son's eyes at the library, as he'd gazed around at the abundant decorations.

"There's every point, as seven-year-old boys do celebrate this time of year, and Bailey deserves the same sprinkle of magic and excitement that every other child enjoys. I know you've both had a couple of tough years; I truly do understand," She placed her hand on Luke's, "Just let me take care of it, okay?"

At the same time, they both noticed that Darcy was staring at their touching hands.

"Am I to understand that you are betrothed to be married?"

Maggie and Bailey giggled while Luke flushed scarlet. Bailey was the first to speak.

"Daddy and Maggie are best friends, like Savannah and me at school. Boys and girls can hang out together without getting married, you know."

Darcy bowed his head toward the boy respectfully. "Thank you, young man, for explaining your customs in this place. I can see I have much to learn."

As the evening wore on, Luke became more convinced that this man was deep into a historical reenactment, albeit a very convincing one. More alarmingly, Maggie seemed to be falling for the charm, the manners, and the myth of the Regency hero right in front of his very eyes.

Early the next morning, Maggie lay cocooned in her warm blankets as snow fell softly outside, staring at her ceiling and replaying the extraordinary events of the previous evening. There came a sharp rap on her front door, and she sat bolt upright in bed. Who on earth could be visiting at this early hour?

Darcy stood on her front porch, just as immaculate as he had been last night, but with the addition of a grey wool overcoat, which she recognised as one of Luke's.

He inclined his head towards her perfunctorily.

"Forgive the prematurity of the hour; however, given my current circumstances, I found it impossible to sleep. I am of the opinion that you must be the one to shed light on how I may return home, given that you were the only person I met in the large stone residence."

Maggie smiled. "That is actually where I work. It's not a residence, but a library, built in 1747, and open for the community ever since."

Darcy blinked. "I cannot fathom letting villagers and the general populace into one's library; what an extraordinary place this is." He extended an elbow. "Please, Miss Claus, would you do me the honour of a promenade through the village?"

Moments later, they made their way slowly up the street into the township, with Darcy exclaiming at many of the sights, not least being the prevalence of the horseless carriages, before Maggie directed him toward the park and the ice-skating rink.

Darcy was utterly transfixed.

"Ah, I have skated on the ice myself in Hyde Park; however, not nearly this many women and children were enjoying the sport. Do you know that might be just the diversion I require today? Shall we?"

Maggie needed no further urging. Strapping on hire skates, they gleefully took to the ice to join the early morning skaters, and after a few initial wobbles, there followed a blissful hour. Finally, cheeks reddened from the cold and the exercise; Maggie had pulled up onto the railing to take a breather when Darcy attempted to skate to a stop beside her. He skidded awkwardly, grasping the railing on either side of her to avoid falling, their faces just inches apart.

She caught her breath. She had registered his striking good looks yesterday; however, this close, he was breathtaking, dark curls framing his perfect bone structure, with a strong aquiline nose and deep hazel eyes fringed with dark lashes and blazing with intensity. He, in turn, was taking in her denim-blue eyes, tumbled auburn waves, and tiny freckles marching across her flushed cheeks. He was raising a finger to collect a snowflake from her eyelashes when she blinked and pulled back.

He cleared his throat and moved a suitable distance away from her. This was not how a gentleman should behave, especially with an unchaperoned lady. Time for this activity to end as he skated briskly across to the kiosk.

Maggie caught up to him, sensitive to his abrupt change in behaviour. Of course, the real Mr. Darcy would be all about propriety, time she took a leaf out of his book to set him at ease.

"Mr. Darcy. Would you be so kind as to escort me to the markets where I may purchase a Christmas tree?"

He nodded in agreement and smiled fleetingly before holding out his elbow once more.

"To the market, we shall go."

As with all small towns, a stranger is sure to invite notice and perhaps gossip. When the stranger is the epitome of tall, dark, and handsome and is escorting the town librarian who had seemingly sworn off men many years hence, the gossip is inevitable.

Rumours and conjecture had spread around the town like wildfire by noon; that lovely Maggie was perhaps finally off the (book)shelf, that she and the dashing mystery man had been seen selecting the finest Christmas tree together, shopping for ornaments and gifts, and that perhaps wedding bells were going to soon be ringing.

"Can somebody please help Bailey hold the ladder?"

Maggie was precariously wobbling above the decorated Christmas tree, a glittering gold angel in one hand and the other gripping the top of the ancient stepladder. She peered through the ice-frosted window and spotted Darcy standing in solitary splendour on Luke's front porch, stock still and smouldering into the distance. The snow-covered outlook from here was quite pretty, but she was sure it wasn't a patch on the view from Pemberley; the poor guy was probably quite homesick by now.

"Got it!" Luke rushed in from the kitchen, flinging off his oven mitts on the way, then steadied the ladder, giving his son a kiss on the head as he did so.

Angel securely positioned atop the tree, Maggie carefully dismounted, and she and Bailey surveyed their handiwork as Luke folded the ladder.

"Bails, would you do the honour?" Maggie pointed at the power switch for the tree lights.

The boy bounced up and down excitedly! "Sure!" He squeaked, high-fiving Maggie before positioning himself next to the switch. "Okay, here we go, three, two, one..."

The lights blinked on, twinkling through the lush green branches and making the tinsel and ornaments shimmer. Bailey was entranced, and watching him, Maggie felt quite nostalgic, but then she saw that Luke looked stricken as if he might burst into tears.

She slipped her arm around his shoulders.

"The tree is for him," she whispered, "And so is the Santa stocking and the gingerbread you're making. He needs the magic. You're doing amazing, I promise."

His hand reached across and sought hers where it rested on his shoulder.

"You're the amazing one, Mags; I honestly didn't have it in me. So, thank you."

Bailey appeared in front of them with a poorly wrapped gift, with a red glittery M scrawled on the front.

"Daddy, can we give Maggie her gift now, or should we wait for Christmas Day?"

Maggie looked at Luke, eyebrows raised, and she saw that he both blushed and frowned in unison.

"Luke, that's naughty. We don't usually do gifts for each other anymore."

He shook his head. "I bought it weeks ago, and now I wish I hadn't, given the circumstances." He glowered at Bailey. "Well, you may as well give it to her; go on."

Bailey silently handed it over yet couldn't contain his glee as Maggie slowly unpicked the tape looped around the parcel.

Finally, the gift came free, and an antique book fell into her hands. It was an extraordinary, cloth-bound copy of *Pride & Prejudice*, with a gold peacock on the cover, dated 1895.

"It's the most beautiful book I've ever seen! How on earth did you find this? Oh, thank you, thank you so much!" Holding the book as carefully as a baby bird, she hugged Luke and kissed him on the cheek.

Once Bailey had satisfied himself that she loved the gift, he skipped off to the kitchen to decorate the gingerbread men, and she and Luke found themselves alone.

"Maggie. There's something I need to tell you." Luke had stopped frowning but was still blushing. He brushed a curl away from her face. "It's something I should have said much earlier, but I-"

The front door slammed. Almost guiltily, they both jumped and pulled apart as Darcy strode into the room.

"Miss Claus, I believe you made a promise to show me your place of employment once more while you oversee the preparations for the upcoming ball, if I wasn't mistaken?"

There was a sudden flurry of activity, of coats and gloves and beanies being gathered, and later, Maggie could have sworn that Luke nearly pushed her out of the door.

Christmas Eve morning arrived clear, bright, and peaceful. An enchanted world lay outside Maggie's window, immaculate drifts of pillowy white snow and delicate snowflakes falling slowly like feathers.

It's the ball, finally, she thought gleefully to herself. She could see the red dress hanging from her closet, the glow of the lustrous red satin, and the flowing folds draped from the boned bodice and puddling silkily on the floor.

The ping of a text.

Sorry, M, the babysitter cancelled on me, so I can't make it tonight – L.

Unexpectedly, hot tears pricked her eyes. She had barely spoken to Luke over the past fortnight, save for collecting Darcy, and often Bailey, for various festive activities. Initially, it had just been assumed that he would be her escort for the Gala Ball, yet things had taken an awkward turn with the arrival of Mr. Darcy. Who, of course, had immediately assumed that he would be escorting her to the ball and had insisted on securing a set of formal tails for the evening.

You promised. She typed back.

That was before. Luke replied.

Nothing has changed. Maggie wrote furiously.

EVERYTHING HAS CHANGED.

She tried to reply, but a notification came that Luke had switched his phone to 'Do Not Disturb.'

Hours later, dressed to the nines with her auburn curls pinned up and zipped into the dress which cinched her waist and gave her an hourglass figure, she was still huffing around the house.

Infuriating man! Intolerable man! He promised! She was stomping up and down her hallway in unfamiliar high heels, huffing away, when a sharp rap sounded from her front door. Darcy!

"Good evening, my lady. May I say that you look radiant?" He proudly escorted her into the waiting cab and even more proudly into the grand foyer of the library. Beautiful by day, the building had transformed by night, lit by a million twinkling fairy lights and festive wreaths draped from every surface. An elegantly dressed crowd milled around, with the sound of a band playing a waltz drifting from the next room.

"May I have this dance?" Darcy held out a gloved hand and bowed to her. Maggie nearly swooned. She had dreamed about this moment since her teenage years, and even though she still couldn't rationally account for what had been happening, she was no longer questioning it. Carpe Diem, she said to herself, taking his hand and smiling broadly.

Darcy whispered in her ear as they took to the floor, "And later, I must beg of you a private audience, as there is something I must ask you."

This may have been the best evening of my life; Maggie had thought triumphantly as Darcy escorted her to the refreshments table. Even if a slightly hollow feeling inside hinted that something may be missing.

The champagne in the glass Darcy handed her was fizzing, just like I'm fizzing; she smiled gleefully. This must be what euphoria feels like, the joy simply bubbling up inside you.

"Come," Darcy said, re-taking her hand and guiding her carefully to a private alcove in between the shelves of vintage books. From that moment on, she would always associate the faint vanilla smell of the old books and the sweet, yeasty scent of champagne as the fragrance of happiness.

Darcy took the glass from her and set it down on a small table; he then took both her hands in his. He cleared his throat.

"You must know how ardently I admire you, your most refreshingly forthright nature; even your modern ways have come to seem so natural, like breathing. I, of course, seek to travel home at the earliest opportunity, but Miss Claus, would you do me the great honour of returning with me - as my wife?"

Darcy's hands gripped to her own so tightly that it felt as if he was tethering himself to keep from slipping away. His intense hazel eyes were fixed upon her face, a beseeching expression upon his handsome visage. Neither noticed Luke, leaning desolately against the corner of a nearby bookshelf, frantically running his hand through his hair.

"Mr. Darcy, thank you for your kind proposal." Well done, Maggie triumphantly thought; *I certainly know my Jane Austen etiquette.* "I am much flattered, and it goes without saying that you have been my dream man for more than half my life. The epitome of a romantic hero, perfect in every way-" Ouch. Darcy's grip had tightened further, and he had moved closer, smiling eagerly. Perhaps she had gone too far with the compliments during her elegant refusal.

While Maggie was casting around for the perfect words to let her suitor down gently, she heard brisk footsteps on the marble staircase and turned to see the back of a tawny tousled head descending decidedly away from her. Oh dear, what exactly had Luke overheard, and what must he have assumed was taking place? No time for elegance now.

"Mr. Darcy. Let me speak plainly. You and I are of different times. You are not a match for my world and my time, nor am I for yours. There is simply no world where we could be together – happily together, that is. You are a beautiful fantasy, and I thank you for this magical Christmas. But I must bid you farewell."

Cheekily, she slipped her gloved hand from his grasp and offered it back to him to kiss, which he did in stunned silence.

"Goodbye and Godspeed, Fitzwilliam!" And she skipped off down the steps just as a small man stepped out of the darkness, dressed as a janitor, with the name 'Nick' embroidered on his dungaree pocket.

"Please come with me, sir." Nick gestured for Darcy to follow him and trundled off, pushing his cleaning trolley, with Darcy trailing behind.

Maggie caught up with Luke in the foyer, entirely out of breath and frantic to make him stay.

"Should I congratulate you on your upcoming nuptials to Mr. Fancy Breeches in there?" He asked bitterly, shrugging on his overcoat.

"Luke! If you'd waited a moment more, you would have heard me reject his proposal!"

"I find that very hard to believe. Why on earth would you reject the exact man you seem to have been waiting your entire life for? Don't think I don't remember high school; you wouldn't give me the time of day because I wasn't brooding enough."

Maggie was unused to Luke looking at her this way, and she wasn't enjoying it.

"It sounds ridiculous, but I asked Santa for a romantic hero, an iconic love for Christmas, and I thought he sent me Darcy as a gift. Yes, exactly what I always wanted."

Luke shook his head and turned towards the front door.

"Wait!" Maggie tugged on his sleeve. "It had to be this way; I had to see the truth so I could finally understand the gift that was right in front of me."

He had turned back to her, his face still uncertain, and she grabbed the lapels of his thick wool coat and held on tight.

"It was you. You are the gift. It's always been you."

His eyes had lit up but were still clouded by uncertainty, as if he didn't dare hope to believe what he was hearing.

"I've always loved you. You're my very own romantic hero. Now, kiss me; we're under the mistletoe!"

Luke looked up at the greenery-draped archway overhead, laughed, and cupped her cheek in his hand.

"I love you too." He kissed her mouth lightly. "And now I believe that means we're betrothed. Because clearly, I am in want of a wife."

She laughed and pulled him close for a much more enthusiastic kiss, resulting in Luke's hair sticking up a great deal more than it ever had been.

The End (nearly).

Epilogue

Escorting Darcy to the reading room, which was empty of all other guests and lit only by soft lamps glowing in the corners, Nick indicated he should be seated in the green leather chair. This Darcy did, looking perplexed at the swift and sudden turn the night had taken.

"Kind sir, may I ask the reason for this private tete-a-tete? Did Miss Claus send a message, perhaps?"

The small man nodded.

"That she did, as it so happens. Here it is, and it is time for you to be on your way." Reaching into his pocket, Nick drew out a slip of paper, which he handed solemnly across to him.

Darcy unfolded, then read the note, brow furrowed. His solid form had become shadowy, smudged around the edges, melting away until he was barely the shape of a man.

"What on earth is this Netherfield Park?" His shadow called back into the room.

Nick shouted back across time - "Ask your friend Bingley!"

The End (for now)

About Athena Law

Athena Law lives and writes in the lush Queensland hinterland. She's recently won a short story award in the 2023 Scarlet Stiletto Awards, and her words have been published by MiNDFOOD magazine, the Australian Writers Centre and The Ekphrastic Review, with more stories forthcoming elsewhere. An expert level procrastinator, she has avoided completing her first novel by attempting to train her ragdoll cats to be more affectionate, listening to writing podcasts, and baking her way through her grandmother's recipe book. Say hello on Instagram @athenalaw_writer and online www.athenalawauthor.com.au

Sunshine and Snowflakes

By Rev. Libbii Armstrong

The Salt Lake City Airport was bustling with people, but as soon as Liezel van der Merwe stepped off the South African Airways plane, she had one mission: find her suitcase.

She scanned the baggage carousel before finally spotting it and hauling it off the conveyor belt. With her carry-on on top, she walked towards the airport entrance, checking her phone for instructions to meet her driver.

Her invitation to speak at the prestigious Global Leadership Summit at the Bear Valley Resort in Park City caused excitement and anxiety to bubble inside her.

Suddenly, she collided with a tall man wearing a plaid shirt jacket, blue jeans, and cowboy boots. A leather cowboy hat shadowed his eyes. "Watch where you're goin', ma'am," he grumbled, his American accent thick and heavy.

"Sorry," Liezel replied, her South African lilt filling the air. "Didn't see you."

"Clearly," he retorted, adjusting his hat to reveal his deep brown eyes.

In the collision, a large piece of cardboard had fallen from the man's hands. Picking it up, Liezel handed it back to him with an apologetic smile. "Thanks," he said gruffly, taking it from her.

"My pleasure," she assured him. As he turned away, Liezel saw her name written on the cardboard. "That's my name," she called out. "Are you my driver to Bear Valley Resort?"

He glanced back at her warily. He was clearly more at home on a ranch than at an airport.

"Yes. I'm Jake," he conceded, reaching for her bags.

"No, thank you," she said, pulling her luggage back. "I can manage."

Jake raised an eyebrow, "Alrighty, ma'am. My truck's outside. It's chilly, though. You should put on a jacket."

"Oh, I'm sure I'll survive," Liezel replied, buttoning up her blue jersey over her white shirt and grey pants.

Outside, a blast of winter air hit her. "Good golly, it's cold!"

Jake shook his head as Liezel wrapped her jersey tighter.

Once Liezel and her bags were in the truck, Jake pulled a warm, woolen jacket from the backseat and offered it to her. "You sure you ain't cold? I don't wanna be blamed for you freezing to death."

Liezel rolled her eyes, accepting the jacket. "Ja, well, no, fine," she sighed as she draped it around her legs like a blanket, immediately feeling warmer.

For the second time, Jake shook his head. This woman was going to be a handful, he thought.

"Best get comfortable," he told her. "It's an hour's drive."

Liezel settled into her seat, captivated by the picturesque view of the snow-capped mountains in the distance. As weariness washed over her, she surrendered to the steady hum of the diesel engine, closing her eyes.

At the resort, a porter unloaded Liezel's luggage onto a trolley, escorting her to the front desk. Faith, the resort manager, greeted her but informed Liezel that her reservation was for November next year.

"No, it's for today, 11 December. Here's my paperwork." Liezel gave Faith her reservation.

"Your reservation is for 12 November, not 11 December," Faith said, pointing to the dates on the paper. "11/12."

"Yes, 11/12," stated Liezel. "11 December."

"In America, we write the month first, then the day," Faith said. "But unfortunately, the resort is fully booked."

"So, you're telling me there's no room in the Inn?" Liezel asked sarcastically. "Is there someplace else I can stay?"

Faith began to say that with the conference and holidays, everywhere else was booked but was interrupted by a loud crash as someone collided with Liezel's trolley, causing Liezel to tumble and her bags to scatter.

A hand reached out to help Liezel. She took it before looking up at the person who had knocked her over. Jake!

"Sorry! You alright?" he asked sheepishly.

"Ja," Liezel said, bending down to pick up her bag...at the same time that Jake did the same - banging their heads together.

"Eina!" groaned Liezel, rubbing her head.

"Ow!" groaned Jake, rubbing his head.

Faith sucked in her breath and then slowly exhaled as she got an idea.

"I'm sure there's room at Kingsley Ranch," she looked at Jake. "Ain't that right, Jake?"

Jake stared at Faith, unsure of the conversation he'd just interrupted.

"Right, that's settled," Faith said, taking his silence as confirmation. "Jake runs Kinglsey Ranch with his sister and is also one of our best ski instructors here at Bear Valley. He'll drive you there."

"I guess I'm taking you to the ranch," said Jake, still confused but catching on quickly. He picked up her bags, hoisting them onto his shoulder, his bicep flexing beneath the flannel. No chance he was letting the damsel handle her own luggage this time. After all, he had a reputation to uphold.

"Ja, ok," said Liezel, following him. She couldn't help but notice how tight his jeans were as he walked in front of her. She rolled her eyes, trying to shift her focus away.

Stepping into Kingsley Ranch's lodge, Liezel was instantly captivated by its cozy ambiance. Exposed wood beams crisscrossed the high ceiling, and large windows flooded in natural light. Plush leather sofas invited guests to gather around a stone fireplace. Toward the back was a huge kitchen and dining room.

The kitchen's saloon doors swung open, and out popped a brunette carrying a tray with two cups overflowing with whipped cream.

"Hello! I'm Brandi. Faith called to let me know you were coming. Would you like some cocoa?" she handed Liezel a cup. "Room three is ready. Jake can show you there."

Enticed by the decadent chocolate aroma, Liezel took a sip and followed Jake up a staircase, stopping in front of a large door.

"This is you," he motioned her in. "If you need anything, just holla."

Liezel stepped inside, and he closed the door behind her.

An antique rocking chair sat next to a crackling fireplace. A chest of drawers was underneath a large window. Liezel sat on the bed, bouncing to test its springiness. The springs twinged in response. Her fingers brushed over the quilt, stopping at the down-feather pillows. She kicked off her shoes and sighed deeply as she sank into the mattress.

At breakfast, Liezel told Brandi she wanted to buy warmer clothes.

"Jake's gotta go into town. He'll give you a ride," said Brandi.

"I am?" Jake walked into the dining room. "It's nice that you two are making plans for me."

Brandi handed him a piece of paper. "We're out of a few things. Here's a list."

Jake sighed as he took the list. "I guess I'm going into town. When do you want to leave?" he asked Liezel.

"I'll be ready just now," Liezel replied.

"Alrighty, I'll warm up the truck," he said.

Jake waited in his truck, the engine humming softly while Christmas carols played on the radio. Twenty minutes passed. Then thirty. No sign of Liezel. Growing impatient, he got out and started for the front door just as Liezel stepped out, wearing a pair of cream shoes, a brightly colored boho skirt, a pink blouse, and her blue jersey.

"Thought you said you were ready 'just now,'" Jake chastised.

Liezel laughed, "In South Africa, 'just now' means in a little while, not immediately."

Jake's eyebrows shot up. "Well, if you're ready now, let's go."

He drove them into town, parking on Main Street. "Mind the puddle," he warned Liezel, opening her door and offering his hand.

She took it and tried to leap out of the truck and over the puddle elegantly...but her flowy skirt snagged, turning her elegant leap into a fumbled fall. Her feet landed in the puddle, icy water breaking through her shoes, cold creeping up her ankles.

"Looks like we'll be hitting the shoe store first," laughed Jake.

Liezel scowled, stepping out of the puddle and shaking her shoes to dislodge the icy water.

When Jake opened the door to the Bare Foot Boutique, three rows of sparkling heels, flats, and sneakers awaited her.

Liezel was immediately drawn to the row of heels, enticed by their shiny sparkles. A saleswoman approached as she picked up a 3-inch gold heel.

"Ain't it gorgeous?" she asked. "It's the perfect pair to wear to a holiday party, right?"

Liezel nodded, mesmerized.

"You don't need party shoes; you need winter boots," Jake chided. "Put the heel down and step away. You'll break your neck wearing those in the snow."

"Ah!" said the saleswoman. "I'll show you our most popular boots." She pointed to the back wall, where boots stood in all shapes and sizes.

"Fine!" Liezel contended, returning the heel and walking to the boots, running her hand along the soft suede material of a pair with fur lining.

She sat down to try them on, lifting her skirt and revealing her wet shoes. The saleswoman looked at her quizzically.

"Someone decided to park next to an icy puddle," Liezel winked.

"Oh, it's my fault you stepped into that puddle?" laughed Jake.

"Well, you're the driver; that is your truck," teased Liezel.

The saleswoman looked at them. "You two make such a cute couple!"

Liezel blushed. She slipped the boot on, feeling the warmth surrounding her feet.

"I've never worn boots with fur inside," admitted Liezel. "It feels strange but oh so comfy! How do they look?"

"Like boots," shrugged Jake.

"Oh honey, don't be tryin' to get a man's opinion on shoes," laughed the saleswoman. "They look great on ya. Do you want to wear 'em out, or should I bag 'em for ya?"

"I'll wear them out - at least they're dry," giggled Liezel.

They continued strolling along Main Street, finishing Brandi's list before returning to Kingsley Ranch for dinner.

Brandi had just finished setting the table with mismatched china and Mason jar glasses when Liezel walked in. "Please take a seat. Dinner will be served as soon as Jake finishes cooking it," she raised her voice towards the kitchen, teasing her brother to hurry up.

Liezel sat, admiring the weathered cowboy boot centerpiece of wildflowers. The smell of hearty beef stew, freshly baked cornbread, and pumpkin pie wafted from the kitchen - a far cry from the spicy bunny chow and sweet koeksisters of Liezel's Durban home.

Throughout dinner, Jake and Brandi spoke about rodeos, ranch life, and their part-time jobs at the Bear Valley Resort: Jake as a ski instructor and Brandi as an event planner. Liezel shared stories of her homeland's wildlife and her work as a motivational speaker. But the evening unexpectedly shifted when Jake mocked Liezel's spiritual beliefs as 'new-age nonsense.'

Despite her disappointment, she stood her ground. "In my culture, we believe in the unseen energy that connects us all. It's not 'new-age nonsense,' it's ancient wisdom."

Jake seemed surprised, but before he could respond, Brandi intervened. "Liezel means there's more to life beyond the tangible," she clarified, eying her brother. "And maybe we can learn something from her perspective?"

Touched by Brandi's words, Liezel smiled. "Yes, there is so much to learn from each other if only we embrace the magic within our minds and hearts."

Jake nodded, processing her words as an uncomfortable tension filled the air.

Brandi, always the peacemaker, redirected the conversation. "What are you doing tomorrow, Liezel?" she asked.

"I've got a ski lesson at the resort," Liezel answered, grateful for the subject change.

The idea of Liezel, with her city-slicker ways, trying to navigate a pair of skis caused a snicker to escape Jake's lips. Liezel gave him a quizzical look as Brandi gave him a swift kick under the table.

"Sorry," he mumbled, rubbing his shin under the table. "I just had this image of a South African beach bum trying to become a Park City ski bunny."

Liezel rolled her eyes. She'd had enough of Jake for one night.

"Thank you for a wonderful dinner," she said. "But I think I'll say goodnight."

"Glad you liked it!" Brandi replied eagerly. "Jake will take you to the resort tomorrow morning."

"Great," sighed Liezel, not liking that idea one bit.

Without looking at Liezel, Jake sarcastically said: "Be down by 7. No more 'just now' surprises. Let's be clear with the timing."

"Fine!" Liezel snapped before storming out of the dining room. "See you at 7."

Brandi waited until Liezel left, then turned to her brother: "Why were you so rude? She's our guest, for goodness' sake!"

Jake just shrugged and went back to his pie.

Liezel waited outside the ski school for her instructor, sipping cocoa. Her vibrant ski suit resembled a tropical bird lost in the snowy mountains of Park City.

"You sure know how to stand out everywhere you go."

Liezel spun to find Jake standing behind her, wearing a ski instructor's uniform. She groaned inwardly.

"I like to live colorfully!" she retorted. "Why are you here?"

"I'm your ski instructor," he said, kneeling beside her, helping her put her ski boots on and adjusting the bindings. He offered her his hand as she tried to stand. Liezel ignored it and took a step forward. The boots clunked down loudly. She felt like a penguin waddling on ice.

"How does anyone walk in these?" she muttered.

"You'll get used to them," Jake said, showing Liezel how to step into the skis and find her balance. After learning basic turns and stopping techniques, he suggested a longer run and guided Liezel to the chairlift.

When the chairlift brushed against her legs, Liezel attempted a graceful descent onto the seat. However, she quickly realized that all those extra layers she was wearing prevented any hope of being graceful, and she toppled backward...into Jake's waiting arms. The struggle was real, and the chairlift had witnessed it all.

She laughed, embarrassed. Chuckling, Jake reassured her: "It takes a few tries to get the hang of it."

The view from the top left Liezel breathless! But her excitement faded as she realized the slope looked steeper and the snow deeper.

She looked at Jake, her eyes wide with fear. "What if I fall?" she asked.

"Then you get up and try again," he reassured. "Just remember to have fun!"

Her shrieks of excitement echoed through the mountains as they pushed off the top of the slope. Liezel's first attempt ended with her falling headfirst into the snow, her legs flailing comically. Jake skied over, concerned, only to find Liezel laughing uncontrollably.

"I think I prefer my adventures a little less...frosty," she exclaimed, brushing the snow off her suit.

"And I thought you were the adventurous type," he teased.

"Oh, I am," she responded. "Let's go again!"

Jake laughed, and up the chairlift they went. Liezel had given up trying to sit down on it gracefully. *You can have this win, mountain -* she thought.

Liezel was determined not to fall this time as she launched herself down the slope. The world became a white blur as the cold wind whipped past her, snow spraying up from her skis. Her fear gave way to empowerment.

After skiing, Brandi suggested visiting the Mistletoe Magic Tree Farm to get a tree for Kingsley Ranch. Jake drove them to a snowy countryside farm.

At the entrance stood a charming farm stand adorned with twinkling lights, selling cocoa and gingerbread cookies. Snowflakes gently fell on rows of majestic trees. A campfire crackled in a stone pit.

"I've never had a real tree. How do you pick the right one?" Liezel wondered.

"If it's not real, what kind of tree do you have?" Jake asked with disbelief.

"Well, living alone and with Christmastime being in summer, having a Christmas tree isn't really a priority," Liezel shrugged.

Jake felt sorry that Liezel was missing out on the best part of Christmas - at least in his opinion.

"It should have sturdy branches for ornaments. Otherwise, you won't get the full Christmas effect!" Jake said, running his hand along the fir needles, admiring their texture before settling on a tall, lush tree.

"This is it!" he said, readying the axe he'd brought.

He skillfully chopped it down, playfully hollering 'Timber' as it toppled while Liezel and Brandi clapped in delight. Watching Jake wield the axe and heft the tree onto his truck only deepened Liezel's admiration.

While the siblings bought sleigh ride tickets, Liezel waited by the majestic Clydesdale horses harnessed to the red sleigh.

When Jake reappeared, he was alone.

"Where's Brandi?" Liezel asked.

"She met some friends and decided to hang out with them," he explained. "So, we'll have a peaceful sleigh ride." He grinned. His sister was a chatterbox, and enjoying Liezel's company in peace would be nice.

The driver waited as they got cozy under a warm flannel blanket before clicking the reins. The horses' rhythmic clip-clop echoed around them. Liezel closed her eyes, breathing in the fresh air.

Suddenly, the sleigh jostled, and her head flopped onto Jake's shoulder. His familiar scent of sweat and cedar now mingled with pine and gingerbread. A shiver ran through her, and without a word, Jake slipped off his jacket and wrapped it around her shoulders. Liezel's heart fluttered.

Brandi waited by the campfire upon their return.

"Ready to make s'mores?" she asked excitedly.

"What's a s'more?" Liezel questioned.

"You've never had a s'more?" Jake mocked. "I'll make you one!"

Liezel watched him roast a marshmallow until golden brown. He sandwiched it between chocolate and graham crackers, causing marshmallow and chocolate to ooze over his fingers.

"Here you go," he handed it to her.

She took a bite, her eyes widening in delight. The sweet taste of chocolate mixed with the toasted marshmallow and the crunch of the graham crackers was like nothing she'd ever tasted.

"Yum," she murmured.

Jake smiled, captivated by Liezel's childlike wonder. She took another bite, leaving a deliciously charming mess on her lips. With a mischievous grin, he tenderly erased the evidence of her sweet indulgence. Liezel hoped the fire's glow would hide her blushing cheeks.

Returning to Kingsley Ranch, Jake and Liezel decorated the tree while Brandi made cocoa. Whenever their fingertips accidentally brushed, it sent a delightful tingle down Liezel's spine. Just as Jake was about to lean in for a kiss, Brandi returned with the cocoa.

"Wow! It looks amazing!" Brandi exclaimed. "Now, the lights!"

Brandi and Liezel gasped as Jake flicked a switch, and hundreds of tiny white lights lit up the tree, giving it a magical glow.

Despite the magic of the moment, butterflies fluttered in Liezel's stomach, and she wondered if it was the electrifying chemistry between her and Jake or the weight of anticipation for her summit speech tomorrow that stirred her soul.

The next morning, the day of the summit, Liezel accompanied Jake to the Bear Valley Resort in his truck while Brandi followed in her little SUV. Jake had a full day of ski instruction ahead of him, while Brandi had the summit's Christmas-themed after-party to organize. Liezel, however, had her speech.

As she made her way into the Summit's conference room, Liezel's nerves began to fray, and she felt the familiar butterflies in her stomach. It was her first time addressing an international audience.

Faith welcomed everyone to the event, and each presenter spoke until it was Liezel's turn. Before beginning, she paused to express gratitude to the Universe.

"Let's explore the art of finding inner peace as a powerful tool for bringing people together and making a real impact!" she began.

A deep voice called out from the back when she paused halfway through her speech to sip water.

"How is what you're teaching practical? How can someone find peace when struggling to make ends meet?"

Liezel looked to the back of the room. Leaning against the wall with his arms crossed was Jake. He'd been skeptical of Liezel's work, and as she spoke of inner peace, he wondered if it was all just talk.

Although disappointed again, Liezel saw it as an opportunity rather than an attack.

"We associate tangibility with practicality," she started. "If we can touch it, see it, measure it, then it's real. But what about our thoughts, emotions, dreams? Aren't they real, too?"

She sought Jake's gaze. "You asked how someone can find peace when they're struggling. My answer is - how can they afford not to? When we cultivate inner peace, we also cultivate the resilience to get through any storm. We make better choices, build stronger relationships, and become more effective leaders."

Jake's skepticism faded as he realized that Liezel's words offered more than just a defense but an invitation to open his mind to new possibilities.

Stepping off the stage, Liezel couldn't shake what had happened. Her thoughts tormented her as she questioned her methods, beliefs, and, most importantly, her budding relationship with Jake.

By the end of the day, she'd decided to return home early. She didn't want to be where her truth was constantly challenged or be around someone who didn't believe in her.

Leaving the conference room, she bumped into Brandi.

"Hey," Brandi smiled. "Sorry, I missed your talk. I've been busy preparing for the Christmas party tonight. You're coming, right?"

"No, I've to pack. I'm leaving for South Africa tomorrow. Could you give me a ride to the ranch, please?" asked Liezel.

"I thought you were staying a few more days?" asked Brandi, confused.

"My plans changed," answered Liezel. She didn't want to explain that her brother was the reason her plans changed.

"Oh," said Brandi, sensing something had happened but not wanting to pry. "I need to finish setting up. You can take my car. I'll ride home with Jake. But it's already snowing. Can you drive in the snow?"

"Ja, I'll be fine," Liezel took Brandi's keys. "Have fun at the party!"

Outside, a dusting of snow-covered Brandi's car, and Liezel felt odd sitting on the left side.

In South Africa, the steering wheel was on the right, and driving was on the left.

"Just stay on the right," she reminded herself as snowflakes stuck to the windshield, obscuring the road. She soon realized she was driving in the middle of the road, not in the right lane.

Suddenly, a deer darted in front of the car, causing her to swerve. The car hit black ice, spinning out of control. Fear consumed her as the car crashed into a snowbank and was buried under an avalanche of snow. Only the taillights remained visible.

"What's up with Liezel?" Brandi asked Jake when he arrived to help decorate for the Christmas party. "She's not coming to the party because she needs to pack. She's cutting her trip short and leaving for South Africa tomorrow."

"Where's she now?" Jake swallowed.

"Back at the ranch, I guess," Brandi shrugged. "She took my car."

"You let her drive in this snow?" scolded Jake.

"She said she'd be fine," Brandi replied.

Jake glanced outside at the snow falling. He grabbed his cell, dialing the ranch. No answer. He dialed Liezel's number. Also, no answer.

"I'm gonna find her. Call me if she comes back. I have to talk to her." Jake hurried to his truck. There was only one road from the resort to the ranch. If anything happened to Liezel, he would find her on that road.

As he carefully turned a corner, he spotted two flashing red lights. He cleared a path to the driver's door and jiggled it open. Liezel sat slumped over the steering wheel.

He unbuckled her seat belt and lifted her up gently. Carrying her to his truck, he wrapped her in a blanket and turned up the heat.

Remorse consumed him as he waited for Liezel to wake up. Questioning her like that was a mistake; his skepticism had taken over. He feared he'd jeopardized their growing romance.

Liezel's eyes fluttered open. "Where am I?"

"Take it easy," he said. "You're in my truck. You drove into a snowbank."

"I did not drive into a snowbank," Liezel insisted. "A deer jumped in front of me, and I slammed on brakes, but then the car started spinning. It spun *itself* into a snowbank!"

Jake chuckled. This was the strong, independent woman he had fallen for.

"Why are you here?" she asked.

"Brandi said you'd decided to go home early and were going to the ranch to pack. I was worried about you driving in this snowstorm.

When you didn't answer the phone, I came looking for you," Jake explained.

"Your question earlier," her voice mirrored her inner turmoil. "Did you ask it because you don't believe in my work or because you don't believe in me?"

Jake looked at her, realizing the magnitude of his actions.

"Believe in you?" He echoed. "Liezel, I believe in you more than anyone I've met. Your strength, passion, and unwavering dedication...it's awe-inspiring."

His voice dropped to a whisper. "And your work? It's not that I don't believe in it. I questioned it because I wanted to understand it better. But I realize my timing and approach were wrong. I'm sorry, Liezel."

Liezel pondered his words. "When you questioned me, it felt like you were questioning my spirit. But now, I realize your intentions were genuine. You wanted to understand me, my work, my spirit... And that means more than you can imagine."

Their hands intertwined, igniting a spark as if the Universe endorsed their deep connection.

"Jake," Liezel murmured, her voice barely rising above the soft purr of the truck's engine. "I believe in us."

Her words echoed in the truck, radiating warmth and promise amidst the winter chill. Sitting together, watching the snowflakes dance, they knew their journey of love had just begun, and it was more magical and beautiful than either of them could have ever imagined.

The End.

Story Inspiration and Details:

This story is a shortened version of a longer novella. For the complete tale of Liezel and Jake, delve into the captivating novella of the same title.

About Rev. Libbii Armstrong

Once upon a time, in a realm of romance, adventure, and leather, Rev. Libbii Armstrong emerged from the sizzling South African heat to become an international bestselling author and leather artisan living in the cool U.S. of A. She is the CEO of Protea Rose Media, a copywriting and publishing agency, and chief creatrix at Celtic Bazaar, where she sells her unique handmade leather accessories. Libbii's diverse talents and experiences have led to appearances on TV, in print and digital media, and as a featured event speaker. When she's not crafting leather, researching genealogy, or planning her next adventure, Libbii pens paranormal romance, urban fantasy, and rom-com stories while surrounded by her beloved coven of rescued cats, a very talkative African Grey parrot, and her sexy beast of a husband...living happily ever after.

Connect with Libbii:

https://www.facebook.com/libbiiarmstrong

https://www.instagram.com/libbiiarmstrong

A Little Girl's Christmas Wish

By Beth Walker

She made the decision to marry Raiden while sitting in his shop wearing her pretty pink dress. She just knew he was her soul mate. She could see his legs sticking out from under his old truck. He had on old boots, and one sock was sticking out the top. It had a hole in it. Even in the school's mechanic shop, he always talked to her like she was a real person. The problem was she was only fifteen, and he was almost eighteen. There was no way her dad would agree to it. She would have to wait. She could wait. She could wait forever.

Then tragedy struck. Raiden joined the military. He was waiting for the bus that would take him away from her. He had no real family, so no one was there to say goodbye. People in town said he was slow, and the military was his only hope to become something. She knew better. She also knew he would come home one day and marry her. Even with the war, he just had to! The icy rain fell like a misty veil, coating the world in gray. The whole world seemed to be reflecting her sorrowful and fear-filled heart. She wore her gray and pink dress because it matched her feelings. The world seemed to have lost its color. How could it have color if Raiden was no longer here? She ran up to him and threw her arms around him. He smiled at her, and her heart felt like it would shatter. Before she could chicken out, she kissed him full on the lips. She kissed her husband goodbye before he even knew he was her husband. He stood there in shock as she ran from him.

With tears blinding her, she ran to the center of town. The weather had sent everyone running home, so there was no one to witness what was about to happen. Only the giant Christmas tree was standing as a sentinel to the magic about to happen. She fell to her knees before it. She took all her longing, sorrow, and heartbreak within her - and bundled it up, casting it to the Universe. With every ounce of faith she had, she wished on the star at the top of the tree. *"Let him know I love him more than there are stars in the sky. Keep Raiden safe, and bring him home to me."*

The Universe honors that much energy. It always has, and it always will. Magic does not always work quickly. Sometimes it takes a long time. The old tree was taken down the next Christmas, and another was put in its place. Then, another after that, it went on for eight years. She never entered into a serious relationship. She just waited. Wishing every year, the same wish, *"Let Raiden come home to me."* She wished it until it just became a habit that had no real power behind it. She continued to wish for it even after she stopped believing it would be possible.

Raiden stood looking out the wall-to-wall window of the hotel suite. Chase sat in the reclining chair, sipping the dark tar he called coffee. Chase had come with him on this mad adventure with no judgment. He had left his beautiful wife and two-year-old child for Raiden's insanity. Chase was more of a brother to him than if they had been born in the same womb. They had gone through boot camp together. Then, they watched each other's backs during the hells of war. When they got out of the military, they started a security business. Using their war hero reputation, they developed a security company. First, just private services, and then they invested in high-tech security machines. Now, they both had a healthy net worth that allowed them every luxury they could want.

The only issue for Raiden was that everything he wanted was just one thing. He was completely insane for even thinking it was possible but obsessed over it almost daily. He wanted to return the kiss she gave him the day he left. He wanted to marry the girl who had kissed him. Now, he was going to go, "Get it out of his system." That is how Chase's beautiful wife Jenna had put it. "Just go get it out of your system. Then you can move on with life." That weekend, she had waved to Raiden and Chase as they drove away to do just that.

Chase stood up, pausing as the pain in his knee shot up his leg and into his teeth. "That never gets old," he complained. "You think it's too early to get going?"

Raiden observed the dark blue skies and shook his head. "If we leave soon, we should be there at about lunch. It will probably only take us an hour or two to find her. It is an incredibly small town. We should be on the road and back here before nightfall."

"I'll hit the shower then and meet you in the lobby." Chase limped to the bathroom.

Raiden shook his head sadly. The knee injury Chase got from the war never quite healed, right? It caused him constant pain. Some nights, it kept his friend up until well after the sunrise. Raiden's own old wounds ached with sympathy. He meditated for a moment on each one of them. His memory echoed with the distant cries of the injured, sounds of gunfire, and their battle cry. *"Jump into hell with both feet and come out in heaven."* Hell does not let go without leaving permanent scars to remind those who visit. Both men suffered from mild forms of PTSD. Raiden frowned as he made his hand move each finger, feeling the strain in them. No, hell did not let you leave without reminders that stayed with you forever.

It didn't take them long to get on the road. Now, they were driving slowly into town. How many years had it been since he had been home? This was the definition of insanity. His therapist had suggested he do this. Get this - whatever it was- out of his system. Chase and Jenna had wholeheartedly agreed. He scanned the streets with a critical eye. The town still had the same old Christmas decorations hanging from the street lights. It looked ridiculous to him. Chase gazed out the window. "It's quaint. You didn't lie when you said it was small."

Raiden just nodded. Chase was the kind of friend who would do anything without question, and Raiden always tried to return the loyalty. Chase even knew about the ring. He knew about the crazy dream where he asked a girl who had not seen him for years to marry him. Chase never said it was a crazy dream. He just nodded. He was here to catch Raiden when he crashed and burned. Raiden knew he was going to crash and burn. It had been almost eight years, and in a town like this, there was no way she was not married. This was a genuine suicide, doomed to fail, end-of-the-line mission.

His eyes focused on a woman walking out of the town deli. His lungs forgot how to work, and it almost seemed like time stopped. She was wearing a pink dress. She had always loved the color pink. Her lanky limbs had thickened, and her hips had filled out to a pleasing shape. She was not the girl who had surprised him with a goodbye kiss. The kiss he obsessed over not returning. She had grown into her beauty and became a woman. She was walking down the street, swinging her lunch bag at her side. Suddenly, Chase's scream broke into his frozen reality, "Brakes! Hit the brakes!"

Raiden slammed the brake pedal. He looked up to see how close he came to hitting the big truck in front of him. Relief crashed into him. "Thanks, man, that would have been costly."

Chase nodded, "Where is your head, man?"

Raiden looked at the woman walking further down the street, and Chase followed his gaze. "That her?"

Raiden nodded, "What should I do?"

Chase laughed, "Well if you are going to stalk some estranged female from your past, do it right. Park the car, and we will follow her."

He parallel-parked, and they jumped out of the car. They briskly walked until they could see the woman turn the corner. Raiden said, "I know where she is going. She always loved it when we snuck out of school and had lunch by the Christmas tree." He slowed his walk.

When they got to the town's center, he could see her sitting on the steps of the City Hall with a sandwich. Chase nodded at him to proceed. Chase knew he would either be a best man today or, more likely, the best friend who sat with his buddy in the local bar. Either way, he was here for Raiden.

Raiden approached the young lady slowly. Just for a moment, he took in her beautiful form. She had an oval face tilted up, staring at the tree with round brown eyes. She was classically beautiful. He could see the reflection of the girl she had once been in her bow-shaped lips, soft cheeks, and hopeful eyes. "Hello, Mary," he whispered softly.

Mary looked up with a pleasant smile on her face. It froze in place, and wonder crossed her face. She whispered, "Raiden?"

Time stopped. The very soul of the Universe held its breath to focus on the moment now happening.

Raiden rubbed the back of his neck. He looked around, realizing everything was exactly as he had imagined. She was sitting looking up at him; the tree was standing behind him, and the sky was a crisp blue. A cold wind gently blew around him. Wrapping around him like the insanity he felt. He looked at her and thought about that past battle cry. *Jump into hell with both feet and come out in heaven.'* He was facing hell. He knew in the core of his being that when she refused him, he would fall into that hell. It would be a long time before he climbed out of it. He took a breath and embraced the insanity, asking, "Are you married, Mary? Is there anyone else?"

Just like in his imaginings, she shook her head. He pulled out the ring box. "Would you marry me? I know it is insane, but would you?"

He waited for her to laugh at him. He expected her to flat-out tell him he was insane, and who did he think he was? She didn't. She nodded, saying softly, "Yes, Raiden. I will marry you. I will marry you this very hour if you want me to."

He was shocked for a moment, but just a moment. Then, he did what he had wanted to do for eight long years. He kissed her back.

Chase smiled. He was going to be the best man.

Time moved forward again, but now the Universe was a little happier.

I would like to say that Mary and Raiden lived happily ever after. Life doesn't work that way. They lived mostly happily. Their lives were full of miracles, pain, awkward moments, arguments, and Love. So much love! Little girl's Christmas wishes always come true.

The End.

About Beth Walker

Beth Walker writes with her own vision in mind. She likes for her stories to be more than her. She hopes to write something one day that is so good people remember it years later for its greatness and not by her name.

Firenze, My Love

By Jen Taylor

It was December of 1987 ~ what feels like a lifetime ago. The setting was Firenze, Italy, also known as Florence. I was just 20 years old, and little did I know what a life-changing trip this would be.

At the last minute, I decided to study abroad for the semester in Italy, a country I had always felt attuned to. I was in a magical medieval setting, and, unbeknownst to me, love was just around the corner waiting for me. One of the unique aspects of studying art history in Florence was being able to have class IN FRONT of Michelangelo's "David," Botticelli's "Venus," frescoes in Santa Maria Novella, and the doors of The Duomo. The food was amazing; I had gelato every day! The pasta was fresh with tomatoes that tasted like tomatoes! Cappuccino each morning with brioche or "un salato." I fell in love with Firenze and allowed myself to be present with all of my senses, smelling the freshly baked focaccia from the local fornaio, tasting the foam on my morning cappuccio, gazing at the cypresses, which held a sad yet elegant beauty for me. I felt the rain on my face and hadn't felt this alive in many years. I was able to be my true self - to start over, as no one knew me there. There were no preconceived ideas of who I was nor expectations of who I was supposed to be. Being in a new city and country allowed my soul to breathe freely, uninhibited by my last 20 years.

I had been dating an American guy from my school program. Like many American men at that age, he didn't know what he wanted, whether he was gay or straight, whether or not he wanted to be a priest. As a Capricorn woman, one thing I was not was indecisive. I knew what I wanted and always had. I was growing weary of his indecision. During this holiday week, we could not stay with our host families, so I had planned to visit an old flame in Livorno. Unfortunately, that did not go as planned, and I ended up at the Santa Maria Novella train station without a place to stay for the night.

Across from the station was a small mercato (market). -I had noticed him before. Tall and thin, with beautiful high cheekbones and dark, sad eyes. His eyes drew me in, and I felt the connection before speaking to him.

"Hi," I said.

His response was in Italian, "Ci conosciamo?" (Translated, "Do we know one another?").

"No, we don't, but I would like to," was my quick response.

Gianni introduced himself, and we talked for a good hour. He was a fantastic listener, and he witnessed my sadness over the recent disappointment of my ex-lover. I was happily surprised at how easily I was able to talk to him. He seemed genuinely concerned and mature - unlike some of the other guys I'd met of late. In the short time I knew him, Gianni had helped me forget my ex. I was transported to the present moment of this cold November day, focusing only on his big brown eyes, sweet smile, and lips I wanted so badly to taste. The topic of needing a place to stay for the holiday week surfaced, and he stated that he lived with his mother, father, three sisters, and cat, but I was welcome to stay. I thanked him but reminded him I was from New York and did not trust anyone.

By the end of our conversation, Gianni had asked me to dinner. I was excited and nervous. The butterflies in my stomach were fluttering. He didn't speak much English, but I didn't care. An evening with him for dinner meant spending more time with him; that was all I cared about at the time. It was a frosty night, bitter cold without snow. It was rare for snow to come to Florence.

As I rushed to get dressed - I had to buy heels because I hadn't brought them over with me when studying abroad. It had never occurred to me that I would need them, especially for a date.

He was sweet and reassuring, and I was falling hard. Dinner was lovely. It was filled with conversation and finding out new things about each other. But I was cautious about letting him kiss me. I knew what Italian men wanted from American women and wasn't about to give in so easily. By our third date, I could not resist his lips. We were in a nightclub called Bella Blu, and I reached over to kiss him. That kiss was unforgettable and ignited the magic of love at full speed.

Our first weekend away was in Venice ~ the city of my dreams. It was my first time there, and it literally took my breath away. To be in one of my favorite cities in the world with my new Italian love seemed like my very own fairytale. We savored a lovely Mediterranean breakfast overlooking the Grand Canal. Gianni and I wandered the canals and winding streets of Venezia ~ losing ourselves in its old-world charm. We enjoyed "pranzo" at a trattoria near Piazza San Marco and enjoyed the glass blowing in Murano. I took my first-ever gondola ride tucked safely in his arms. Never in my wildest dreams had I imagined a love affair such as this. Those memories held me over for our return to Florence, back to our "everyday lives." We had grown so much closer that weekend. We had privacy and room to explore Venice and one another's psyches.

For our next date, Gianni asked me to meet him at the "semaforo" on Via dei Servi near The Duomo for our next date. I didn't know what a "semaforo" was. He explained it was red, green, and yellow, and it changed color - for the traffic. "Ohhhhh! A traffic light!" I remember someone asking if I spoke Italian. Gianni didn't really speak English. I responded that yes, I did. How else do they think we communicated?

Over Christmas break, I did end up staying with Gianni and his family (his three sisters, mom and dad, oh, and cat!). It was Christmas Eve, and Florence was decked out in its very own holiday splendor. Traditionally, Italians celebrate Christmas Eve more than the American Christmas morning tradition. At midnight, we would open gifts. Gianni's mom always assembled a beautiful nativity on the first floor of their duplex. Raffaella was preparing fish and making homemade pasta from scratch. She was from Emiglia Romagna and one of the best cooks I knew. I was elated to celebrate our first

Christmas together - Gianni took me by Vespa into the center to find some last-minute gifts. We explored Florence by night in its magical crisp winter wonder. I tried hard to stay present without worrying what the future would hold. I allowed myself to surrender to his deep chestnut eyes and warm embrace.

Christmas at the Fani household was extraordinary. Despite our differing religious, cultural, and linguistic backgrounds, I had never eaten so well or felt so welcome. I wasn't a big fan of fish, but it was delicious, and Raffaella definitely had the Midas touch, a simple food that titillated my tongue. We spent a beautiful night together and woke up next to one another in his family home on Christmas Day. The day after Christmas in Italy is Santo Stefano, and also a holiday. Gianni took me to Piazzale Michelangelo, which provides a spectacular view of the whole city. My heart felt full and overflowed with a joy I had not felt for many moons: this place, this man, this love.

New Year's Eve is my birthday, and I would usually spend it with my mother, whose birthday is January 1st. I spent it with Gianni, his sisters, and their boyfriends this year. His eldest sister, Patrizia, and her fiance,' Ugo, had rented a house out in the country. The fog was so dense that night that one could barely see the dividers on the road. Alessandro, Gianni's little sister's boyfriend, drove carefully with the door open a little so he could see the markings on the road. That ride was both frightening and exhilarating. We arrived at the house and enjoyed a delicious homemade dinner: bruschetta and caponata for appetizers, and pasta Sicilian-style (Ugo's relatives are Sicilian), and plentiful Chianti. That birthday would be unforgettable - I was now

21 and would be able to drink legally in the United States, although Italy allowed their kids and teens to drink in moderation with meals.

That dreaded day was nearing the end of the semester when I was supposed to head back home to New York. My heart ached with the thought of being far away from him. When I thought about it, my heart felt like it was breaking. I thought of calling my parents, who lived separately, to ask for their advice. My mother, of course, insisted I come home and finish college. My father suggested returning to finish with the option of returning back to Italy after graduation. This idea soothed and excited me at the same time. It was not really a *"goodbye - addio,"* but a *"see you soon - arrivederci"* when I thought about it in those terms. I could live with that much easier. As sad as I felt about our impending separation, I had a sense of hope that things would work out. Destiny seemed to hold us in her arms.

We had to live separately for six months. Those were some of the longest months I'd ever experienced. We wrote letters almost every day and called when we could. Gianni found a magical pay phone where he didn't have to pay. Eventually, the time came for Gianni to visit me at school. I was living in Swarthmore, Pennsylvania. That year was a cold, snowy winter, and Gianni had never seen so much snow. He slid and fell while walking through the drifts near my home. It was funny to watch him slide and fall like a little kid.

We spent days snuggling by the fire, watching Columbo reruns; he came to some of my classes with me and helped me translate *Inferno* by Dante, even though it was written in old Italian. The time for his departure was drawing close, and our conversations turned to more serious matters.

How would we go forward?

Would I go back to Italy?

Would he come here?

How could we be together?

I leaned on his shoulder and cried. It seemed like such a daunting task to be from two different countries and to speak two different languages. Just the language issue seemed like an insurmountable task. *How could he come to New York City if he didn't speak the language? Could I move to Firenze?* I felt anxious about it but tried to push these feelings to the back of my mind.

How could we ever make it happen?

Matteo held me and reassured me that we would find a way. *"Non ti preoccupare, cara Jenny,"* he said. *"Un modo lo troveremo."* (Translated: Don't worry, dear Jenny, we will find a way). That reassurance was a small reassurance in the cold reality that he was about to leave, but I took all the warmth of comfort I could get from it. I hoped for the best and was determined we would make it work somehow.

Gianni returned to Firenze, and we were both devastated. I tried to live my life, focus on my classes, and engage in some kind of social life, but I continuously felt that I had left a part of me in Florence. My mother warned me how hard it would be to have a relationship with someone of a different culture who spoke a different language and was of a different religion. I saw it as a challenge, and nothing would stop me from doing my utmost to make it work. Gianni felt the same way, and thankfully, his parents were open to the idea and supported us fully.

After much thought, we decided I would return to Firenze, to my love, and live there. We would live there for three years. Years later, in the year 2000, we would return with our son, Giancarlo. His first words would be in Italian.

The End.

About Jen Taylor

Jen Taylor is the editor for Girl on Fire Magazine's "Wine Down with Jen," where she uses her 23+ years of experience as a New York-based spiritual psychotherapist to bring you cozy couch conversations you would have with your best friend over a glass of wine after work. Jen specializes in challenging subjects, and nothing is off-limits for the convo with her. She has a unique twist of blending astrology into her guidance that will even have the stars lining up in your favor. When not writing for the magazine or seeing clients, Jen enjoys traveling, photography, spending time with her kids, and a good cup of coffee. Jen is a multiple best-selling author in a collaboration series, her own series *Letters to Myself*, that debuted its first book in 2023, and working on several books to drop in 2024. To connect with Jen away from the magazine or her books, she can be reached at mailto:jentaylorscw@gmail.com

A Typewritten Love

By Kerri-Ann Sheppard

Sasha Reid and Christmas did not go together unlike mistletoe and stolen kisses. If there was ever someone who was like Scrooge, it was her. Christmas had been a very formal affair when she was a child and, from her perspective, really boring. There was no fun, and her parents had the attitude that children should be seen and not heard. Christmas was an excuse for the adults to drink to excess, overeat, and ignore the children.

Her various aunts and uncles had children and would all descend on Reid Manor for Christmas. As an only child, Sasha found the other kids annoying. They only ever saw each other at Christmas, making them strangers despite being family.

This was her first Christmas without her parents. Both had passed away within days of each other in February. She had no children of her own and was currently single. No joy on Christmas for her, and she was fine with that, more than fine, actually. She was looking forward to having some much-needed downtime and reading, reading for pleasure rather than to pay the bills.

Her work colleague, Amelia, had invited her to join her family at Christmas. She had been thinking about it. The idea of being utterly alone on Christmas also didn't sit well with her despite her Scrooge status. Sasha gave into Amelia's unrelenting pressure and said yes, I'll go to your party. Thankfully, Sasha didn't need to worry about buying any presents for anyone, which was another chore she detested. Her parents had always expressed bitter disappointment with any of the gifts Sasha had carefully thought about and purchased for them. She went to great lengths to select things she thought they would like, whether it was a book, a tie, or a scarf. She had spent a lifetime trying to win their approval; it had failed, every single time. Not having to buy presents for strangers was a huge relief. Of course, she would bring a bottle of wine and some after-dinner mints; she couldn't turn up empty handed.

Amelia and Sasha had been working together at the publishing house for almost two years. Working as editors gave them the freedom to work from home, and to a large degree, they could pick and choose the hours they worked as long as the work was done. Their friendship had deepened over numerous Zoom calls and emails. Sasha now considered Amelia to be like the sister she had never had. Many a glass of wine had been drunk after work hours, of course, while they discussed the works they were reading from the slush pile. Sometimes, one would ask the other for a second opinion on writing which had caught their eye. The question always being, *"Is this as good as I think it is? What do you think?"*

They both also harbored desires to write their own novels. Amelia had been working on a psychological thriller for several years, although between children and her husband and work, her writing was progressing much slower than she would have liked. A few pages here, a few pages there, whenever she could spare the time. Sasha had been working on a Christmas romance; the irony of it was not lost on her. How was the person most uninterested in Christmas writing about Christmas as though it is the most magical time of year?

Sasha had arrived in Grandcrest and was staying at a quaint bed and breakfast just off the main street in town. She could leave her car there and walk around town easily. She relished the opportunity to be able to explore with no agenda. When she traveled with friends or her last lover, she felt she had to hurry and couldn't take her time. She loved looking at gardens and buildings and bookshops above all. Watching people was always fascinating, especially thinking about the secrets people had, didn't share with anyone, and dared not speak out loud. Making up stories in her mind about strangers and the lives they led kept the creative cogs in her mind working overtime. Occasionally, she would overhear conversations and wonder about the actions that came before and what the consequences of those actions and conversations were. Writing her own stories allowed her to dictate the outcomes of conversations and actions as much as the characters she wrote about allowed her to. Sometimes, a character would introduce themselves rather unexpectedly, or another would act in ways she hadn't anticipated. That was part of the process of writing that excited her, the unknown and the way stories and characters would unfold before her eyes.

On the main street of Grandcrest, the old church had been converted into a bookstore. Snow covered the waist-high stone wall surrounding the building. The cobblestone path had been cleared and led to the heavy oak wooden door of the church. Inside the door was a small alcove allowing people to wipe their shoes and leave their umbrellas. If Sasha had been looking for magic, then walking into the bookshop, she would surely have found it.

Emerald-green velvet sofas and armchairs were scattered throughout the central area of the store. An enclosed fire was roaring and keeping the space warm. Shelves lined the walls and created different sections within the open cavernous space. There was an area with large floor cushions and low shelves encouraging young readers to take a book and enjoy it.

A small cafe was set up in one corner, serving hot beverages and decadent-looking cream-filled cakes. To the left of the café, there was a single table and chair. On the table was a vintage typewriter with round, silver-edged keys and a black folder containing pages of text typed on the previous days and weeks. A man in a cream-coloured cable knit jumper was tapping away at the keys as though his life depended on the words pouring forth. He looked like he was in that ever-elusive writing zone that Sasha only occasionally achieved.

Sasha ordered a hot chocolate and a brownie with cream. Walking past the typewriter table, she nodded at the man typing and took the folder. Sinking into the sofa, Sasha put her bag next to her and opened the folder. The opening page outlined that the store owner had typed an opening sentence several months ago as an experiment. Each day, customers typed several pages of text. Word had spread around Grandcrest about the anonymous story being written in the bookstore.

Sasha started reading, and her editorial hat went on immediately. This story was something unlike anything she had ever read. While she had been reading the previous pages, the man at the typewriter had been replaced by a woman. Sasha continued reading, and another woman replaced the one at the typewriter. Other shoppers in the bookstore seemed to be patiently waiting their turn to sit and write. There was no way to tell who had written which part of the story or how many words each person had written.

Sasha walked over to the typewriter and grabbed the newly completed page. She read it and then added it to the folder. Her imagination was running away from her as she was thinking about what she would contribute to the story. There was never any doubt in her mind about whether she would contribute to the story. It had captured her heart in a way that she thought was long gone and impossible. Over the course of an hour, Sasha had observed at least eight people sit down at the typewriter and tap. A couple of people sat there and read the pages from earlier in the day and it looked like they added a line or two.

Her cup was now empty, and the typewriter was still being used by someone else. She left the bookstore, vowing to return the next day. Glancing around the space one last time for the day, she saw the man who had been at the typewriter when she first arrived. He nodded in acknowledgement and flashed a warm smile at her, making her cheeks flush a delicate shade of pink.

The next day, she returned to the bookshop. Ethan, the man from the previous day, was already at the typewriter. Sasha sat down at the table closest to the typewriter, watching and waiting for the chair at the typewriter to be vacated. She wanted to be the next person at the typewriter; she wanted to read what he had written. Shaking her head, she felt like a hormone-driven teenager, not the nearly fifty-year-old woman she was.

At the exact moment that she pulled her notebook out of her bag, he left, and someone else sat down. "Argh," she said.

The following day, as Sasha arrived, the man she had seen on her first visit was leaving the bookshop. He said hello and flashed that gorgeous smile at her. Her lips curved upwards, hinting at a smile. Sasha chided herself for being silly and reacting like a lovesick high-school girl, gushing happily at the thought that he had indeed smiled at her.

Over the last few days, Sasha had returned to the bookstore several times, some days even twice a day. She had checked out the children's books, the cookbook section - not that she liked cooking at all, and the gardening section, especially anything to do with flowers. This store had a selection of titles that would rival the bookstores in any big city. Whoever was doing the buying, obviously had good taste and knew books. The ambience, the typewriter, and the man at the typewriter were all drawcards to the bookstore, not that she would ever admit that to another soul. *Was her grumpiness towards Christmas wearing off,* she wondered?

The next day was Christmas Eve. She arrived at the bookstore earlier than usual, hoping to see him. When she took her seat and didn't see him, her heart sank. Maybe, she hoped he would arrive while she was there. Today, she also needed to find a book. Overnight, she received a message from Amelia about a Christmas tradition that they had only started in the last few years. Each adult needed to bring their favorite book from childhood. They would wrap their book at Amelia's place, all using the same wrapping paper, making it a book lucky dip experience.

Only the children received presents from the adults at Christmas. And Sasha was grateful that she didn't have to buy any presents for children; her own childhood seemed so long ago, and the things she longed for then seemed insignificant to her now. This tradition that Amelia and her husband had started was reigniting a joy for Christmas that seemed to be lacking amongst their friends. After the children had had their fill of gifts, the adults would each be given a book from under the tree and unwrap it. Sasha was glad that she had found the bookshop and knew exactly what book she would buy.

This morning, Sasha was quick and managed to get to the typewriter before anyone else had. She quickly scanned the current and previous pages, reflecting on how the story had progressed since she had written last. Headphones on and her favorite music taking her to that inspirational zone where the words flow through her and out onto the page. The barista placed her flat white on the table, and she typed. A page and a half later, she left her contribution for the next person to continue.

While she was typing, Ethan walked into the bookstore and saw her typing there. He took a seat at what had become her regular table. He waited there for her to scoop up her bag and her cup and free the typewriter for someone else.

Sasha saw him sitting there, and a smile spread across her face involuntarily. He nodded for her to sit down, and she did. His smile and the cheeky wink felt inviting and ignited feelings in her that had been lying dormant for a long time. It had been a couple of years since she'd had a partner - her parents being unwell had consumed a lot of her time when she wasn't working. She was feeling ready to venture into the land of dating again. And maybe she would get her Christmas wish.

Sitting across the table from Ethan, she couldn't shake the sense of there being something familiar about his face, perhaps a familial resemblance. She wracked her brain, trying to make a connection, but none was forthcoming. They fell into an easy conversation about books, of course, and Christmas movies.

It had been easy chatting with Ethan. Hours vanished into the midwinter afternoon. Realizing the time, she made excuses to leave, saying that she still had one last present to buy.

He asked, "What do you need to buy?"

"I need a children's book for this Christmas party that I'm going to. It's a lucky dip thing for the adults."

"Do you know which book you are after?"

She replied, "Yes, I do. It's my childhood favorite."

"Oh, you do have to tell me what it is now. Please, with mistletoe on top," he said with a cheeky grin spreading across his face.

"Oh no, there's no mistletoe here, so I guess I don't have to tell you," she said, winking at him.

She grabbed her bag and headed towards the children's book section. Ethan followed, hot on her heels, curious about the book she was about to select. He grabbed a random title and said, "Is this it?" Sasha shook her head and laughed.

He grabbed another book, and she shook her head again before he could say anything.

She had found her title and pulled it from the shelf while he was replacing his random title. He didn't see the title. She made her way to the counter to pay. She handed her book to the shop assistant. Ethan tapped her on the shoulder and pointed up. They were standing underneath a sprig of mistletoe. Her eyes lit up when she smiled at him. Their lips met for a moment. Sasha could feel the heat rising on her face.

"Merry Christmas, Ethan," she said.

"And same to you too, Sasha. I hope to see you again."

She nodded and stashed the book in her bag.

Walking back to the bed and breakfast, Sasha wished she had asked for his number. She was staying for several more days, so maybe she would be lucky enough to run into him again.

She hoped she would be lucky like that.

Early mornings and Sasha were not on good terms. Mixing Christmas Day and an early morning was sure to deliver the worst things she could imagine. Now that the day was here, Sasha was wholeheartedly regretting having accepted the invitation. Everyone else would know everyone, and yet again, she would be on the outside. The only small consolation Sasha could find was that she adored Amelia and would also like her extended circle of friends and family.

Buzzing the doorbell on the grand, snow-covered ivy building, butterflies were fluttering wildly in her belly. Thankfully, Amelia answered the door. Sasha wrapped her arms around Amelia in a big hug.

"I thought you might not have come," said Amelia to Sasha.

"Oh, I thought about it; I'm not a fan of the whole commercial thing," Sasha replied and handed Amelia a bottle of rosé.

"Do you have a book to wrap?"

"Sure do. I'm hoping no one else has picked the same one as me," said Sasha.

Amelia showed Sasha to a small reading room off the main foyer where she could wrap the book. Sasha could hear animated voices of children and adults down the hallway lined with tinsel and mistletoe. Wrapped present in hand, she walked the few steps down the hall and wished she had a strong drink in her hand to quell her remaining nerves. The room to her left was large and a roaring fireplace was keeping the room intoxicatingly warm. Near the entrance way to the room was the most giant Christmas tree she had ever seen in real life. The perfectly pointed tip was decorated with a cut crystal star, which seemed to shimmer and sparkle. A ladder would have been needed to put the decorations on those top branches, Sasha mused to herself. Pink and silver decorations dangled amongst the branches, and underneath the lower limbs were a dozen or so identically wrapped yet slightly different sized gifts. Sasha placed hers with the others and ventured further into the room.

Several cheerful children dashed through the room, shrieking joyfully. They already had their presents, so the adults could relax, enjoy conversations, and a meal without being asked when the children were going to be allowed to open presents. Sasha could feel her shoulders dropping into a more relaxed state. Perhaps this wouldn't be so bad, she thought. Amelia had spared no expense in decorating the house. Candles were flickering despite the early hour of the day. Mistletoe hung from every doorway and was under almost every light. Mental note: look up before standing in the one spot for too long.

The other guests were close to the fire. Some men were kneeling and holding long sticks with marshmallows at the end, while others watched as the marshmallows roasted. Sasha felt like she was walking into a fine example of the perfect Christmas Day. Amelia turned and saw Sasha admiring the scene from the doorway. Amelia promptly whisked her into the kitchen for further sisterly interrogations.

"Spill the news, Sasha. It's written all over your face," said Amelia.

Pretending to not have any idea what Amelia was talking about, Sasha smiled and fiddled with the beaded bracelet on her wrist.

"I've got nothing to tell," said Sasha.

"I don't believe that for a moment. You have a gorgeous radiance about you that's new, and it suits you."

"I have just been having a wonderful time here in Grandcrest," said Sasha.

"I've lived here a long time and never seen anyone glow like you are after a few days here. I know that look. Who is he?"

Sasha told Amelia about the story she had been reading that was being typed at the bookshop in town. Amelia knew of the story, of course, but hadn't been to read it. Lazing about in gorgeous bookstores with in-house cafes was a mere memory these days. Her own life was full and she was content despite being tired. She had all the things she had ever wanted. Seeing her dearest friend find that same contentment would be her own Christmas wish come true. Sasha continued telling her friend about the time she had spent reading the story and her contribution to the story. She wasn't quite ready to tell her about Ethan just yet.

"Enough with the romantic ideals of the story you've been reading. I get it; it's magical and whimsical and has made you feel like you are part of something bigger. Truly, that's wonderful. You're holding out on me, Sasha Reid," said Amelia.

"I'm not sure there's anything further to tell Ams," said Sasha.

"Please, just tell me about this person who has you speaking in overtures of giddiness at Christmas," said Amelia.

Sasha elaborated on the man she had met, the coffees they had shared, and their long and easy conversations. Her descriptions of his physical appearance were vague and omitted the details like the deep forest green of his eyes or the silver flecks in his hair. Patting her cheek with her cool hands, she tried to hide the color rising in her cheeks.

"What's his name? He sounds dreamy as can be, Sasha," said Amelia.

"You'll probably know him, given it's a small town and all."

"Oh, I don't know everyone. I'm not in everyone's business, you know, just the people I care about," said Amelia.

"Ethan," they both said at once.

Sasha stared wide-eyed and wished the ground would open up and swallow her. His name was out of her mouth when she saw him entering the room. Hopefully, Amelia wouldn't assume that Ethan was the man she'd been talking about. Sasha knew her friend would be watching every move now. Amelia smiled broadly and wrapped her arms around her big brother.

"Merry Christmas, Ethan, you're late," said Amelia.

"Timing was never my strong suit; you know that, Melly. Merry Christmas," said Ethan.

Ethan and Amelia were clearly lost in a moment of friendly sibling teasing. Still as a statue, Sasha hoped she wouldn't be noticed and wasn't sure whether Ethan had fully recognized her from a side-on profile.

"And who is this with us, Melly?" said Ethan as he turned to face Sasha.

"Sasha Reid," said Ethan and Amelia at the same time.

"That's my name," said Sasha, unable to keep the color from creeping into her cheeks.

At that same moment, Ethan realized that Sasha was Amelia's work friend, and Amelia worked out that Ethan was the man Sasha had been talking about. Amelia quickly grabbed the platter of food they had been preparing as they talked and she left the room; giving them space to talk.

Sasha hadn't looked up since she'd been in the kitchen. Ethan pointed up above her head to the mistletoe, as he moved in closer to Sasha. Sasha did not stop him and felt her breath frozen in time; as they gazed at each other for long moments.

Overnight, they had both chastised themselves repeatedly and severely for not asking for the other's number or social media contacts.

Ethan placed his hand around Sasha's waist and drew her close to him.

Maybe, Christmas had just became her favorite time of year, thought Sasha.

Their eyes closed as their lips met, a Christmas wish come true.

The End.

About Kerri-Ann Sheppard

Kerri-Ann is a published author, book editor, and solo mama to two special needs children – one of which needs home-schooling – all the while completing her master's degree in creative writing. She achieves each superwoman feat with no outside support other than copious cups of mildly warm tea, chocolate when the kids aren't looking, and kitty cat snuggles on the couch. When successful at getting out of the house solo, she juxtaposes sweaty boxing classes with dreamy yoga nidra. Kerri-Ann has been involved in the development and publication of multiple collaborative books which have become international bestsellers. She is looking to publish her first poetry anthology *'Tattoos and Bourbon'* in 2024.

You can find Kerri-Ann at kaswrites.com

Mr. Merry's Christmas

By Emily M. David

Her breath was hard, the thud of her heart beating in her ears.

Just one more, she thought, and she rounded the block, her feet pounding the pavement with each step.

Breathe in. Breathe out. Breathe in. Breathe out.

Why do I do this to myself? She wondered as she adjusted her headband.

The cold air burned her lungs, but the run felt good. Running in the cold air made her feel *alive-* something she hadn't felt since. Well, since that day.

Alive, she thought, *Alive and well and burning my lungs up with frigid cold air.*

Alive.

As she got back to her front yard, Janna slowed her pace to a slow walk, ultimately landing with her hands on her knees as she bent over to stretch.

Her earbuds turned off right as she leaned into a low stretch, perfect timing as always. The air was grey and gloomy tonight, a sign of impending snow, and she shivered as she opened the house and stepped inside.

She put on a pot of tea while she let the shower steam up and called the Indian restaurant on the corner.

"Yes, it's me, Janna......no thank you, yes I'd like the usual please. And extra naan. No, very spicy is fine.....Oh, and I'd love a second portion for tomorrow; you have my card. Thank you!"

Putting down her phone, she stepped into the hot, steamy shower. She breathed deeply.

Mmmmmm

She could smell the eucalyptus leaves hanging from her shower head as she stepped in and soaped up.

When she finished, she had just dressed and was toweling off her hair when the doorbell rang. She opened the door, signed the receipt, and thanked the delivery person profusely.

Another quiet evening, she thought, turning on the television as she set her table for one.

Always for one.

Always since....

She shuddered and picked up her spoon to dig into her supper. Steam fogged up her glasses. Delicious, just the way she likes it!

Janna woke up to her car coated in a light blanket of white, just enough to make the salt spray up all over the place as she drove but not enough to close school for the day. *A science teacher's dream,* she harumphed, shouldering her bag and balancing her coffee on her way out the door. She hated explaining to sullen teenagers why it hadn't snowed enough to close school that day. For middle schoolers, science was absolute- either it did or didn't. There was no in-between.

She sighed as she plodded down the long hallway to her chilly classroom, but her heart skipped a beat when she saw the cute substitute teacher was across the hall from her today. *I guess Mr. Seeneck called out again; he hates bad weather.*

Mr. Merry was lean and muscley and subbed at her school only occasionally. After he had taken time off to do three tours of duty overseas, he didn't want to return to teaching high school biology, so he moved back in with his aging parents and became a substitute teacher in her district.

She loved it when he was in; not only was he a real treat for the eyes, but he always had baked goods and smelled as though he had dabbed cinnamon behind his ears like cologne. *A real-life gingerbread man,* she mused.

He smiled as he stepped out into the hallway.

"Janna! I made cheesecake squares this morning. Would you like one?"

Would she ever!

"Oh, thanks, please, I mean, yes, you, I mean..."

He laughed jovially as he swooped around, grabbed a tray of gorgeous cakes the size of cereal bowls, and pointed to one in the center.

"I think Blueberry is your favorite?"

Brrrriiiiingg!

Saved by the bell! She yelled a quick thanks as she grabbed her cake and ran to her own classroom. Why must she always look like an idiot when he's around?

No matter, she was married. Sort of. Or, at least, she was supposed to be, and who knows what his story is? He certainly never sticks around long enough to talk about it on account of his being a substitute teacher. He was never around for more than a few days at a time.

She hid the cake in her desk drawer and put on a brave face to teach 37 children about the genetics of pea plants.

As lunchtime came, her mouth watered at the thought of the blueberry cheesecake in her desk drawer. *He always just seemed to know her so well,* she pondered. *It's almost like he paid attention and listened when I spoke or something.*

She rolled her eyes hard. He was a substitute teacher. Who lived with his parents. And she was just NOT interested.

Love wasn't the same anymore.

Not since....

She shook her head, it didn't matter. She struggled through her salad- it was too cold to be eating these torture devices- and savored her Indian takeout- it was always the perfect meal.

As she picked up her cheesecake, she heard Mr. Merry knock on her door and let himself in.

"I hope I'm not interrupting," he said, sliding into one of the student desks.

"Oh- uh- no, never."

"I see you've gotten to the cheesecake- the best part of any meal, if I do say so myself."

"Oh, you do, do you?"

She wondered to herself if he bothered Ms. August nearly as often. The kind old woman would have a conversation with a houseplant if no one else was listening, and she was always thinking of everyone else. According to legend, she had once knitted scarves for every one of her students for the holidays.

"So? Monday then?" His question jarred her back to the present-day moment.

"What, uh, yeah! Monday then."

Mr. Merry smirked as he sauntered out into the hallway and across to his borrowed classroom. *I guess I'm having lunch with him again Monday* she sighed, running to the bathroom before the bell rang.

At the end of the school day, Janna sighed as she slid into her chair. She had papers to grade, but they would have to wait until later; she needed to straighten up her room quickly if she wanted to go for her run before it got too dark.

As she locked her classroom door, she scurried down the hallway to change before leaving.

As she turned the corner towards the faculty bathroom, she heard a familiar voice yelling:

"Hey! Where are you off to in such a hurry?"

"I've, umm, got to run."

"I see that, but where to?"

That Mr. Merry just doesn't quit! she thought.

"Got to go!" she murmured, sliding into the bathroom to change.

She knew she didn't *have* to run so much, and not every day, but she wanted to, she told herself. She could quit anytime.

It was definitely not a problem.

It just wasn't.

She felt every rock and stone under her feet, her heart pounding out of her chest. She rounded the corner, and smacked right into something.

Teetering backward, she heard herself let out a 'yelp' her late dog would have been proud of.

"Janna? Janna.. Janna, it's me. Do you need an ambulance? "

"Janna"

As things came into focus, she found herself looking into the eyes of none other than the annoying Mister Frank C Merry.

"Are you alright there?" he said as she struggled to sit up. "Whoa there, little pony. You could have a head injury."

No, she wanted out of there. If she'd wanted more of Merry's attention, THEN she would have a head injury. Ugh.

"Please, no- I - uh- I've got to- I've got to get back to running."

"No, you most certainly do NOT. Sit there right now, and I'll check you out. Then, I'm taking you either to the hospital or home."

She began to protest, but he produced a flashlight from who knows where and began checking her pupils.

"Alright, it appears that you're fit as a fiddler on Saint Padraig's, but still, I'd like to take you home. C'mon, my car is right over there."

She knew better than to start asking questions, and her head might have been a little sore in the back, not that she would admit that to him. She allowed him to guide her.

After settling into the car, he turned on her seat warmer, tucked her into a blanket, and checked her seatbelt before sitting down in his own seat.

A flashlight? A blanket? Oh right, military training probably prepared him for emergencies. And for being in her way all the time.

She didn't even hear what he prattled on about as he started the car and drove the few short blocks to her house. She thanked him as he pulled into her driveway, and she reached for her seatbelt. When he finally stopped the car, he locked her door, trapping her inside.

Don't kidnappers usually take you away from your own home first? She wondered.

Then, she saw him opening her car door with a key and felt two muscular arms reach in to grab her. She hoisted her out of the car, picked her up, and cradled her as he strode towards her front door.

"The code is 0823," she whispered in a daze.

As he plopped her on the sofa, he drew in a sharp breath, noting how sterile and *white* everything in her house was.

"Nice place," he murmured.

He went to the kitchen, put a kettle of water on the stove and then rummaged through her cabinets looking for teabags. Finding none, he sliced the lemon he found on her counter, opened her spice drawer, and shook a little bit of this and a little bit of that into a coffee filter that he tied shut with some string from her apparent sewing kit.

"Who keeps a sewing kit in her kitchen drawer?" he rolled his eyes.

As the kettle whistled, he poured the hot water into her mug and walked it over to her. Sitting next to her on the couch, he handed her the tea.

"What on earth is this?" she asked. He wasn't sure if she was musing or if this question was accusatory. She was so confusing to him.

"Oh, just something I whipped up for you. It's tea. I'll help you relax and heal."

She sipped slowly, cautiously.

"You may have a concussion, though. When does your husband come home?"

"I don't have one."

"Oh, I'm, sorry. Boyfriend? Girlfriend? Mom?" he grasped at straws.

"No, not anymore, and no, thank you. I will not be calling her, and you won't either."

"Welp, you're stuck with me, then. It's good that it's Friday, and there's no school tomorrow. I'll stay here and keep an eye on you," he quipped.

"No, thank you."

"Yes, thank you. You could have a concussion, and I will NOT be allowing anything serious on my watch. Sergeant Franklin C. Merry, medic and former US military chef, at your service."

She rolled her eyes hard as he said this, but inside, she was grateful.

"Now, the first order of business is to keep you awake, and I do NOT suggest blue light screens as our method of treatment," he took the remote control from her hands.

"There are 2 days until Christmas vacation, and there is not a single decoration in this house unless, of course, you don't celebrate, Ms. Scrooge?"

"It's Soretato, thank you very much! And no, I'm not really into Christmas anymore."

"And why might that be, Ms. Scrooge?"

"Soretato and I don't really want to talk about it..." she trailed off, reaching for a blanket and her mug of whatever delicious poison he had concocted for her.

Taking a long sip, she continued, "It's just.... It's been, well, it's been a while since I've felt like celebrating much of anything."

"Ah, a true Grinch, I see. Well, let's see what we can do about that heart while we take care of your head," as he made a face, presumably to present Grinchy eyebrows.

"Well, if you'd like, there's probably some Christmas sheet music inside the piano bench, not that I play anymore, but you're welcome to do so. I am going to bed."

"Oh no, ma'am you are not! Let's find it then, shall we?"

The piano bench turned up nothing. She had forgotten that she had burned all the sheet music when....when it had happened.

"Alright, plan B then. Where is your storage? Surely you have some decorations somewhere?"

"Nope, I don't think so, and also, I don't want to."

He huffed under his breath and rolled his eyes hard.

"Alright, well, put your coat on. We are going to the store."

"We're doing what? But what if I'm concussed?"

"We need to eat dinner, and I'll just see what I can talk you into."

"Fine, but no Christmas."

"Let's go."

As they wandered through the aisles of the store, he put this, that, and the other things into his shopping cart. He showed her how to select the perfect onion and asked her about eleventy-five billion times how she was feeling.

After the *fancy* food market, he pulled into the parking lot for Bullseye, offered her a caffeine-free latte at the coffee shop inside the entrance, and then bought two anyway when she declined and pressed one into her hand.

He pointed out lush holiday pillows, glittery ornaments, and a big, green artificial tree as they walked around the store.

He wrapped her in a display of garland and proceeded to force her into dancing to the 1980s electronic Christmas music that the store had piped in.

Wrapped up in the moment- and the garland- she felt herself leaning into the music. She threw her head back and laughed harder than she had in what felt like forever. She looked into his eyes, which had lit up like the tangle of C9s she was so used to unraveling after Thanksgiving dinner, and she felt drawn in like a magnet.

There was a physical spark between them as their lips met, and he held her close, afraid to let go.

When she pulled back, she looked surprised and..*pained?*

What had he DONE?

She clammed up and started to untwist herself from the garland but found herself trapped.

He let her loose and watched as she turned away, blushing sheepishly.

Quietly, he put the garland back on the shelf. She motioned to her head and started towards the door.

Their drive home was silent, pockmarked by a few bumps in the road and a few beeps of the horn as traffic built up around them.

As they returned to the house, she unlocked the door and snuck directly into the bedroom. He started to follow her but thought the better of it and settled into the kitchen to begin cooking.

While the onions began to sweat, he knocked on the door to check on her.

"Janna?"

"Just a moment, I'm changing."

He stepped back from the door, unsure of how to respond.

Hearing the oil sizzling on the stove, he turned back to the kitchen and resumed his meal preparation. He was slicing chocolate to top the mousse when she emerged from her room.

Wow. She looked radiant.

She was clearly trying to hide behind fuzzy slippers, pajama pants with cartoon puppies on them, and an oversized long-sleeved thermal, but he couldn't see anything but beauty.

She was toweling off her hair as he pulled out a chair at her table.

"Dinner, madame, is served."

She slid into her chair, unsure of what to do next exactly.

First, he served her a delightful mushroom soup, then a green salad with walnuts and beautiful pink onions. When he put a plate of crispy garlic bread and pasta full of tomatoes, olives, artichokes and more, she was certain it was a plate of gemstones.

Just when she thought she couldn't eat anymore, he placed a gorgeous chocolate mousse in front of her. She was convinced she would fall asleep for days as he put on some music and began cleaning up the kitchen. He implored her to go and relax, but she knew she would fall asleep if she did.

She walked over to the kitchen and began drying the dishes as he stacked them on her counter. The third time she turned around, she felt the world sway slightly.

Steadying herself on the counter, she prayed he hadn't noticed.

He had.

He reacted in a heartbeat, picking her up and carrying her over to the couch. He propped her feet up, fluffed a pillow behind her back, and returned a moment later with a cool towel to place on her head.

She sighed, frustrated with herself, but let him care for her.

When the dishes were finished, he slid onto the sofa beside her and took one of her feet into his hands. Rubbing gently, he asked her how she was feeling.

"Worse than last Christmas," she murmured, sounding tired.

"Last Christmas? What happened?" he didn't expect her to answer.

"She left me," Janna whined.

He gently placed her foot down, picking up the left.

"At the altar. We had been together for a long time, and we were finally going to be married. She showed up, went through the ceremony, and then couldn't say, 'I do.' She ran off, crying like she was disgusted by my very existence. On Christmas Eve."

He inhaled sharply. "Ouch. I'm sorry."

"Mmhmm, it's why I hate Christmas."

"So I see, I would too," he saw her drifting off to sleep. He knew that he could let her sleep some if he woke her up periodically for monitoring, so he moved to the chair, stopping first to cover her with a blanket.

About an hour later, she awoke with a start. "Water!" She gasped, running to the sink. Before he could react, she said, "I'll be dehydrated! I never drank my gallon after my run!"

He started to object but thought better of it. Instead, he poured her a glass of water, added a lemon slice, and gave her a straw.

"How are you feeling?"

"Like I've been hit by a truck, but I think I'm alright. You can go home. You should go home. I'm okay, really!"

"No, I'll stay," he watched her drift off.

When he woke her an hour later to check on her, he had a warm muffin in hand and a cup of steaming cocoa. She knew better than to ask questions, so she bit down into the buttery pillow and moaned with pleasure. She had never known food to taste so good.

She thanked him quietly and left the room. When she returned, she had a 1000-piece Christmas Puzzle in her hands. She unceremoniously dumped it out onto the table, motioned for him to join her, and began sorting out the corner pieces and the framework. Without a word, he sat next to her and began sorting by color. He would let her speak next, decide how much she wanted to share.

After a moment, he stood and tossed a pot of popcorn on the stove. She needed to keep eating to get her strength up.

After several moments of silence, she cleared her throat, "I-" she paused, "I'm sorry. I never told anyone that, except the people who already knew. She really broke my heart that day."

"I can't even imagine what that felt like."

"It hurt. It still hurts. She was the love of my life. She gave me purpose for a life worth living. We were going to adopt children together, go kayaking on weekends, and build a cabin in the woods where we would go for every vacation and school holiday. I thought we were forever, and then she just walked out. I told everyone to stay for dinner because, at that point, I had paid for it, but everyone from her side left. My uncle called members of his golf club to come sit at their tables."

He chuckled at that, imagining a bunch of middle-aged men in golf shorts showing up halfway through a wedding and sitting in someone else's seat.

"It's not funny," she giggled quietly. But now, she could see, it was a little bit funny.

She turned over the puzzle pieces and continued, "By the time I got home, the house was empty. She had taken everything that was hers and most of what was ours. I threw the rest away. I've hardly replaced any of it."

"It's been a year."

"It has, it's been a long and painful year, and it sucks knowing I'm not lovable enough."

"But, you are...." he trailed off.

He stood, added freshly melted butter and salt to the popcorn, and added it to the large bowl he found inside the cabinet above the refrigerator.

She dug in eagerly. "Yumm! I haven't had popcorn in so long!"

He smiled wide as he threw the popcorn into the air and caught it with his mouth.

She laughed hard like she had at the store. Maybe there was still happiness in there, somewhere.

Around four o'clock, there was a knock at the door. As Janna rose to answer it, she wondered who it could possibly be.

She felt the chill of the cold winter air immediately upon cracking the door open. And then she saw *them*.

Them, the familiar pair of Doc Martens that she'd moved from the doormat into the closet so many times. Her eyes traced slowly upward, landing first on the bouquet of flowers and then the piercing blue eyes just above them.

"Take me back, Janna, please! I was wrong! You are the love of my life!"

She stepped backwards stunned for the second time in twelve hours.

Frank started to rise, but thought the better of it and waited in the wings, ready to pounce on cue.

He watched her lean towards the unfamiliar face, her eyes gleaming with tears? Anticipation? He wasn't sure.

Just as it looked like their lips were about to lock, he heard Janna's voice ringing like a bell,

"No, thank you. You really hurt me after you threw me away like a piece of household garbage, and I don't need someone who is going to treat me like that."

She spun on her heel and closed the door firmly behind her. The stranger was clearly stunned, as her shadow darkened the door frame for a few moments too long. As she spun, Janna lost her balance and fell to the floor, sobbing. She drew up her knees and let loose.

Sergeant Franklin C. Merry, science teacher, was at a loss. He didn't know what to do. For the first time since BASIC, since his first day on the line at the mess, since Medic training, since…since, he was at a loss and didn't know how to fix this.

He slowly walked to her, sat beside her, and waited. When she tilted her head into his chest, he wrapped his arms around her. He held her while she sobbed, acutely aware that this wasn't fixing anything. The biologist in him knew it was supporting her catharsis, but the Sergeant in him wanted to play superhero somehow. He couldn't reach the croissants, and he wasn't sure they would be able to fix things either.

He just waited.

Finally, she turned to her side and snuggled into him. After several minutes, he kissed her forehead, calculating the risk versus the reward and hoping it would heroically and magically make her feel better.

She sighed calmly and smiled a little.

When daylight warmed them, he yawned, awakening. He carried her to the sofa and went to the kitchen to start coffee and warm the croissants with a bit of chocolate. When she sat up, her hair looked like the victim of an electrocution. He smiled to himself and poured her a cup of coffee. Bringing a plate with two croissants, he invited himself to the sofa, but she popped up and scurried away as soon as he went to sit down.

After what seemed like an eternity, she returned, fully dressed and coiffed. Maybe she didn't realize it was Saturday?

"Janna, there's no schoo-"

"Good morning! Saturdays are for cleaning! Will you stay to disinfect the house, or will you vacate after breakfast?"

"I- what?" had she forgotten last night? Was her concussion that serious? Maybe he should drive her to the emergency room?

"Thank you for taking care of me last night, but cleaning day is cleaning day, and I must-" he cut her off as he swept her into his arms and leaned in for the kiss. She leaned into him this time, and he pushed a lock of hair out of her face.

"The cleaning can wait." He pressed into her, afraid to let go.

"Fine, but I want breakfast now, please." He laughed and released her to the table. After she devoured seven scones with chocolate, he was washing dishes when she emerged from the bedroom with his coat in her hands. "What now?" He worried, knitting his brows.

"Get dressed; cleaning can wait. I need a Christmas tree to put you under."

His eyes nearly popped from his skull.

"Yes, ma'am!" he gave her a playful salute.

It seemed like Mister Merry would get his Christmas wish that year after all.

And so would Janna, even if she didn't know it until now.

The End.

About Emily M. David

Emily M. David is an English Teacher and Literacy Coach who moonlights as a writer. She lives in New Jersey with her husband where they spend their time updating their home and relaxing with family. Emily also works with private clients helping them to find the best techniques to work smarter, not harder. She incorporates research in brain science, the psychology of learning, and years of experience in education to help her clients streamline their processes and take life by the to-do list. Emily writes and edits for The Furry Journal Online for pet parents. She has been a guest author in Girl on Fire Magazine and this is her first publication with Elite Publishing House.

Find her on Instagram at @EmilyDavid42.

Fighting Spirits Relaxation

By Zachary Shiloh Watts

Christmas is more than just a holiday season. It isn't just about the "Birth of a Savior." It is more than gifts under a tree. I used to think this time was nothing beyond over-commercialized nonsense.

Christmas, for me, is the cold air. I went crazy for the smell of cookies. It is people putting their differences aside. The allowing of grievances to be flushed out. To see how beautiful life is through the eyes of a child.

My name is Jack Leroy Masters.

I have been in my home state of New York for many years. I have been living with my family again over three and a half, to be exact. I don't drive. I have never been on a plane physically.

I am fortunate to have built quite a life for myself. I reversed Type II diabetes when I was thirty-two years old. I have been on my own romantically over four years. I have been featured in numerous books. I have participated in my share of virtual summits.

As 2023 starts wrapping up, I noticed an opportunity. My most known publisher is Amelia Janet Desveaux. Amelia announced that her "Fortune" visibility event was coming to New York City. I read the details.

This was more than just the coming together of entrepreneurs. We were given "Red Carpet Treatment" for "Radiant" family members. We were provided a retreat to relax with friends. We were uniting to uplift others. It was a celebration of the forthcoming year.

I used to cry when Amelia would do events in other states. I had worked a day-to-day job. I was struggling in my business. I only imagined what I would do.

I spent thousands of dollars throughout the years. A significant portion of that money went towards improving myself. I had enrolled in several online courses. Sought teachers who I thought were "better than me."

I found a recurring theme in my life. It wasn't just as an adult. It goes as far as my childhood.

It was a lack problem. I was raised in a biological family that discussed lack of money. I grew up around people who harped about the lack of time because we had things to do in a twenty-four-hour span.

That problem would build as I got older. I would hear half-hearted wishes. There was no big action to change the circumstances. Folks expected the government to help them. The lack didn't just stay with money. It affected our health too.

When Fortune was announced, I felt as if I was rewarded. I felt as if my prayers were answered. I did literally cry. It was proof of my hard work manifested.

I had saved what money I could. I made sure that all of my monthly expenses were taken care of. I booked my room at the New Yorker Hotel. I was building my excitement for Fortune. I practically told everyone I knew that I wasn't missing this.

Among those spoken to was my friend named Erica Faith Tate. Erica was someone I confided in through the last two years. She was a fan of my writing. A strong supporter of my podcast.

We both were raised in dysfunctional families. We each were engaged to be married twice. We have been single prior to the Coronavirus Pandemic. We have focused on ourselves.

When Erica heard of Fortune, she was telling me how she couldn't make it to New York. She didn't have the money to do so. She was always in her shop called 'The Parlour.' She was helping to care for her nieces and nephews until her sisters could pick them up.

Danish Love told me how much she wanted us to meet in person. I really wanted to meet her too. I understood what kept her in her small town. We talked about what we would do when she came to New York City.

As my wait for Fortune was wrapping up, I was invited to lunch by a family friend. Mr. Jenkins wasn't just that to me. He was one of my strongest male influences. If I had an issue with anyone (or anything) in the world, he provided a place for venting. He was one of the seldom few who knew about Erica.

Mr. Jenkins didn't only want to give me food for my body. My dear friend wanted to nourish my soul. He asked me to come into his living room. I obliged him.

Mr. Jenkins said:

"Let me start off by saying, I am proud of you. You have accomplished a lot of amazing things. I am happy and grateful to witness how you have grown.

With that said.. I have not only beheld your growth. I noticed how you pigeonholed yourself. You are obsessed with business. You go grocery shopping. You stopped going to places that made you happy. You don't go on dates.

Why?

You are ashamed of yourself. I'm not saying this to put you down. You know it down in your heart. You feel like you have nothing to offer women romantically. Plus, you let external circumstances of this world cloud your judgement.

You are absolutely wrong, son.

You have a big heart. You are funny. You are one of the most articulate people I know living. You should open yourself to the world. Not just be here in New York City.

I know how big this Fortune thing you're going to is. You see this as an opportunity to expand your reach. To obtain interviews for your podcast. To be interviewed by others yourself. To network with people who can lead you to potential clients.

Life after that is up to you. I would love for you to be happier. To do more. I want you to get out of NYC. How? I can think of one way (or more so person, to be exact).

You have spoken highly of this young lady named Erica. She is unfortunately not going to be at Fortune. I know that upsets you. Sounds to me that she could use a good friend. Someone to send her some holiday cheer (not just online).

You yourself need some joy this holiday season. I don't want you to spend another Christmas at home. You've done that too long. You've been shacked up in your mother's basement (since your previous romantic relationship ended). You are continuing this unhealthy pattern of being alone.

I have a gift for you. I was gonna wait until Fortune was over to give you this. You are going to her exact location. You will spend an exact week out there.

Do I make myself clear, Jack?"

It took me several minutes to respond. I wound up crying in front of Mr. Jenkins. Everything he said was on point. I expected nothing less of him. I eventually thanked my friend for his support. I promised him that I would spend time with Erica.

Time passes, and then Fortune takes place. It is December 12 through 14.

I go through my morning routine. I take a shower (after I am done working out at the gym). I dressed myself in a red and black flannel shirt, black striped suit pants, and panted leather shoes. I left Staten Island to get to the New Yorker Hotel by 3 PM.

I stand outside of my destination. I take it in that I am returning somewhere I haven't been in over a decade. I pray over myself. I do the same for all who are going to and leaving this historical establishment.

I notice there is a line for check in. My excitement for rising. As I got nearer, I noticed a woman in front of me. We have about six people ahead of us. She was calmly waiting.

Her hair was short in length. The color was majority brown. There were some lovely grey streaks.

She was wearing a black and white flannel shirt. She had on a sequin skirt. Her ears held two angel's wings drop earrings. Her feet were blessed by black boots (that went up to her knees).

The wait to check in passes as seconds becomes minutes. I am still taking it in that I haven't been in this enchanted place for over thirteen years. I felt like I was in a storybook.

The pretty young lady makes her way to the recently occupied desk. I made mine with the next. We both checked in successfully. I felt my excitement kick into a higher gear.

I am a very observant man. People have told me that I am a great listener. As I was checking in, I swore I heard the name to the woman in front of me. I finally knew why I felt a sense of warmth from her.

The woman's name was Erica Tate. I was losing my junk positively. I wanted to say something but played it cool. I didn't want to embarrass my friend.

I make my way to the elevator. So does my even more recognizable friend. As we wait, I feel like a little child on Christmas day. I am in awe that Erica Faith Tate is here in New York City. My belief is that she's attending Fortune as I am.

Erica asks:

"Excuse me, sir? Did I hear your name is Jack Leroy Masters?"

I answered:

"Yes, I am, beloved."

Erica asks:

"Do you recognize me?"

I say to Danish Love:

"Hi, Eri! It's great to finally meet you face to face. Welcome to New York City."

Eri replies:

"Hi, Lee! I'm so happy to see you. I'm excited to be here. I feel like I am dreaming."

We give each other a hug. The embrace was cozy. I felt as if I was home in my friend's arms. I swear she felt the same about being in mine.

The elevator has made its way to the lobby (as we unfold our bodies). We are all alone in the elevator. I'm blushing at her. I believe she's taking me in. We both get off on the same floor.

I am jazzing out (after leaving the elevator). I am wondering what room Eri is in. She is walking in the same direction as I am.

We arrive at our individual rooms. I feel my energy increase. Why? Danish Love is right next door to me.

I get into my room. I unpack my belongings. I had a little snack. I drank some water. I wrote in my journal about the check in. Once the writing was done, I banged the table enthusiastically then chanted (up to three times):

"Yes, hun, yes"

I believe I heard the laughter of a familiar woman. I had to calm down a little bit. I allowed myself to actually lie down on my bed. I closed my eyes. I had a 30-minute nap.

I woke up. I exercised a pinch. I did push-ups against a wall. I used these four grips strengthening devices. I splashed some water on my face.

I did a 15-minute meditation. I followed that up with the Emotional Frequency Technique. I tapped on my left hand with my right. I went around the other focal points. Did as such a round of three times.

The opening of Fortune was at 7 PM Eastern Standard Time to 10 PM. It was on Forty Second Street. Fortunately, I knew how to get there. That happens to be in Times Square.

After a brief prayer, I would leave where I was staying. Erica wound up leaving about the same time (as I did). We exchanged glances with each other. We made our way to the elevator together. As the ride continued, I thought to myself:

"I know we just met physically. I don't want to come on too strong. I would love to hold her hand. I would be blessed to escort her to Fortune."

I told Danish Love what was on my mind. Her smile turned even brighter. She said to me:

"I was hoping you'd ask. I am not familiar with this area. You are."

I gently put my left hand in Eri's right. We got off in the lobby. We made our way to the Fortune venue. As we walked together, I gave Danish Love a little bit of a tour.

I showed her places I used to go to. She was taking in the different scenes. I could tell how much fun my friend was having. It was as if she waited her whole life for this moment.

When we arrived at Fortune, Amelia Janet Desveaux really didn't disappoint. It was a true "Red Carpet" affair. I knew what I was walking on. So did Danish Love. I didn't know about Eri, but, my dopamine level increased slightly.

We walked through the door. We gave our coats to the receptionists. We were asked to go to the ballroom. We walked to there (hand in hand). We said, "See you later," then went our separate ways.

I heard a grand, leveled voice exclaim, "Lee San! Lee San! How are you?" Only one person I could think of would call me that. I witnessed this woman of Japanese descent come my way. She is with her beloved Sensei husband.

Natsumi Watanabe has arrived. I matched her vibrancy. I reply with "Hi, Natsumi Chan! I'm Flowtacular. Thanks for asking. How are you?" She tells me how much fun she's been having. I am introduced to Watanabe Sensei.

There was one very important person I was looking for. The hostess of this event. My mentor. My friend. That is Amelia Janet Desveaux.

I see this woman in a button up shirt. It was yellow, gray, and white. She wore flower earrings. Above black heels were white pants. I could hear this solid Southern accent.

I couldn't stop smiling. I waited over three years to meet her. She featured me in her books four times. Helped me to publish my solo book. I heard the voice say:

"Hello, Jack Leroy Masters! How are you?"

I replied, "I'm doing well, Ameliakins! How are you?". We chatted a pinch. I gave her a hug. I make my way to my table.

Sometime after dinner is enjoyed by all attendees, soft music starts to enshrine the area. I can see all of the couples I know come together to dance. As they slow dance, I can feel the pure love that every person has for their partner.

My eyes catch the sight of a dear friend. She is watching the others from a distance. She is swaying a bit. It's Erica.

It's been a pinch since I interacted with her. I walked up to Danish Love. I said:

"Hi, Eri. I saw you standing by yourself. Thought I would join you.

I'm not just here to stand together in some corner. Not only to chat. Would you like to dance with me?"

She tried to persuade me that she was shy. How she didn't have any rhythm. I looked her in those crystal blue eyes then said:

"I'm by your side. Nobody else matters to me right now. I want to dance with you. You held my hand on the way to this venue. I ask you to take it again. Please know you have nothing to fear".

She lights up like a Christmas tree. Her right hand has reunited with my left. The first slow dance is over. The second song begins to play. We joined our friends on the dance floor.

I tell Danish Love, "This is how we dance. It's not a big commotion. Just going in circular motions together."

As the dance continues, I am on Cloud Nine. I thought of all our chats. How I wanted to do this. Be in an environment like Fortune.

Once the dance is done, out of my mouth comes:

"You did well. I really enjoyed myself. Thanks for dancing with me. I appreciate it.

Would you like to get out of here? We still have another two days. I would love a change of scenery."

We grabbed our coats. We walked the late evening streets of Manhattan. We took in the beautiful starry sky. We made a trip to Rockefeller Plaza. I took a picture of Eri under the famous tree lit up on Television (after Thanksgiving) every year.

As we headed back to our hotel, it started to snow. Eri said she wanted to talk to me. Asked if I would come to her room. I was wondering what she had to say. I did oblige her.

We get to Eri's room. We put our stuff down. I sit in the chair. Danish Love sits on her bed. She says:

"Thanks for a great evening, Lee. I have received unexpected tours. We were able to hang out with people we have known for years.

I said earlier that I wanted to tell you something. I'm not just here for fun. I came to New York not only for Amelia's help to gain visibility.

My older sister, Rebecca, called me some days ago. We had lunch at her house. She and our younger sister, Tabitha, wanted to have a chat with me. They noticed how I was doing.

I look sluggish. I have no time for myself. I am always at my shop. I am constantly under stress. As you know, I look after their kids until they're able to take them home.

My sisters are right. I'm sure you could tell as we have talked the last several months. My health has been declining. I tried to deny it. This is partly why I never left Montana.

I really wanted to visit you. You have been a great friend. You are always around for me to talk to. You never truly judged me. I didn't meet you face to face, but I always felt like a Queen.

I have always admired you. How you take your health seriously. I have not only told you this. I talked to my sisters about my adoration.

I told them about this event. How I wanted to go. Your attendance. How I felt that I couldn't close my shop for more than a day. Etc., etc.

Rebecca asked me how much I wanted to be part of Fortune. I began to cry. Tabitha held me in her arms then said they had a Christmas surprise for me. I was to go to Fortune. I was to spend the whole time away.

We went to our favorite hair salon. I felt changes were coming, not just for you. Not only Amelia. Our friends. I could sense shifts beginning to manifest within me. I wanted to reflect that on the outside.

I cut my hair. I packed what I wanted. I booked my flight to New York. I prayed that I would run into you at this exact hotel."

As I heard Danish Love's story, I saw her cry before me. I felt every single word she said. I swear it was like I was listening to myself. I wiped her tears.

I replied:

"Your story was amazing. I didn't tell you this. I had a chat with my friend, Mr. Jenkins. I thought you weren't gonna come out here. I will tell you the truth. I was a bit sad.

Mr. Jenkins reminded me of some things. I have accomplished a lot on my end. Christmas is quickly approaching. He told me that I spent Christmas alone for far too long.

I was to go to Montana. I was to have joy beyond Fortune. To get my tushy out of where I have been my entire life. To be with the woman I talk to other people about most. To add some holiday joy to her life. That was you.

I was gonna message you on Facebook once this was done. Let you know I was coming to see you. I was ready to experience life outside of New York, New Jersey, and Pennsylvania. How much I valued you as a general person.

I thought today was going to be special. I was correct, plus then some. I want to help you better your health in any way I can. I don't want to wait until I come for my Montana stay. As I said before, we left Fortune (for tonight), we have two more days there.

You are my friend. My co-author. Let's make not just this coming Christmas special but all Christmases beyond it.

I love you, Danish Love".

We both got up. We came together for a hug (which seemed to last longer than the previous ones). I looked Erica in her eyes. She looked me in mine.

We wound up closing our eyes. We felt our heads move toward each other. Our lips touched calmly.

I saw Erica as a Queen.

I would take her out to dinner (every night after we were done with Fortune). We went to the real-life Bubba Gump restaurant (for Night 2). We went to Applebee's (Night 3).

We explored the Museum of Natural History. I went there at different times. Eri taught me about some people behind the exhibits when she was with me.

One of her biggest dreams was to go on a horse and carriage ride. I saved that for Eri's final night in New York City. She let out a high-pitched squeal (when she heard we were going for the horse and carriage ride).

Fortune ended on an excellent note for us. We (along with our friends) all gained stronger visibility. We generated actual clients. Made or were featured for interviews. We were recommended for whatever services we provided.

I kept my promise to Mr. Jenkins. I would get out of New York City. I headed to Montana for an exact week. I was picked up by Danish Love. We went to some of her favorite places. The one she felt I would be drawn to was a shrine.

I went on to meet Erica's family. I felt welcomed straight from the beginning. They thanked me for helping Eri better her health. She was more alive than they remembered her to be.

Eri began exercising more. Danish Love allowed 'The Parlour' to be closed only on Sundays. She reduced her working hours by an hour (so she could have an actual hour or two for herself). My bestie woke up every day with a new zest for life.

A year would pass. I traveled to places in and out of America. Eri left Montana to be with me. We got married and live happily ever after.

The End.

Story Inspiration:

I have been a published author for numerous years. I have channeled my life. I have three published letters. I have written an interlude. I have written over eleven books on how I manifested my dreams.

This is the first book where I, Zachary Shiloh, am not the main focal point. I am not writing the story by my real name. I am living through a character named Jack Leroy Masters. Leroy was a thought I had for my second go in a book series called Rebel Romance.

He began manifesting for this exact moment. He birthed his world after the "loss" of my father. His story answers numerous questions of the real-life Zachary Shiloh. As he gets ready to come forth, I am celebrating my life.

I have not just accepted that my father has been gone over four months. I have been on a great path unknowingly over four years. Went from an overweight Type II diabetic who was losing everything that matters to a man who believes he is manifesting his life.

About Zachary Shiloh Watts

Zachary Shiloh Watts is an all-life New Yorker. He was born in Brooklyn, NY (during the winter of 1987). Has resided in Staten Island (since 1997). He is the proud middle of three children.

His favorite season is Spring. His favorite color is red. When talking with Zach, he tends to not cuss. Should he curse then it goes with what he is conveying (at the time). He loves being in nature. Weight trains 3X (or more) a week.

When he isn't working, Zach is pursuing his wildest dreams. One of them happens to be his love of writing. He has the honor of saying he is a Best-Selling Author. His next book releases are his second memoir called In *The Midst of CHAOS: MANIFESTING Life With The Infinite* and a co-authoring in Poetry called *Flowers*.

Another passion is the expansion of what he calls BLK Lion's Airspace. What is BLK? BLK is short for black.

BLK Lion's Airspace is The Flowtastic Zone where LOVE shines brightest. Home of the BLK Lion's Domain interview segment (where Universal Grounding is partaken). He discusses Universal Laws (more so Law of Attraction), writing, health and whatever else keeps him highly vibrational. His podcast has been around since June 16, 2019.

The most important thing to Zachary Shiloh is his online coaching business. It was known as Love's Roar from 2020. One half of what was called Fear To Love's Roar in Summer 2021. Since April 28, 2022, it roars as Mind Over Matter Unlimited.

Mind Over Matter Unlimited isn't your typical weight loss. It is where health resurrection MANIFESTS. It STARTS in the MIND. What FOLLOWS will AWE you.

Please contact and support Zachary Shiloh by using the provided links:

https://www.facebook.com/BLKLion130/
https://twitter.com/BLKLion130
https://www.instagram.com/blklion130/
Zacharys.watts@yahoo.com
Zacshi130@gmail.com

An Unforgettable Stop in St. Pocono: A Heart-Warming Tale

By Alicia Thorp

Rae, a beautiful woman, had just turned 30 and was the mother of a young son. When she became pregnant, the father, who wasn't ready to settle down, told her he had accepted a job overseas. For three years, Rae raised her son in her hometown with the help of her parents, but she yearned for more. In search of a better life for herself and her son, Francis, who was only a small child at the time, Rae decided to leave her hometown and move to the West Coast, where they spent five years. As Francis approached his eighth birthday, Rae felt a pull toward home. As a single mother, Rae recognized the special bond that existed between Francis and her parents, his grandparents, and wanted to ensure that their bond remained strong as Francis grew up and her parents grew older. She made the decision to move back home.

To make the journey back to the East Coast more meaningful, Rae decided to homeschool her son and make a road trip out of it. Just after Thanksgiving, they began their journey home in hopes of beating the weather before it got too cold to cross the country. The weather would still be cold in passing, so she made sure to pack warm bundles of clothes they had not been used to wearing in their warm West Coast home for the past five years.

Mile by mile behind them, they were on the home stretch, just a few nights away from home. Usually, Rae and her son would stop at motels to rest for the night, but it was forecasted to snow, and Rae knew she had to start looking for a place to stay for a few nights. As Rae pulled into a gas station to fill her gas tank, she googled *'lodges.'* Instantly, cute towns started to pop up on her search. Out of nowhere, a warm memory struck her, and she recalled that, as a child, there was a mountain town she had visited once. Rae was hoping that the village from her memory was near where she was now. She was just in luck. Rae found a reservation, quickly booked the room, and now had a weekend reservation that would keep her off the roads during the snow that was going to be arriving soon.

Following the route plugged into the navigation system, they arrived at the next town. Rae was captivated by the picturesque scenery and magical atmosphere. That instant warm feeling buzzed through her like electricity. The town of St. Pocono, this little town was inviting and so welcoming. Snow lightly fell as she searched for the lodge. The atmosphere was euphoric and instantly put a smile on both Rae's and her son's faces. Little did they know this stop would be where they made memories that would last a lifetime.

St. Pocono was decked out for Christmas. Rae and her son were even more captivated by the festive atmosphere than anything. There were twinkling lights and festive decorations in every corner of the little town. Everywhere they looked, they could see the spirit of Christmas. Garland and wreaths with the most enormous red bows hung on the lampposts. People smiled and laughed as they shopped for gifts and enjoyed holiday treats. Rae rolled down the car window just a bit to hear the beautiful town's hustle and bustle. The air was filled with the scent of gingerbread and hot cocoa, and the sound of carolers and holiday music filled the streets. The town was alive with magic and a perfect winter wonderland; Rae could instantly feel the joy and kindness in the air.

As she pulled into the lodge and parked her car, Rae took a moment to absorb her surroundings. A beautiful wrap-around porch sat perfectly around the mountain lodge, a grand red velvet chair was being decorated, and sparkling icicle lights hung from the roof, all of which created a breathtaking display. As she led her son Francis towards the lodge, they were met by Logan – a charming man who held the door open for them. Rae was momentarily distracted by the man's warm, brown eyes, which left her feeling both awestruck and flustered. Was it the town's spirit that had her feeling giddy, or was it this perfect stranger before her?

After settling in that evening, she and Francis set out to explore the lodge to see what all the commotion and bustle of the small lodge was about. Rae let Francis sit and play with the other kids in the lodge just as she and Logan crossed paths again. This time, Rae took the opportunity to strike up a conversation with him. Logan was cheerful and kind. She soon found out that Logan was the owner of a local holiday warehouse store, the biggest one for miles around, and he was a Christmas enthusiast. Logan's enthusiasm for Christmas was contagious, and Rae couldn't help but get swept up in it. Rae was momentarily distracted as she saw a familiar face out of the corner of her eye. Blinking her eyes to make sure they were not playing tricks on her, Rae was overjoyed to see Grace, her cousin whom she hadn't realized had moved out of their hometown and into the town of St. Pocono. Grace was always eccentric and artsy in the best way. When she told Rae that she spends all year perfecting the decorations that are hung with care all over the town, it made sense that she was the mastermind behind the lodge's stunning holiday decorations. As Rae and Grace started to catch up excitedly over conversations of time long past, Logan excused himself and went off to finish hanging up the lights on the porch of the lodge.

For nearly an hour, Grace and Rae gleefully chatted away. At that time, Rae discovered that Logan was single. Grace even told Rae that she witnessed Logan light up with such cheerful chatter as he spoke to Rae, something she hadn't seen since his split from his fiancée a few months back. Rae was blushing and happy to know this bit of information. Rae knew that Grace had to return to work, so she set off to explore the lodge more by herself.

Rae wandered, awestruck by the magical Christmas tree in the back courtyard. Not only was it impressive in size, but it was also full of beautiful decorations. The tree was adorned with gorgeous red, green, and white garlands, ribbons, and bows. The gold and silver Christmas ornaments were mesmerizing. It was going to be beautiful once they did the tree lighting ceremony and could see the lights sparkle in the night sky. The sight of it was like a daydream, perfect in every way. The tree's beauty is a testament to the love of Christmas in the town as well as a great showcasing of Grace's creativity and dedication, as she has clearly put a lot of effort into making it as magnificent as possible.

Rae was jolted out of her dreamlike state when she heard a phone ringing. She saw Logan just a few feet in front of her; she must have missed him in her fixated love of the decorations around her. Logan looked as if he was about to say something, but his attention immediately went to the phone ringing in his hand instead. He apologized and excused himself so he could answer it. As a gentle breeze blew, Rae returned to a state of calm, watching the ornaments sway.

Logan came back and seemed a bit flustered from the phone call, but Rae didn't want to pry. He wanted to let Rae know that Santa had arrived and was ready to start his story for the kids on the front side of the wrap-around porch. Francis had followed the other kids and was already out front to see Santa, so Rae quickly made her way to the front of the lodge to be with him.

The sight was like something out of a Christmas movie. Santa was sitting in his grand red velvet chair, surrounded by children, eagerly listening to his story. The porch and front lawn of the lodge were decorated with tinsel, lights, and ornaments. You could smell the outdoor firepits and the sweet scent of marshmallows roasting.

Looking around, Logan was standing near the doorway, watching the excitement from the crowd with a smile on his face. Rae walked over to him and asked if he wanted to join her and her son. He hesitated for a moment but then nodded and followed her to the group.

As Santa finished his story, he asked the children what they wanted for Christmas. Francis eagerly raised his hand and told Santa what he wanted: a train car. Francis was always mesmerized by trains. He would tell his mom that he loved how fast they were, not like cars, and how they seemed to move so effortlessly. Francis did not see many trains on the West Coast and was awestruck every time he saw someone with a train set. Logan nudged Rae and whispered that he had something in his store that Francis might like.

After Santa's story, the children were given a chance to sit on his lap and take a photo. Francis was thrilled to have his picture taken with Santa and even more excited about the prospect of getting Christmas presents in just a few weeks. The night was perfect and came to a close. Rae and Francis said their goodbyes and made plans to see Logan after breakfast so he could show them what he had in his warehouse for Francis. As Rae and Francis went to sleep that evening, they were warmed by the Christmas spirit and the beautiful town of St. Pocono.

The next morning came, and excitement still hung in the air. Logan arrived shortly after breakfast and invited Rae and Francis to his store, which is only a few blocks from the lodge. As they walked, Rae couldn't help but notice the town's charm and its people's kindness. Everyone was present in the moment, waving to one another, laughing, and spreading holiday cheer. As Rae arrived at Logan's store, she couldn't help but notice it was a treasure trove of holiday decorations, ornaments, and gifts. Francis was in awe of the displays and the variety of toys and trinkets. It was just like Santa's workshop!

Logan took them to the back of the store and showed them a train set that he thought Francis would like. Francis was ecstatic and couldn't wait to set it up in the room at the lodge. Logan refused to take any money for the train set, saying it was Francis's Christmas gift.

As they walked back to the lodge, Rae couldn't help but notice Logan texting on his phone and then putting it in his pocket as if he had just received some bad news. Rae and Logan were so new to each other that she didn't even think to ask him for more information. She was captivated by the town and its infectious holiday spirit; nothing seemed like it could ruin her mood.

Back at the lodge, Rae and Logan helped her son set up the train set. While Francis sat and played, Rae sat by the window, watching the snow gently fall outside, and felt content. Logan and Rae found themselves in the flow of conversation, and she was so drawn to him and couldn't deny the attraction that she felt.

As the night wore on, Logan said his goodbyes and left. Rae watched him walk away, feeling conflicted and unsure of what to do next. But one thing was sure - St. Pocono had captured her heart, and she knew she didn't want to leave just yet.

Rae was scheduled to leave town soon but wanted to spend time with her cousin Grace before leaving. Together, they worked on last-minute decoration projects for the big tree-lighting ceremony that evening. Rae was also curious about Logan, so she made sure to ask about him.

Grace had nothing but good things to say. Logan was always known for his kindness, gentle demeanor, and trustworthiness. Grace let Rae know that his previous fiancé left him because she wanted a different kind of life, and he was heartbroken. Despite the heartbreak, Grace could tell how much Logan admired Rae's energy and joy. It was a match that Logan had been dreaming of, and unknowingly, it was a match Rae had been dreaming about as well.

Grace generously invited Rae to stay with her for a few more days as the lodge was booked, and their stay there expired. Grace suggested that Rae explore the town and go on a real date with Logan. Rae was thrilled with the idea and eagerly accepted the offer.

As the Christmas tree lighting came closer, the town was in a buzz, almost in a euphoric state of peace, joy, and love. Rae and Francis made their way to the Christmas tree lighting ceremony.

The anticipation for the tree lighting ceremony grew as the sun began to set. Soon enough, the crowd gathered around the tree, eagerly waiting for the switch to be flipped. The mayor of the town stepped up to the podium, and the crowd erupted in cheers and applause, eager for the ceremony to begin. As the mayor finished his speech, the crowd grew quiet in anticipation. Suddenly, the switch was flipped, and the tree lit up in a rainbow of colors. The sight was breathtaking, with each light twinkling like a star in the night sky.

Logan found his way to Rae. They started talking about their love for the holiday season, and Rae could open up about how much she missed being surrounded by family during the holiday season. They talked about their favorite Christmas movies, and Logan shared the best local places to buy Christmas cookies for her and her son. Rae mentioned how she was staying in town a few more nights with her cousin, which warmed Logan's heart. Just as the ceremony was coming to a close, Logan turned toward Rae and asked her if she would like to go on a date with him. Rae's heart skipped a beat as she looked into his eyes and eagerly accepted his invitation.

Just then, everyone could hear the sound of carolers in the distance. They walked towards the sound and found a choir of children singing classic Christmas carols. It was a magical moment and the perfect way to end the evening and kick off the holiday season.

As everyone said goodnight and goodbye, they headed in different directions, but both Logan and Rae felt a sense of excitement and possibility for what the future might hold. Anything seemed possible with the magic of the holiday season and the promise of a new romance.

The next afternoon at Grace's, Francis was playing with his train, and Rae was waiting in anticipation of her real first time out alone with Logan. Grace had suggested a cozy restaurant nearby that served delicious local cuisine. Rae was excited to try it out and spend more quality time with Logan.

When Logan arrived to pick her up, Rae noticed his warm smile and kind eyes. They chatted on the way to the restaurant, and Rae felt comfortable and at ease with him.

They ordered some of the local specialties at the restaurant and talked about their interests and passions. Rae was impressed by Logan's dedication to his work, the community, and his love for the town. She shared her own experiences as a freelance writer and her passion for traveling, all while missing the comforts of home.

Logan and Rae ended the night with an evening walk around town to see the Christmas lights and decorations. It was a magical experience. The charming streets were filled with the festive spirit of the season, something she couldn't see herself getting tired of. As they walked, their hands gently clasped together, and they held hands as they strolled through the illuminated pathways.

Stopping at a small cafe for some hot cocoa, Rae felt a spark between them that caught her off guard. Looking into Logan's eyes, she realized she was falling for him. The warmth of the cocoa matched the warmth in her heart, and she couldn't wait to spend more time with him.

Upon returning to her cousin's house and getting ready to call it a night, Grace approached Rae in the living room. Grace inquired about Rae's date, but she had some news of her own to share. Living in a small town has its drawbacks, as everyone's business seems to become common knowledge within seconds. Grace revealed that Logan's former fiancée had returned to town that night and was waiting for him at his old place, which they once shared. This news left Rae feeling uneasy. She now questioned her feelings and even thought about getting back on the road to head home, as having someone not ready to commit to her brought back memories from years past.

The next morning, Rae went to grab her morning coffee and, to her surprise, saw Logan and his ex-fiancée at the coffee shop. Feeling embarrassed, Rae turned around quickly, but not before Logan caught sight of her. Shortly after, Logan called and explained that his ex-fiancée had returned unexpectedly despite their break-up. He assured

Rae that nothing had happened between them. In fact, his ex-fiancée left to stay with a friend and was set to leave town that afternoon. Logan and his ex-fiancée agreed to meet at the coffee shop so he could retrieve his keys. Logan was honest about his relationship being over and expressed his desire to move forward. Even though Rae's feelings were hurt, she decided to give Logan another chance and stayed in St. Pocono for a few more days.

The rest of that day, she spent time with her cousin and son. Grace showed her some local museums, and they went to an outdoor ice rink. Grace showed Rae a few scenic trails and suggested that she and Logan go there together as she had two more days planned for her visit. Upon returning to Grace's house, they found a stunning bouquet on the doorstep with a note from Logan, filling Rae's heart with the warmth of the Christmas spirit.

Over the next two days, Rae and Logan continued to see each other. They spent time taking scenic hikes and enjoying the local cafes. They enjoyed chatting away at the lodge the most. As the last magical winter night approached for Rae in St. Pocono, they met up for one last time. Rae strolled through the streets, adorned with twinkling lights, and the sweet smell of chocolate chip cookies filled the air. Soon after, snowflakes began to fall, creating a truly enchanting atmosphere.

When Rae found Logan at the lodge, the snow gently landed on Rae's cheeks as her hand met his, admiring the town's Christmas tree. Logan looked at her with care, and they gazed into each other's eyes. The holiday spirit enveloped them both, and they knew this was the moment they had been waiting for. Slowly, they leaned in, their breaths mingling in the chilly air, until their lips met in a sweet and tender kiss.

The world around them seemed to fade away as they lost themselves in the warmth of each other's embrace. It was a moment they would never forget, a moment of pure magic and joy wrapped up in the holiday spirit of the charming Christmas town.

As they pulled away from each other, their hearts filled with love and happiness. They knew this was just the beginning of a beautiful journey together, one that would be filled with many more magical moments.

As the next morning approached, Logan arrived at Grace's home to say goodbye to Rae and Francis. Although it was a sad goodbye, for now, they know it won't be forever. Logan had plans to travel after Christmas to visit Rae so they could celebrate the New Year together. Rae was comforted, knowing that they would see each other soon. Rae and Francis felt bittersweet as they set off on the final leg of their journey to Rae's hometown. They created unforgettable memories in St. Pocono and the start of something beautiful was just beginning. Rae cannot wait to see what the next chapter has in store.

The End.

About Alicia Thorp

Alicia Thorp is a mom of three, wife, 3x Amazon Best Selling and International Best-Selling Co-Author, lifestyle editor for Girl on Fire Magazine, and a Social Media Marketing Coordinator & works with Adults with Developmental Disabilities.

By learning the essence of life/work/family balance, Alicia has a successful Lifestyle Business where she coaches other moms with her signature program, Dash of Faith, to do the same. You can and should have it all.

Follow her, shop her looks, or get more inspiration on Instagram at www.instagram.com/alicia.thorp/

DM her the word WISH for a free PDF download of the Dash of Faith Success Method.

Christmas on the Cape: A Season for Second Chances

By Roberta A. Pellant

Summer Sparks

On a balmy Fifth of July evening on Cape Cod, amidst friends' laughter and the distant fireworks pops, two souls wandered into a new chapter of their lives. Stefan, a newly single father, had been coaxed into attending the party by friends who insisted he needed to get out more and to shake off the gloom of his recent divorce. Bee, equally resistant to the idea of socializing, found herself at the same gathering through a similar conspiracy of well-meaning friends.

As twilight painted the sky in hues of fading gold and deepening blue, their eyes met across the deck. There was an undeniable charge at first glance, a spark neither could quite comprehend. Perhaps it was the fading sunlight dancing in her eyes or the gentle strength evident in his stance, but something compelled Stefan to move toward her, navigating through the throng of people.

He positioned himself by her side with an almost territorial sense of purpose, effectively shielding her from any other would-be suitors.

Their conversation began tentatively, with the typical pleasantries exchanged between strangers. Yet, as the sky erupted in vibrant colors from the fireworks, a day later than most, so did their dialogue, bursting with shared laughter and candid revelations about their recent painful divorces. The connection was immediate and profound, but both were quick to shield themselves with disclaimers about not being ready to date.

Their meeting seemed destined to be a single page in their stories, a brief chapter of connection before retreating to the solitude they each believed they needed. Yet, the universe had other plans.

As summer waned, Stefan and Bee kept crossing paths. The small-town charm of being on Cape Cod meant their circles overlapped, whether they wished it or not. They found themselves thrown together in benign activities: boating trips with mutual friends, group gatherings on the beach, and casual encounters that slowly chipped away at their resolve to keep their distance. With each meeting, the joy of their newfound friendship blossomed like the hydrangeas lining the Cape's quaint cottages in Maushop.

Their first kiss came unexpectedly after a sun-soaked day trip to Martha's Vineyard. Amidst the quaint shops and cobblestone streets, they found themselves alone, their friends having wandered off. The kiss was a crescendo of all the unspoken tension between them, natural as the tide coming in. But the moment ended as quickly as it began, leaving them both reeling. In the confusion of their abrupt parting, Stefan forgot to ask for her number, and Bee, flustered by the intensity of her feelings, didn't offer it.

Fate, however, refused to let the story end there. After weeks of an aching void filled with thoughts of *'what ifs,'* Stefan found Bee's work email address after a quick Internet search. Their digital correspondence quickly reignited the embers of their connection, and soon, those embers blazed into love. Emails became calls, calls became visits, and the fear of hurt was overshadowed by the joy of falling deeply for one another.

A Cape Cod Conflict

But as the crisp autumn air settled over Cape Cod, so did the reality of Stefan's family dynamics. His two children, still tender from the upheaval of the divorce, clung to the promise their father had made: no new romances. His siblings, protective of the children's feelings, met Bee with a coolness that frosted over the warmth she brought into Stefan's life.

The trouble had begun subtly with Stefan's family. His siblings, protective of their niece and nephew, viewed Bee as an interloper. They had quietly disapproved of Stefan's newfound happiness, fearing it was too soon for the children to understand and accept another woman in their father's life. When Bee wasn't invited to join their Thanksgiving celebration, it was a clear sign of their rejection. To her, it felt like a cold wave had doused the warm embers of their summer romance.

Stefan tried to mend the rift, explaining to his family the light that Bee brought into his life. But his words hit a wall of resistance, his family's worry for his children's well-being acting as a barrier and defense to his requests. The children, young and confused, could feel the tension, and in their innocence, they, too, began to pull away, their laughter dimming.

The rejection stung, opening old wounds of distrust and fear in both Stefan and Bee. The pressure and the pain were too much; they split, their relationship succumbing to the harsh realities of disapproval and broken promises.

With Thanksgiving passing in a blur of tension and unspoken words, the relationship between Stefan and Bee became strained. The festivity of the holiday season couldn't lift the weight of unacceptance that hung over them. Their love, still so young and fragile, was buckling under the pressure.

In a moment of despair, they decided to step back from the brink. It was a mutual decision, heavy with unshed tears and unspoken fears. Stefan dove back into single parenthood, while Bee threw herself into her work, her heart quietly breaking with each Cape Cod sunset she watched alone.

December arrived with its promise of new beginnings, and the magic of Christmas just around the corner. Stefan and Bee, each lost in their own worlds of *'what could have been,'* tried to move forward. Stefan went on a few half-hearted dates, pushed by friends who wanted to see him happy again. Bee, too, accepted the dinner invitations of a few men, but none could ignite the fire in her heart.

During these long, frozen nights, Stefan realized what he had lost. The laughter that filled his home, the brightness that shone in his children's eyes when Bee was around, and the peace he felt in her presence was irreplaceable. It was time to stand up to his family, to thaw the ice with the heat of his conviction. It was time to trust again, not just in love, but in himself and the possibility of a happy future for his children.

Stefan stood on the porch of his weathered Cape-style condo, a structure that had weathered many storms, much like himself. Inside, the laughter of his children echoed, a bittersweet reminder of the joy that had briefly returned to their lives with Bee's presence.

His journey back to Bee would require more than just courage; it would require a grand gesture, a leap of faith fitting of the holiday spirit that was beginning to take hold of Cape Cod. And it would lead him to the moment when Bee, with twinkling lights reflecting the strength of her resolve, would turn the tide of their love story with a Christmas commitment.

Bee, for her part, wandered the chilled beaches alone, her heart as turbulent as the gray Atlantic waves crashing onto the shore. She reminisced about the summer days spent sailing and the evenings wrapped in Stefan's embrace, both now distant memories as the December wind whipped around her.

Cape Cod was quickly transforming into a holiday card scene, with lights twinkling from the houses and the first snowfall dusting the sand dunes in white. The year-rounders wrapped themselves in scarves and mittens, greeting each other with smiles and season's greetings, but for Stefan and Bee, the festive cheer couldn't penetrate the frost around their hearts.

As Christmas approached, Stefan's family planned their annual holiday gathering. It was a tradition that Stefan had always cherished, but this year, the thought filled him with dread. He envisioned the house filled with merriment and music, but Bee's absence would leave a hollow space beside him.

It was a frigid evening when Stefan's resolve began to thaw. His daughter, Megs, climbed onto his lap, her eyes filled with wisdom beyond her years. "Daddy, why doesn't Bee come over anymore? I miss her." Her innocent question was a jolt to his heart, a painful reminder of what they had lost.

The realization hit him like a wave: he missed Bee not just as a lover but as a part of their family. He missed her laughter in his home, her warmth beside him, and the way she had made them all feel complete. He could no longer let the opinions of others dictate the course of his heart.

Christmas was supposed to be a time for love, for family, and for taking chances. Stefan knew what he had to do. He had to fight for their love, to bring back the woman who had unknowingly become his partner in every sense.

The next day, with a determination that surprised even himself, Stefan gathered his siblings together. The snow outside was a soft whisper compared to the fervor in his voice as he spoke of Bee, of their love, and of the happiness she brought not just to him but to his children. He spoke of second chances and the true meaning of family and togetherness during the holidays.

His siblings listened, the walls around their hearts crumbling as the snow continued to fall gently outside. It was the season of miracles, and as they watched their brother, they began to understand the depth of his feelings.

Meanwhile, Bee sat in her teeny apartment, the Christmas lights she'd hung up casting a soft glow against the windowpane. She tried to lose herself in a book, but the words blurred together, meaningless against the backdrop of her longing for the one true love of her life.

It was a simple knock on her door that changed everything. Bee rose, her heart in her throat, and opened the door to find Stefan, his breath misting in the frosty air, his eyes alight with hope.

"Bee," he began, his voice catching with emotion, "I can't promise you every day will be perfect, but I can promise that I will fight for us every day if you let me. My family... they understand how much I love you, and they accept it. Please, come to Christmas dinner. Let's start our forever."

Tears welled in Bee's eyes, her heart soaring as she stepped into his embrace, the cold forgotten. They stood there, under the spell of the twinkling stars and the soft glow of holiday lights, two souls intertwined.

As they prepared to face their future together, Cape Cod lay draped in white, the snow a silent testament to their love rekindled. With its message of hope and love, the holiday season had woven its magic around them, promising a new beginning and a chance for happiness that would outlast even the longest winter.

Their conflict had been a tempest, but as every Cape Codder knows, after the storm always comes the calm. And for Stefan and Bee, the calm had come in the form of a Christmas miracle, their love the greatest gift of all.

The holiday season was now a beacon of their love, a symbol of new beginnings and everlasting warmth amidst the cold. As they prepared for the festivities, with the support of Stefan's family slowly returning, the joy that had once filled their hearts during those summer days found its way back, stronger and more resilient against the cold ocean winds.

The Christmas Commitment

Cape Cod in the waning days of December was a portrait of idyllic winter beauty. The usual golden sands were now a soft ivory, and the expansive ocean, which in summer sparkled under the sun's caress, churned with the deep blues and grays of the winter tide. The holiday season was more than a mere date on the calendar here; it was an embrace that the small coastal communities of the Cape welcomed with open arms and open hearts.

In each window of the weathered shingle homes, wreaths made of ocean-tumbled driftwood and evergreens were hung with care, twinkling with fairy lights as dusk fell each day. The snow, which had been falling in lazy, thick flakes for days, lay undisturbed in places where human footsteps had yet to tread, pristine in its wintry blanket.

For Stefan and Bee, each flake of snow and each burst of chilly air were reminders of the fragility and beauty of starting anew. They found themselves wrapped in the layers of a holiday season that was less about the ribbons and bows and more about the bonds of trust and the hope that love, like the evergreens, could be everlasting.

After the turmoil of their respective divorces, the idea of spending another Christmas alone had seemed inevitable to them both. Yet, fate, with its capricious whims, had other plans. Their journey from a summer spark ignited under fireworks to a deep, if uncertain, affection had been riddled with the potholes of past pains and familial expectations.

Stefan had faced his own share of inner turmoil, having to balance the promises made to the bright-eyed children who looked up to him with the yearning of his heart for Bee's companionship. His exuberance over finding love again was tempered by the promise he'd made to his children, a promise that felt like an anchor as he struggled to reconcile his role as a father with his own needs as a man.

It was a battle waged in silent thoughts and sleepless nights until the moment he chose to share his heart's truth with his family. The initial conversations were fraught with resistance, his siblings skeptical of any new addition to their close-knit circle, wary of any more upheaval that could affect the delicate balance of the family, especially the children.

But love has a way of seeping through the smallest of cracks, and Stefan's unwavering belief in Bee began to soften the hardest of hearts. In time, the staunchest of opponents in his family started to see the light that Bee brought into Stefan's life, a light that was gentle and healing.

Their walk on the beach that brisk week before Christmas was filled with introspection and the muted sounds of a world hushed by snow. They strolled side by side, sharing the comfort of their joined hands as the ocean laid out before them in its wintry splendor. The cold was sharp but exhilarating, and as they reached the snow-frosted pier, a blanket of tranquility enveloped them.

Bee, who had always found solace in the steady lapping of the waves against the shore, felt a kinship with the relentless sea – both of them had witnessed storms but stood steadfast. She turned to Stefan, her eyes clear and certain, even if her heart was a tumult of emotion. She'd come to realize that the sum of all her fears paled in comparison to the possibility of losing what they had found in each other.

"Stefan," she began, her voice barely above the whisper of the ocean wind, "I never imagined I could find this... with you. That I could feel... whole again."

Stefan, his cheeks reddened from the cold, smiled at her with a tenderness that spoke volumes. "Bee, I've stumbled through darker days, each one a step toward you. Without knowing it, you've been the beacon guiding me home."

There, on that frozen pier with the Atlantic whispering their backdrop, they shared words of commitment and love, the kind of love that was not loud and flamboyant but quiet and steadfast. It was a promise made not under the traditional mistletoe but under the vast expanse of a December sky, a vow as infinite as the stars that began to peek through the velvety night.

"I want to be with you through every season, every trial. I want to wake up every Christmas morning knowing you're by my side," Stefan confessed, his words hanging in the frosty air, crystalline and sincere.

Bee's heart swelled, the walls she'd built over the years crumbling in the wake of his earnest declaration. "And I want to be there, Stefan. To be the one you share your hopes and fears with, the one who stands with you when the world seems too much to bear alone."

Their kiss was a seal on the silent covenant they made to each other, a kiss that spoke of past sorrows and future joys. It was a moment marked not by fanfare but by the profound understanding that they were embarking on a life journey together, a journey neither of them had planned but both desperately wanted.

In the days leading up to Christmas, the mood in Stefan's home transformed. His family, once reluctant, now extended open invitations to Bee, including her in holiday traditions and family gatherings. The change was not instantaneous but grew day by day as they witnessed the authenticity of Stefan and Bee's feelings for one another.

The children, ever the barometer of truth, accepted Bee with the uncomplicated love that only children can offer. They included her in their games, asked for her help hanging their stockings, and shared the innocent magic of their Christmas excitement. Bee's presence became interwoven with the tapestry of their lives, her laughter and kindness enriching the already festive atmosphere.

Christmas Eve dawned, a canvas of pearl-gray skies and gentle snow that seemed to cleanse the world in anticipation of the night's joy. The house was filled with the scent of pine and the sounds of merriment as family and friends gathered, drawn by the warmth of the hearth and the promise of companionship.

Stefan and Bee moved among their guests, their happiness a tangible thing that seemed to light the room brighter than any bulb. They found moments of quiet amidst the chaos and shared glances that said everything words could not. As they stood hand in hand, heralding the arrival of Christmas Day, they understood that the true meaning of the holiday was found in the love they shared and the blended family they were creating together.

The Christmas of that year would forever be etched in their memories as the beginning of a new chapter. And as they stood, surrounded by the people they cherished beneath the gentle glow of the moonlight on the snow outside, they knew that every future Christmas would be a milestone, a marker of the life they had chosen to build together on the shores of Cape Cod.

The End.

About Roberta A. Pellant

Dr. Roberta A. Pellant is an MBA Professor, Consultant, 7x Entrepreneur, #1 International Best-Selling Author, Keynote and TEDx Speaker. She is a certified professional development trainer and is sought after for her executive leadership coaching. She was Vice President of Knowledge and Communications at US Capital Global, a corporate finance company, and former owner of BumBoosa© Bamboo Products, before it was acquired. She has been featured in Wall Street Select, Yahoo! Finance, Market Watch, and International Business, and on ABC Chronicle. She is considered a top business expert across several industries and works with women entrepreneurs to increase their month over month revenue with a proven 9 step framework and Mastering Business $uccess program.

Learn more at: www.robertapellant.com

Diamond Haven

By Magnolia Tiberii

"AHHHHHH!!!!" I heard a loud shriek coming from my employee's mouth.

Running out of my office, nervous to see what awaited me, I asked Emily what happened.

"Sorry! Sorry! I didn't mean to scare you, Gia; it's just that the Christmas decorations have finally arrived!"

Laughing, I agreed with her, "It's fine, Emily; I get the same excitement this time of year."

"Being able to see the Christmas decorations firsthand is the main reason I took this job, right, Gia?"

"I figured! But I am so glad you did; I don't know what I would do without my best worker and best friend!"

I opened Gia's Decor about three months ago. I have been an interior designer for about five years now. Opening a decor and furniture store has always been a dream of mine, and seeing it finally come together is the best Christmas gift I could ever receive. Since I opened not too long ago, I don't have the ability to have as many employees as I would want; that's why my best friend Emily has been a God send, helping me get the store all together. Plus, she shares my love for Christmas, which is always a plus. Living in New York City, if you want to keep your business open, you must go big or go home during Christmas. Everywhere you turn on the streets of New York, it looks like Christmas has thrown up.

"So! Should we start displaying it?" Emily says with her huge blue eyes bulging out.

"I don't know, Emily; it's already 6:10. Maybe we should start tomorrow morning?"

"Oh, c'mon, Ebenezer Scrooge! We closed ten minutes ago, no one is going to be in the store; it's the perfect time to sprawl out and get to work! C'mon, we can order Chinese food and play Christmas music...I know you want to...."

"Fine! But only because you called me Ebenezer Scrooge, which is the most insulting thing I have ever heard!"

"Great! I'm glad you came to your senses, Mrs. Clause."

Laughter came out of me, "Much better, Emily. Ugh. Where do we even begin?"

Emily and I are staring at what used to be our marble-tiled floor, now covered with every Christmas decoration you could imagine. Lights. Christmas Trees. Throw pillows. Ornaments. Garland. Sparkles, lots and lots of sparkles.

"Okay, well, I'm going to start by putting the wreaths on our front doors. How about we start from the beginning of the store to the end?"

"This is why I hired you, Emily, the brains of the operation! Perfect, you do that, and I'll work on stocking our shelves with some ornaments. That way, I can get being on a ladder out of the way. You know me with heights!"

"Oh, do I ever; Gia and heights were never friends! See you soon. Wish me luck trying to get these wreaths up with all this snow on our front step."

Ughhhh...Why did I have to be so afraid of heights? I never understood how people are completely fine with getting on ladders. I'll just try to focus on all these pretty ornaments we got in. As I fill our shelves, I am reminded of my childhood when I come across one specific ornament; there's only one of them. It's a red angel with a slot in it that can be filled with a picture. I used to have one just like it when I was little, and in it was a photo of me and my mom. When we moved to a different house when I was 17, we lost the ornament because I never found it again. My mom passed away last year. Another reason why I really wanted to open up Gia's Decor. She and I used to talk about this dream of mine for so long. If only she was here to see it happen with me. I continue filling the shelves and trying to ignore memories, so Emily doesn't catch me crying when she returns from hanging the wreaths outside.

DING DING DING DING DING

"Ugh, Emily, that's right, we keep forgetting to have someone fix that doorbell. Whenever someone comes in, it rings like a hundred times," I explain, my back facing the doors.

"It's so annoying it sounds like an alarm clock!"

"Emily?"

Hmm. Why isn't she answering me? I turn to face the doors hesitantly, trying to still keep my balance on the ladder.

Woahhhh, oh boy, oh boy...HELP!

In seconds, I am off the ladder and into Emily's arms.

Wait, these arms feel quite muscular to be Emily.

I turn and lock eyes with someone who looks nothing like Emily.

Jet black hair with an ever so slight curl, a full tight beard, a nose that I thought only existed on perfect sculptures, he's about 6 feet, broad and burly. He is wearing a long black peacoat with a burgundy cashmere scarf. The only thing this man and Emily have in common is their big, icy-blue eyes.

Oh! That's right, Emily ordered us Chinese food. I've never seen a delivery driver this handsome before, I think to myself.

Barely getting my words out, I say, "Hi! Oh gosh, I'm so sorry. Thank you for catching me. I'm pretty clumsy when it comes to being on ladders, ha-ha! Give me one second. I'll go get my wallet so I can pay you!"

"Okay, so how much do I owe you?"

"Man, you Americans are funny. Do you always pay your customers looking for help?"

"I'm sorry? Are you not the food delivery guy?"

He was chuckling, "Apparently, you Americans assume, too. What? Just because I look Italian, you think I have food with me?"

"No no! Oh gosh, I am so sorry. See, my friend and I are getting our store together for Christmas, and see, well, since we are closed and will probably be here all night, she ordered Chinese food for us.. And.. well... yeah, I'm so so sorry if I've offended you."

"Offended me? Sweet-a-heart, please don't apologize. I am here for help. I was wondering if I could talk to the owner or someone in charge to help me. I am from Italy and just moved here for a few weeks while completing a work project."

I'm sweating. Did he just call me sweetheart? Excuse me, he actually called me "sweet-a-heart" with his endearing Italian accent. Stumbling to find my words, "Oh yes of course!" I stick out my hand for a shake. "I'm the owner! I'm Gia. So, what exactly do you need help with?"

Ah. Gia. You must have some Italian heritage down the line.

I bashfully giggle, "Well, yes, actually I do! How did you know? My mom was Italian."

"Well, your dark curly hair, olive skin tone, and big brown eyes helped, but I also have about ten cousins named Gia."

He's noticing my features. I stop myself before I start to drool. Ahem.

"So, what exactly were you looking for help with? Umm..."

"Milo. Sorry, I am not good at remembering American customs; my name is Milo. Well, like I said, I just moved here. I will be here in New York for about two months. I'm an architect, and I am working on the hotel we just built about a block away. Since I've noticed you are very hated in New York if you don't decorate for Christmas, I was looking to hire an interior designer to help me decorate the hotel for the season."

I gulp deeply, where the heck is Emily. I need her here to help me get words out of my mouth.

"Yes, of course! Well, I am the interior designer here, so I will be the one helping you with the project. I can take your information now, and we can get started!"

"Actually, I have already taken too much of your time. I notice you are closed, and I don't-a want to keep you here longer than you have to be; your husband is probably getting worried."

"Oh, no worries, no husband to get home too, haha," I say, imagining how red my cheeks are.

"Well, in that case, how about we meet tomorrow for dinner to exchange ideas?"

"Sure! I'd be happy to, how about Carmine's? 7:00? It's an Italian restaurant, so hopefully, it reminds you a bit of home."

"I like a woman who takes charge," he says as his one eyebrow raises ever so slightly, and he squints at me with his piercing blue eyes. "I will be there. Ciao signora."

He walks toward the door and glances back at me over his shoulder before returning to the blistering cold.

I try to find my breath again once he leaves. This was the last thing I was expecting tonight.

DING DING DING DING DING.

"Brrrrr. We have got to get that doorbell fixed!"

"Yeah no kidding! Emily! Where have you been? You'll never believe what just happened."

"Ugh, well, the lights on the wreaths weren't working, so I had to take them down the block to borrow batteries from Mr. Jenson and…"

"Okay, okay, okay, yeah, that's great. GUESS WHAT JUST HAPPENED? So, I was up on the ladder putting away the ornaments and…" my voice trailed on to recount the whole incident.

That night, Emily and I talked about Milo as we finished up the entire store. At midnight, we had our Christmas wonderland all complete.

"So! Do you think he'll make a move on you tonight??"

"Emily!! It's just dinner, and we are discussing how to decorate his hotel for Christmas." I roll my eyes at her and look at my closet.

"Sureee… that's why you have been taking an hour to figure out what you are going to wear! Look at you. I've never seen you blush so hard!"

"Trust me, that man can make anyone blush. Emily, you should see his eyes," I say, flopping onto my back on my bed and staring at the ceiling.

"He better kiss you tonight."

I pull up to Carmine's with butterflies in my stomach, keeping my eyes wide open at the passenger window, searching for a dark, handsome Italian man.

Knock knock knock

Startled, I look out my window to find Milo and his gorgeous white smile.

"Ciao Bella! I am ready to taste this want-a-be Italian food!"

I laugh as he opens my door and guides my hand out of the car.

"Wow, you do that dress a favor," he says with a smirk.

I smile inside, excited to tell Emily that we chose the right dress when we picked this gray sequin dress with feathers at the bottom of my sleeves.

We sit at a secluded table right by the window, joined by candlelight and roses on the table. It isn't snowing tonight, but there are so many stars out, and the air is crisp.

"So, Gia, I need your help making my hotel look like Christmas City. I really want all the guests to be speechless when they enter my hotel. I am only good at constructing buildings, not decorating them, so when I saw your store near me, I thought you'd be perfect for the job. I am going to be completely transparent with you: building this hotel in America, in New York City, has been challenging. It's been quite expensive, so I will have a tight budget. I am hoping that's something you can work with?"

"Yes of course! I work with tight budgets all the time; that's no problem at all." I take a sip of my wine, trying to relax enough so I can talk to this stunning man.

"I was going to mention that as my friend Emily and I were taking inventory earlier today, we realized we had a lot of extra Christmas decorations. There are ones that we really don't have enough room to put on our floor, so I was going to suggest we could use some of that for your hotel! Or even your apartment; I know you said you'll be living there for about two months, so it might be nice to have a little Christmas spirit in your own home."

"That-a won't be necessary, Gia; I appreciate it, but just the hotel."

"Oh c'mon! It'll be fun, plus I have so much extra stuff I have nowhere to go with it, please, you have to take some for your home."

Suddenly, there is a shift in energy when Milo's face drops, and what was once a bright white smile now looks like he is trying to bite his tongue from saying something he wanted to.

"I'm sorry if I crossed a line; I just figured its free decorations taking up space at my store, so…"

"Please, Gia, you don't have to apologize. I really appreciate the offer, but how about we just stick to the hotel for now, eh?"

I shake my head in agreeance but can't help but wonder what I did wrong.

The rest of the evening was a dream. We got many appetizers to split and shared our meals; we talked and talked for hours until the restaurant was closing and had to kick us out.

As Milo walked me to my car, he leaned his hand against my door as he began to explain,

"Look, Gia, I just wanted to apologize for before; you had no reason to apologize; you are just a sweet-a-heart..."

Ugh, there he goes again with that word.

"And well, the truth is I don't want any Christmas decorations at my apartment because I am not really a big fan of Christmas. You see, growing up, we moved a lot and were never in one house for longer than three or four months. Every Christmas, we were trying to get settled into a new home, and I would think about how by the time the next Christmas rolled around, we probably would be in a new house again. Christmas is that reminder of never having a place to truly call home. So yeah, I am sorry if I came across as rude or ungrateful; that wasn't my intention, G."

I should be responding to his heartfelt explanation, but I can only think about how already has a nickname for me, G.

I gather myself and respond, "Milo, it's all good; I'm so sorry to hear that, especially because I have had the opposite experience with Christmas. Christmas is my absolute favorite time of year, and every Christmas is so special to me and flooded with memories. It makes me sad to think you've never had that. I'm so sorry if I brought up painful memories."

"You have been nothing but caring and patient G. Hey, listen, I will stop by the store tomorrow so we can go through some of those Christmas decorations for the hotel."

"Sounds Great, Milo."

He is staring at me intensely like he's looking through my soul with his eyes. His hand is still leaning up against my car, trapping me, but not where I feel unsafe; quite the opposite, I feel incredibly safe entrapped in his burly arms. He leans in closer and closer.

I can't believe Emily was right, I think to myself.

"MISS! MISS!"

You've got to be kidding me. Milo backed away to run to the waiter, calling my attention to give me the leftover food I had forgotten on the table. Ugh, stupid Gia, you probably won't even wind up eating the leftovers! I wanted that kiss.

After our waiter interrupted the moment, Milo and I hugged, said our goodbyes and separated ways. The rest of the night, I kept thinking about seeing him again. I thought about how he opened up about his childhood and how much I was beginning to fall for him.

DING DING

We finally fixed our doorbell, so now it only dings a normal amount when someone walks through our door. I have been looking up all day at the door, waiting for Milo to come in, but so far, it's just been regular customers.

DING DING

Milo?

Ugh. No, just some old man.

I walk into the back room to prepare some decorations for when Milo arrives.

A few moments later, hands that smell like cigarettes and cologne cover my eyes.

"Good evening, G," I hear in a low and raspy voice. Finally. Milo.

I squeeze him and feel like a teenager again, giddy to see him.

"So, I have some good and bad news. I have to travel to The Catskill Mountains, about two and a half hours away, to meet a co-worker helping me with the hotel this weekend. The good news is…I can bring a guest, and I was wondering if you'd care to join me?"

Next thing I know, I'm packing my warmest clothes to go to the mountains with Milo.

About three hours later, we made it to the Catskill Mountains; there was a little bit of traffic but nothing terrible. It is absolutely beautiful here and the perfect getaway from the city. Our deck balcony overlooks the snowy mountains, and the snow acts as a barrier to any outside sounds. It feels like Milo and I are the only ones on this earth.

Milo hands me a glass of wine as we sit on the deck, staring at unblemished scenery.

RING RING

"Hey Milo!"

"Ciao Giuseppe!"

"Listen, I'm so sorry to do this to you; I'm sure you already made it to the Catskills, but unfortunately, I have a family emergency and won't be able to help you with your hotel this weekend. Is it possible for us to reschedule? Again, I'm so sorry, Milo. I feel terrible!"

"No worries, Giuseppe, it gives me an excuse to come back to the mountains. I hope all goes well with your family, talk soon."

"I knew I could count on you, Grazie Milo."

CLICK

"Well, G, I'm yours for the whole weekend. That was my co-worker Giuseppe; he has a family emergency and can't make it this weekend. So that just leaves me and you. I guess I could call around and see what activities there are to do here?"

"Ugh, that stinks; I hope Giuseppe's family are okay. Hmmm. Actually, calling around won't be necessary. I have a few ideas myself!"

"Ohhhhh really? And just what may that be?"

"Okay, Milo, hear me out. Before you get too upset, I've been thinking..."

"Yes... I'm listening."

"Well, I know you said you're not much of a Christmas person, but you talking about your childhood made me think of mine. See, my mom just passed away last year, and well, she always knew how to make Christmas special. We did every Christmas spirit activity you can possibly think of! We baked cookies, watched our favorite Christmas movies, ice skating, gingerbread houses, you name it, we did it! It wasn't the activities that made it special, though; it was the love and the memories with whom we did it. Anyway, I think that's why Christmas has always been so special to me, and knowing that you've never had that upsets me. Sooo... my proposition is that you give me just this one weekend to show you what Christmas is all about. And if you hate it, we never have to do it again! Just give me this one chance, pleasseee..."

"Question. Do we get to eat the cookies?"

"Haha, yes, of course! That's the best part."

"Then you have a deal, Miss Gia."

"Good morning, Milo! Time to get our Christmas on!!"

"Oh gosh, what did I get myself into?"

"C'mon! Wakey wakey! First on our list is ice skating!"

"Sweet-a-heart, Italians weren't made to be on the ice."

...

That Saturday, we spent the day ice skating, baking cookies, and building a snowman. All of which Milo was surprisingly good at. I've never felt like I've known someone for so long when I've only known him for about a month.

"Amore! This is a waste of food. Why are we putting a perfectly good carrot on a snowman?"

"Haha, Milo! Its tradition, you have to!"

"Oh, mamma mia. This is a sin. Here I go."

"Yay!! Our snowman is complete! C'mon, you have to admit that's a pretty good-looking snowman."

"Yeah, yeah, yeah, he is pretty good looking," Milo says as he stares deeply into my eyes, making me blush.

"Ahem, let's go inside! Now it's time to decorate the tree with, of course, some hot chocolate."

Milo lit one of the most perfect fires in the fireplace. We made hot chocolate and completed our tree. All that's left now is the tree topper!

I climb the ladder and begin to top our tree with the most beautiful gold star.

"Hey, Milo, do you mind looking for more strands of lights? There's one strand on here that seems to be out."

"Sure thing, G. I'll go see what I can find," says Milo as he walks away.

WOAH WOAH! NOT AGAINNN! HELP!!

Suddenly, I am wobbling off the ladder, and I fall into Milo's arms again, only this time I know who it is. It certainly isn't Emily, and it certainly isn't the Chinese food delivery guy; it's the man I am deeply falling for.

Literally and figuratively.

"We have to stop meeting like this, G," Milo says as I am scooped into his arms, and he looks down at me.

I swear Milo's piercing blue eyes are staring straight through me. This time, I can't seem to look away. He brushes away a curly piece of hair out of my eyes and keeps his eyes locked in on mine.

"G, I just want to tell you this has been the best weekend of my life. And you were right, Christmas isn't all that bad. Thank you for showing me joy lies within the memories you create with the people you love. And that's you. I love you, G."

He glances at my lips, then back into my eyes, then back onto my lips, and kisses me, just like you would expect an Italian man to kiss.

Afterward, I manage to get the words out, "I love you too," and we go back to continuing our Christmas-filled weekend.

The next day, we did some more Christmas-filled activities but mostly talked about how to make Milo's hotel unique and how to perfectly decorate it for Christmas. The grand opening is in a week already. We talked till three in the morning. We talked about Christmas of course. We talked about life, our childhoods, our fears, our loves, and our memories. It was perfect. This weekend has been perfect. He is perfect.

On our car ride home, I notice Milo being quieter than usual. I ask him if everything is alright, but he responds with a subtle shrug and says, "I just have a lot on my mind with the hotel opening soon."

My overthinking kicks in, and I can't help but think he isn't telling me something. The rest of the car ride is quiet. We listen to some music, but the majority of the time, I just sit in the passenger seat, watching the scenery go by. A few hours later, we have made it back to the city. Milo drops me off at my apartment first. He gets the door for me and heads to the trunk to get my luggage. As I fumble for my keys to get into my apartment, my stomach is gnawing as if someone gutted it out like a pumpkin.

He gets the door for me and walks me up the stairs to my apartment.

"Milo I…"

"Listen, Gia, something is going on. This weekend was perfect; honestly, you showed me what I thought no one could. You gave me a new love for Christmas and created new memories. I loved every second, and I'll never be able to thank you enough for it."

I sigh, hoping there isn't a "but" coming soon.

"But,"

Ugh. There it is.

"But Gia, I'm not sure it was enough for me. I've always been on the run, moving from place to place. It's what I am used to and what I am good at. My two months is almost coming to an end here, and I don't think I can stay. I'm going to have to move back to Italy. I'm sorry, G. I just can't do this. Here, with you, staying in one place."

My heart has sunk. I try to bite my lip as hard as I can so that I don't cry as I make my way up to his eyes. I take a deep breath and get out the words I don't want to say but know I need to.

"It's okay, Milo, I understand. It must be hard to live a different way when you've been like this for most of your life. Thank you for this time spent together and for letting me join you on this project."

I pick up my bags and try to get in my apartment as quickly as possible.

He looks at me one last time and says, "Gia, I would really love it if you still came to the grand opening. You were every bit of this project as I was. I still want you there."

"I'll be there." I promised as I disappeared into my apartment.

Today is the grand opening. I go back and forth in my head, "Should I go? Should I not go?"

It's the right thing to do. I have to go.

I put on this long red dress with a long bow in the back, hoping it'll make me feel better and make this night go easier.

When I pull up to the hotel, I see the big sign at the entrance covered in cloth as we await the name reveal. Milo is standing in the front of the hotel, greeting everyone as I try to hide in the crowd.

As everyone settles in, Milo announces he will be revealing the name now. He climbs a ladder and whisps the cloth covering the words

"DIAMOND HAVEN." As he is up on the ladder, I can no longer hide within the crowd. We lock eyes. I thought I could do this. But I can't. The moment he locks eyes with me, I want to hide again. As everyone claps and admires the hotel, snow begins to fall, and it is the perfect chance for me to get away.

I start running in the snow with my big red bow trailing behind me as I try to find my way to the car.

"G! G! Please, Gia, wait up!"

Ugh. I almost reached the car when I heard Milo calling my name. I don't want to stop, but I do.

As the noise of panting gets closer, I start to feel bad and wait for Milo to catch up to me.

"G. Please. I need to talk to you. I messed up, okay. I got scared and wanted to flee. This whole time, G, I've been trying to figure out what to name my hotel. Everything has been going perfectly except the name of it. And last night, Diamond Haven hit me."

"Milo, please, I should get home, and you should enjoy the grand opening."

"No Gia, please just let me get this out. I named it Diamond Haven because of you. All my life, I wanted a place to call home, to have a haven. But for me, that was rare, as rare as a diamond. But you, G, coming here to New York, finding you, and having that weekend with you. You feel like home, Gia. You are home. And you are so rare. Please forgive me; there's nowhere else I'd rather go than be here with you. Before you say anything, I have something for you."

I unwrap this beautiful dark green wrapping paper to find an ornament. A red angel with a slot for a picture in it. Just like the one I had when I was a little girl. The one with the picture of me and my mom. Instead, this time it had a picture of me and Milo. Tears come streaming down my face.

He gently brushes his hand against my face and kisses me as the snow falls around us.

"Welcome home, Milo."

The End.

About Magnolia Tiberii

Magnolia runs her own interior design business. She works virtually, helping people all over the United States create their dream home. Magnolia graduated from the New York Institute of Art & Design. She has also had the opportunity to write in another collaboration book as well as is in the midst of her own solo book! On her days off, you can find her enjoying her hobbies, such as painting, reading, enjoying the outdoors, and spending time with her family! Magnolia's favorite place to be is anywhere on a beach, and fitting enough for this book, her absolute favorite holiday is Christmas! Magnolia is also a huge mental health advocate and hopes she can do her part to be a friend to anyone she comes across paths with!

You can connect with Magnolia on Instagram: @magnolia.designinc

Christman with Blueberry Girl

By Lisa Stamey

Violet's Pov

Violet and the hotel owner stand together overlooking the damage to *The Cybill*, the historic 10-room beachfront art deco hotel that was one of the first hotels built on Miami Beach. The owner says, "I can't believe all the damage Hurricane Aiden has done, and the insurance is likely unwilling to give us enough to restore it to its original wonder. As a family, we will think about whether we want to rebuild no matter what, or do we tear down and build something new or just sell the land? So, Violet, please tell the staff that we will pay everyone to enjoy the holidays with their families while we decide the next steps."

Voilet sends an e-mail to the staff:

Hi Team: You have paid time off through the beginning of the year. Please enjoy your time with your families, stay safe, and look for any e-mail around Christmas regarding the next steps.

Due to the hurricane, the owners of her rented carriage house have decided to sell, and they got a cash offer on the first day, so they need to break her lease. She is sad to be losing these fabulous Miami Beach views. Lucky for her, her parents have just as lovely beach views at their home on the beach in Edgewater. It's a small community on the

Georgia coast, so she will go there and wait to see what her next steps are. It is not the fast-paced beach of Miami, but the smell of the marsh and the giant live oaks with all the Spanish moss are home no matter how long she has been away.

Violet's parents are so excited that she is coming home and hope she will help with the hardware store they would like her to take over so they can retire. Still, they have yet to tell her this lovely new surprise. They keep telling each other they will talk to her when the time is right.

Oliver's Pov

Oliver is sitting at the harbor club discussing the last of the details for the sale of his app called Viewfinder; the new owners are noticing that he has brought them a fabulous view to conclude the purchase of his company. Oliver says it feels only suitable to sell with this fantastic view; that is how he got the inspiration for the app all those years ago. The app helps you crop out to get a perfect memory and auto-tag the location of anyone you have a saved picture of on your phone. So, while giving the world an ideal view, you stay more in the moment with the people you are within the photo. Oliver's parents are leaving for their month-long cruise at Thanksgiving. Oliver has been talking to Aunt Laura, and she has finally convinced him to come home for Christmas since he no longer has work as an excuse. He was unsure if he was sad to leave Northern California, but he is sure he'll return by the New Year. His life is in California.

Oliver's parents were both schoolteachers, just like Aunt Laura, who had been enjoying their retirement up at the lake house for the past couple of years, and Aunt Laura had been visiting them more now that they've been coming to Edgewater. Aunt Laura passed away just after Thanksgiving, forcing Oliver's parents to communicate via Facetime with him since they were on a cruise to Australia. Since, they'll be home in time for Christmas, they all have agreed to plan a Celebration of Life Party on Christmas Eve, when they come home to Edgewater. Oliver just needs to ask around who can help put it together.

Aunt Laura was the most beloved schoolteacher and a person who was always willing to lend a hand. She delivered one of her famous pies to the Diner and checked in on Bill before she passed away, enjoying the ocean view from her porch. Bill, who owned the Diner, had gotten Laura's recipe for the pie years ago, but he loved it when she brought one in that she had made herself. Somehow, they always tasted a little extra special. Bill and Laura had a secret crush on each other in high school, but he went off to college and met Tracy. They had built a great family together. They moved home once Tracy had become sick with cancer. Laura had been a great friend to the family for years and was like a second grandmother to Bill's grandkids.

Violet's Pov

Violet had moved back and got settled into the home at Edgewater during early November. Surviving Thanksgiving; she was now starting to miss the fast-paced life of Miami. Everyone that she knew was married in the small town. Her parents are starting to wonder if she will leave and head off to another big city if the hotel in Miami decides not to reopen. She's been posting a ton more on Viewfinder, trying to impress her old friends that her life is super exciting here in Edgewater. Only the perfect food, outfit, hair, or view would be good enough.

Oliver's Pov

From the will, Oliver knows he has inherited Aunt Laura's beach cottage, 50% of the boat, and part of her 1st Love Blueberry company. As Oliver drives into town, he sees the Diner and wants a familiar home-cooked meal. Bill sat in the corner at the family table, helping his granddaughter with her math homework. His daughter Katie is working behind the counter. Oliver is greeting with people giving him huge hugs, telling him how sorry they are that Aunt Laura is gone, and how much she has meant to all of them. Oliver tells Katie this is the best meatloaf and mashed potatoes he has had in a long time; West Coast home cooking differs from the South. Katie insists that he takes a piece of the blueberry pie home and have it later.

Violet is sitting at one of the tables right behind the counter. She's so busy trying to find the best angle to take her selfie with her pie that she doesn't realize she's pushed her chair into the walkway. Just as Violet hits post on Viewfinder, Oliver turns around and bumps into her chair, sending his blueberry pie all over her and her white silk blouse.

Oliver thought: *'These tourists needed to live in the moment, not on their phones.'*

Violet's first thought: *'Who does that guy think he is? He did not even say he was sorry.'*

Violet is so flustered that she doesn't realize it was posted as a video before she closes her phone.

They both head to get into their cars and thinking: *'Thank god this night is over. I'm just gonna go home.'*

They arrive home at the same time, pulling into their driveways that are right next to each other. The only thing between them is Aunt Laura's HUGE blueberry bushes. Neither one notices the other; they look at their phones as they walk in the house because their Viewfinder app is going crazy. When they get inside, they realize the video of their earlier accident has gone viral.

Oliver's Pov

Since Oliver founded Viewfinder, he has had many followers on his page – *1stview*. Oliver's brain is still in CEO mode, so he starts stressing over how he will deal with this PR situation and who is *VIVI9090*?

Violet's Pov

Violet is so embarrassed that she wants to just crawl into a hole but is glad only her Miami friends know she is VIVI9090. Back home in Edgewater, she is known as Lottie, so she has another account that her family and friends follow, LottieEW. For the next few days, she stays around the house, or when she goes out, she wears a baseball cap and jeans like in high school. Hoping the disguise is enough for none of the Edgewater friends to recognize her from the video. The idea that the person at the dinner was a tourist that was working for her.

Oliver's Pov

Oliver is so busy working at Aunt Laura's house. If he sells it, he needs to up the curb appeal. He doesn't think about who VIVI9090 is but has noticed Lottie next door and thinks she looks just as down as she always did in high school. Is she dating anyone? Plus, he needs to connect with the CEO of 1st LOVE Blueberry to see what they want to do about the boat; he knows he can run the company from anywhere.

Oliver and his childhood friend, Sam, agree to meet for dinner at the coffee shop at the pier. Sam tells Oliver you have got to try the turkey sandwich with the blueberry jam; it is a Charlie special, and all the locals know to ask for it. Charlie explains that when he first moved to town, some locals needed to be sure of his extensive city menu, and he was having difficulty getting business. Then Aunt Laura brought him some for her blueberry jam and told him to play around with it. She also told him she would come twice a week and always bring a friend. "I was still busy even after the season was over," Charlie bragged. Charlie continued to explain, that first Thanksgiving, he decided to host Aunt Laura and some of her friends. "I added cranberry sauce and served your grandmother's blueberry jam instead of cranberry; it was a huge hit. This sandwich is a nod to that night when your Aunt Laura got me some of my most loyal customers; some come over twice a week just for this sandwich." Charlie was beaming as his re-created the story for Oliver. Sam says I must be your best customer because I come in daily.

Over lunch, Sam tells Oliver that he is the CEO of 1st LOVE blueberry syrup company, and they are employee-owned, with Oliver's Aunt Laura controlling 50% with 1st LOVE blueberry company. Oliver says well, I inherited 1st LOVE Blueberry company with 1st Blueberry Girl. All Sam knows about 1st Blueberry Girl is that she was to learn she was 1st Blueberry Girl this Christmas. If she could identify the three unique ingredients, she would get her part of the company.

Violet's Pov

Violet is covering for her parents one day at the hardware store when Oliver walks in to get supplies. Oliver was telling Violet how he feel like her when Aunt Laura busted her under the blueberry bush eating blueberries in her younger years. "I've eaten so many blueberries since I've been at her house. That's all she has in her freezer, but they still don't taste as good as when she would make them for us," Oliver laughed. Violet feels a tad terrible about the viral video, so she grabs some jars of 1st LOVE muffin mix and reminds him he just needs to add fresh fruit. Oliver asks Violet if she knows who made the muffin mix? Violet does not but promises to ask her parents. When she asked her parents at dinner that night.; they told her it was a former student of Ms. Laura next door and Anna, who lives near the marina in the yellow house.

Oliver's Pov

Violet and Oliver meet outside in the morning and Violet suggest they go over the marina she had gotten a lead that they needed to follow up with there.

173

Oliver has not been over to the marina since his parents sold the casino boat to Aunt Laura so that they could build a cabin and retire. Oliver has mixed feelings about the boat. He was home during the school year, but never had friends come over because it was weird to have your friends see how tight money was in the off-season. They had to sleep in the small cabin at the bottom of the boat because the money they made during the season was for retirement and Oliver's college fund. Oliver loved the summers when he got to live with Aunt Laura. He went every summer since he was underage to legally be on the boat when it was officially a casino. He kept himself so busy during the school year he just was there to sleep. Just hanging out with friends just happens at Aunt Laura's. When they got to the yellow house, Oliver recognized the home of David, who always repaired the boat for his parents. Anna was his granddaughter.

Aunt Laura and his parents were retiring, and with no parents and two siblings, Anna's family was going to need the extra money now that the casino boat was not going to be running. Aunt Laura paid David to maintain the boat, and Anna used the ticket booth rent-free now as the shop to make the muffin mix. Violet and Oliver went over to the shop to chat with Anna. She explained that she was unsure why, but Aunt Laura said she called her 2nd blueberry girl. Ms. Laura had taught her how to design the mix and helped her find places within about 2 hours of Edgewater to sell the muffin mix. She also added that everywhere that purchased the muffin mix got a complimentary bottle of syrup sent to them, but just like Edgewater, people just loved it. Sales reached big enough that she had to start hiring staff to help her make it. Most of the places, in the beginning, were all shops of former students of Aunt Laura. But since Anna had followed Aunt Laura's lead and started an online store, she has people from all over the world buying her mix.

That evening, many of their classmates would meet at the beach, have a bonfire, and pretend it was cold rather than almost 60 degrees. Violet was having a great time and thinking about how her friends in Miami would never just go to the beach like this last minute. They all wanted to know precisely who would be there, and if the who's who list needed to be bigger, they would not show. While they were all catching up, it came up that Oliver was the creator of Viewfinder, and everyone put it together that it was he and Violet in the viral video of the blueberry pie. Violet wanted to crawl under the nearest dune. As soon as people were not looking, she made a run for it. It had taken a long time to get over the last bonfire she had attended with Oliver. Senior year, when they had all been playing spin the bottle down at the beach, Oliver had to kiss her. However, the rules were it had to be on the lips, and how long was equal to how much you would miss them. She and Oliver kissed for over 5 seconds, the amount of time everyone who was not dating kissed each other for. They laughed it off, saying it was 5 seconds for all the years they had known each other. That night, she wrote him a note to tell him how she felt. It was true they had never dated, but they were best friends. They knew each other's dreams and crushes (or so he thought), but they both had felt the chemistry of that night.

Oliver's Pov

Oliver had never seen the note. Oliver looked for her at the beach party she had escaped from and found her spinning her beer bottle while sitting in the sand. All he could think about was *'I wish I told Lottie that night just how good that kiss was.'* But all he did was just silently sit down and wait for her to speak.

She said, "Sorry again for making you lose your pie. I would bake you another one, but you know how badly I am in the kitchen."

Oliver said, "That's okay. I made my own," and at that moment, the bottle stopped and pointed at him. He said, "Can I kiss you like I should have kissed that night senior year ?" She was expecting a 5-second kiss. He surprised her again; this time, it was a kiss that said you are my person. He then said you want to go to the house for pie.

They walked up the boardwalk hand in hand and sat up all night eating pie and catching each other up on everything since high school.

The next day, Oliver's parents stop by the boat on their way in, and they see a bottle of syrup and a note to Violet. It does not make sense because they don't even think that Violet has ever been to the boat other than maybe when it was a casino boat. But it is in Oliver's favorite spot to watch the world go by. Everything with Laura had meaning, so they take a picture of how they find it and stop at the hardware store to get some muffin mix since Oliver still cannot find his aunt's recipe book.

Violet's Pov

Violet is working, so they give the syrup and letter to Violet. She goes to her thinking place on the beach and reads the letter.

My Dearest Violet,

I will never forget finding you under my blueberry bush with your fingers just purple from all the juice. You had been determined to discover which bush tasted like the blueberries you and Oliver had in the kitchen the morning before. You both had claimed they were the best blueberries you had ever had, but when I made them, as Oliver had fixed with me the previous morning, neither of you said they were the same. Then, one day, you were telling your mom about all the fancy sugar I had at my house that she did not have, so she came over to look at all my fancy sugar just so she could buy them for you. But none of those were correct; you said it was sugar that you grind. It all clicked, and I figured out your additions. Those things made my syrup so unique, and you will always be my 1st Blueberry Girl.

I know from our chats that you are wondering if you want to return to Miami, so I want us to fix up this old boat and have you run it as an event space. Our community needs a place to gather all year round to enjoy our fantastic views. With your hotel experience and that blueberry cocktail, we could help everyone have a longer busy season. Also, when you have figured out the three ingredients and let Sam, the CEO of the Syrup company, know, I would like to officially transfer 1st Blueberry Girl, which is currently a blind trust. I run 50% of all my profits from the syrup to create scholarships for our best and brightest of Edgewater to legally turn control to you since you are my 1st Blueberry Girl.

Also, you have been inspired by Oliver in ways you don't know; ask him why this view is so important to him the next time you see him. I have asked him to come this Christmas, but with work, you never know if he will have the time. I did a little checking, and Oliver never saw your letter in high school.

Love

Aunt Laura

Violet looks up and sees Oliver working on the house. His Aunt would love to see the care he has for it. But I wonder if I'm leaving. He sounds like he is going after the house sold, so how do I tell him I'm the mystery girl his aunt connected him to in her will? I'm in the kitchen, so I must get his help.

So, she goes up to the house and tells Oliver the entire thing but leaves out the part about the letter.

Oliver is a little confused, but since he is starting to fall for her again, he does not want to do anything to scare her away and has a huge thanks to his aunt for bringing him back into his life.

So now, as they go, they ask Charlie if he will help with food for the Celebration of Life, and they ask if Aunt Laura ever did anything different to blueberry jam. He said yes, she always asked me for the pink peppercorns. They both think that it is a good help. The letter talks about the three sugars, two that you grind.

Then they saw Bill at the dinner and asked if they would make a couple of pies. And they ask him if Aunt Laura did anything different when she ate his pie; he said she always put salt on it. Again, she had said the 3 sugars were the clue.

Finally, they went to ask David to see if he would help with the lights on the boat and Anna if Aunt Laura did anything different to the muffins that were not listed on the jar.

Anna said she always sprinkled cane sugar on the muffins before she baked them. So, that one made sense. Now, they would just need the other two pink sugars.

So, they are all set to have Aunt Laura's life Celebration on the boat on Christmas Eve; it was fitting he always held a Christmas Eve party for her friends and family.

Violet asks Oliver's parents where they found the letter.

They point to the big window at the back of the boat. Violet thinks to herself after everyone leaves, *I will ask Oliver about this.*

As everyone is leaving, you start to see snow flurries. It never snows at the beach in Georgia, so everyone is rushing home, hoping to wake up in the morning to a white Christmas. When they are all done, they pull up two oversized chairs and look out the window. Violet asked Oliver the importance of this view; there had to be a reason Aunt Laura left my note and bottle of syrup right here. Oliver looks over with a questioning look and a shy smile. He said that is where my heart was every night. She looks hard out the window and realizes it is the point where she and Aunt Laura live. Violet realizes that Oliver has loved her just as long as she has loved him, so she leans over and gives him a huge kiss, one to tell him he is her person. They find a life raft that is the only soft thing around, so they both want to watch the snow as they fall asleep.

The following day, Violet could smell the coffee, and she knew there were still a couple of blueberry muffins in the gally; she hoped Oliver would bring them up with the coffee.

She went to turn the Christmas tree lights back on and realized that there were two presents under it, one for each of them and both from Aunt Laura.

Oliver went first; he opened it up, and it was Aunt Laura's original recipe book that he had lost after she gave it to him as a graduation present. Lottie held her breath to see if he would find the letter she had left in it all those years ago. It was right where she left it in the blueberry lemonade recipe. Oliver read the letter; it was everything his 18-year-old self-needed to hear to let all those old childhood worries go.

Now, it was Violet's turn. It was the crystal-like dishes that had been on Aunt Laura's kitchen counter when they were little. Violet was just in shock. She could not believe she was given the three sugars for Christmas.

Oliver starts laughing at her and saying, "I do love you, but you are the clueless person in the kitchen; the only one is sugar. The other was her salt and pepper shakers; you remember how her kitchen was all pink, even the salt and pepper were pink."

Then Violet said, "Well, that morning we had the best blueberries; you put two spoonsful of sugar and two twists of the shiny sugar (now I know that was salt). Still, I did not understand why you did not use the last sugar, so when you went out of the room, I ground the pink ball of sugar one time (now I know it is peppercorn). Those are the ingredients: cane sugar, Himalayan Sea salt, and pink peppercorns."

They Facetime Sam on the way to Christmas lunch; Lottie had made the deadline and figured it out before the end of Christmas, but then Sam swore them to secrecy, and as far as everyone was concerned, Lottie had finally figured out the 3 sugars, and these were just Aunt Laura's old hand-me-down sugar bowl and her salt and pepper grinders.

The End.

About Lisa Stamey

Lisa has loved writing for a long time, but is debuting her first published piece of fiction in *Wish Upon a Star*. She hopes it is just the beginning of the many words she wants to write and share. When she is not hanging out with friends and family she may be cooking, crafting, supporting local artist, or being a community activist and high school mentor.

Wonderful World of Riverville

By Paula Eberling

As I finish packing the last box, I take one last look. It's been a good home. I will miss the kitchen the most. I run my fingers down the cabinets and remember the many hours of stripping, sanding, and painting that went into them. It's been five years since I divorced, and with my mom's passing, I have no heartstrings holding me here anymore. It has been a long journey to healing my heart. In my desperation to forget the pain, I decided to move. No attachments, no commitment, no broken heart. Time for a new start. I sigh heavily and brush the tears from my eyes. Well then, here I go. Off to Montana, to another fresh start.

As I close the back door, I feel a rush of sadness. "Goodbye," I whisper. My heart is heavy as I walk to my car. I keep telling myself it will work out.

I throw the rest of my belongings in the trunk and jump in the car. I grab a CD out of the glove compartment. It's my mom's Christmas CD. Of course, it's moms, I mutter as I slide it into the CD player. I feel as if Mom is reminding me that the Christmas spirit is all around me. Nothing like Christmas music to set the mood. I haven't celebrated Christmas since Mom passed. She died on Christmas Eve, and I lost my love for Christmas the night she died. The music seems to relax me.

I cross my fingers for good luck and begin the drive. Riverville is an eight-hour drive, and it's beginning to snow.

The drive is long, and I have enjoyed jamming to my collection of CDs. My throat is sore from singing, but I feel giddy. As I park my car, I have a sudden rush of anxiety flow through me. *What am I doing? I just sold my home, boxed my life up, and took a job off Craigslist. What if the owner of the business is a serial killer? What if I hate my job?* I tell myself it is going to be okay.

I throw my head back and let out a whimper, "What are you doing?" I drop my head onto the steering wheel, attempting to pull myself together.

My fit of chaos is interrupted by a knock on the window. I am shocked to see a man bent over. He has a concerned look on his face. "Hey lady, you okay?"

I stammer a bit and slowly open my car door. "Hello, I'm fine; I uhh, well, I am new in town. I think this is the address to my apartment. I just pulled into town and am a bit overwhelmed."

"Yes, Ma'am, I suppose you are a bit overwhelmed. My name is Jacob; I presume you are Destiny. I am glad you found the address. I am the owner of the coffee shop, and I have been waiting for your arrival. If you're up to it, I can show you around."

"Of course, oh my gosh, I am so embarrassed," I mutter. "Yes, I would love for you to show me around".

"Alright then, shall we?" Jacob says as he extends his hand to me.

As we shake hands, I notice his warm smile. He seems genuine, and his eyes are soft and welcoming. I can smell wood smoke in the cool, crisp air. Oh, how I love the smell of wood burning.

Jacob notices me taking in the smell and giggles as he says, "You wanna go in, or you gonna stand here all night and smell the air?" I blush a little and apologize as I hurriedly go into the shop. "So, Destiny, what do you think?"

"Umm, you can call me Des, and I love how quaint it is. The shop is very welcoming, and I love that you have a bookstore here. The equipment looks new, and you have a great coffee-making inventory."

Jacob is beaming with pride as he looks around. "I think coffee and books go hand in hand, don't you?"

"I suppose so," I say as I look around, taking it all in. "If you don't mind, I am a bit tired. Can you show me where I will be staying?"

"Of course, where are my manners? You must be tired; please follow me." Jacob leads me to a back door and up some stairs. "Your apartment is up here. It's not big, but I think you will find that it has all the comforts of home." Jacob opens the door and gives me a quick tour. "Alright, Miss Destiny, I will leave you for the night. We are closed on Sundays, so you should have some time to settle in and find your way around. Here's your key. I will see you sometime tomorrow."

My hand brushes his hand as I take the key. I feel a chill run through me as I tell him goodnight.

"Night, Miss Destiny. "

"Good night, Jacob. Thank you for showing me around."

I unpack my bag and take a quick shower. The water feels heavenly. My tired body welcomes the heat. I finish up and throw my robe on. I notice a door in the bedroom. I open the door and am delighted to find a small balcony. The air is crisp and cool. I inhale deeply. It feels good. Maybe this is my chance to let go of the past, to heal my grieving heart. Mom would love it here. I look up to the sky filled with brilliant sparkling stars. Twinkling lights of heaven dancing in the sky. I take a deep breath and feel my body release the tension. Yes, this might work out. I step back into the warmth of the room and slip my pajamas on. The bed is soft and smells of freshly washed linen. I feel my eyes becoming heavy and soon drift off to sleep.

I wake up with the sun warming my face. The room is cool, and I pull the blankets up around me. I drift off to sleep again and am woken up by a knock on my door. Who could be here this early in the morning?

I throw my robe on and open the door to a smiling Jacob holding a steaming cup of coffee. "Well, good morning, Miss Destiny. I thought you might want something warm to wake you up!"

I squint my eyes at him as I mutter good morning. "I thought you were closed on Sundays."

With a childish giggle, he says, "We are closed; I just thought you might like a warm cup of coffee to start your day. When you are ready, come on down to the kitchen and I will make you something to eat. I know the fridge is empty, so I thought you might be hungry after your travels."

I'm not much of a morning person, and I am somewhat agitated with Jacobs's happy chirping. Who wakes up this happy?

"You gonna take your coffee," he asks. "Thank you. I will be down in a bit." As I close the door, I can see Jacob walking down the stairs, bouncing like a tigger humming a tune, not a care in the world.

I go to the balcony and take in the crisp air and warm sun. I sip on the coffee Jacob made me. It's pretty good. Imagine that the Tigger makes great coffee. I smile as I think about him bouncing down the stairs.

"There you are. I thought you might have gone back to bed," Jacob says as I enter the room. "I threw together a quick breakfast for you. Do you like waffles?" Jacob places a plate of waffles in front of me adorned with strawberries and whipped cream. "I want you to make this kitchen your own. The coffee shop is your space. You can do what you like with it. I will be here every day, minding the bookstore and retail side. Make yourself at home. Tomorrow is going to be busy. I will see you in the morning if you need anything, let me know."

I spent the afternoon digging, cleaning, prepping, and getting to know my space. It's nearly supper time; I suppose I should head upstairs for some downtime. As I pass by the bookstore, I notice the Christmas tree near the fireplace. The tree stands tall, adorned with twinkling stars. Simple but beautiful. My fingers touch the branches, and I choke back the tears.

My thoughts are interrupted by Jacob asking, "Miss Destiny, are you doing okay?" I can feel his eyes intently watching me. His cologne fills the room.

"I'm sorry, I was just admiring your tree. It reminds me of my mom."

"I do love Christmas he says with a warm smile." Jacob stands beside me, gazing softly at the tree.

I notice the stubble on his face, how it frames his strong chin. I catch myself staring at him, watching him, and listening to him tell his story of the great Christmas tree hunt.

"So, you pick your trees out?"

"Yep," he says with a grand grin. "Do you want to go Christmas tree hunting for your tree?"

"Me? Oh no, not me. I haven't put a tree up since my mom passed. She died on Christmas Eve, and I haven't had the spirit of Christmas like I used to."

"I'm sorry for your loss, Miss Destiny. I truly am."

I hear his words, but I tune his genuine kindness out. "It's fine. It's easier this way, and I just don't celebrate Christmas."

Jacob is staring deep into my eyes. I can feel his compassion without him speaking a word. Soft, kind, and staring deep into my soul. I feel my chest become heavy, and I quickly dismiss myself before I become a puddle on the floor.

How can this man, this stranger, stir so many emotions in me? It's been years since my divorce, and I swore off love. I will never let anyone hurt me again. How did he even get out of me that I don't celebrate Christmas? I close the door to my apartment and head straight to bed. Tomorrow is a new day.

It isn't long before I find myself right at home. Making coffee, serving people, and keeping myself busy. It's been two weeks since I arrived. Riverville is a busy little tourist town but holds a quaint hometown feel. It's almost closing time.

As I flip the closed sign, Jacob comes up behind me. "Hey, Des, you wanna go for a Christmas stroll? Christmas stroll? Yeah, Riverville has the best Christmas stroll. Christmas caroling, beautiful trees, hot cocoa, and a winter stroll under the stars. Doesn't that sound enticing?" Jacob's grin runs across his face, and his eyes sparkle as he describes the festivities.

I want to go, but the flutters in my heart make me nervous. I am attempting to make every excuse not to go. "Jacob, I need to clean up the shop. I'm not sure how long it will be." Jacob is quick to respond, saying two pairs of hands make the work lighter. I roll my eyes and realize he won't take no for an answer. "Fine, I will accompany you. We better get busy cleaning."

We made record time cleaning. Jacob's enthusiasm is enlightening. This guy is always smiling. Jacob extends his arm, "Shall we?" I have no words for the joy that fills me. We slowly stroll through downtown Riverville. The shops are adorned with Christmas lights, garland and mistletoe. We stop for some hot cocoa and listen to the Christmas carolers. The weather is perfect, no wind, and the crisp, cool air makes it easier to snuggle in closer to Jacob as he leads the way.

I can feel Jacob pull me closer to him. We walk arm and arm, silently enjoying each other's presence. As we approach the shop, Jacob tells me he has a surprise for me. Waiting in front of the shop is a large hay trailer full of carolers and townspeople. "I hope you don't mind, but I asked them to wait for us. I thought you might like to take a tour near the lake this winter eve."

"I would love to!" Jacob helps me up onto the trailer of hay. We take a seat, and Jacob snuggles me under the winter's moon. The ride was full of song and laughter. The moon's reflection danced across the lake, and the snow crunched under the horses' hooves.

We make our way back to town. It's getting colder out, and snow is beginning to fall. Jacob leans into me and cups my chin with his hand. "Destiny, thank you for accompanying me this evening." I can feel the warmth of his hand under my chin. The touch of his hand sends chills down my spine. I can feel a flutter in my belly, and my heart is pounding. Jacob leans in close to me. I can feel the breath of his words on my lips as he's speaking. I quickly thanked him for a wonderful evening and awkwardly repositioned myself on the straw bale to avoid eye contact.

We arrive at the shop and wave as the carolers head on their way. "Miss Destiny, I have one more surprise for you."

"Another surprise? Jacob, it's been an eventful night. I can't wait to see what it is."

Jacob motions for me to come into the shop. "Des, I hope you don't mind, but I put your surprise upstairs." Jacob grabs my hand and leads me upstairs and to the balcony door.

We enter my apartment, and Jacob leads me to the balcony door. "Des, I wanted to share some Christmas spirit with you. You have said that you don't celebrate Christmas. I know your heart is healing from a past love, and I know your Mom passed on Christmas Eve. I hear you humming the Christmas tunes playing during the day. I see you giving out cand canes to the children when they come into the shop. I know deep down the Christmas spirit lives in you. I wanted to share my Christmas tradition of having a tree from the mountains that surround Riverville."

I watch as Jacob opens the balcony door. There before me was the most beautiful Christmas tree. The lights twinkle, and pinecones adorn the tree. "It's beautiful, I whisper."

"I see you out here every morning drinking your coffee, and I see your star gazing at night after a long day of work. I also put a chair up here for you and a patio heater so you won't be cold."

"Jacob, why would you do this for me?"

"Destiny, I have been alone for a long time. When I placed the ad for a Barista and baker, I didn't know that you would be walking into my life. I do just fine by myself, and I don't need a woman to fix me. But, you make everything feel alright. The townspeople love you, and you blend into this magical place. I just wanted to give you the same kind of magic that you give me every day. I see you running, and I see you holding people at bay because you don't wanna get hurt. You should feel joy and should be loved like you deserve to be loved. Destiny, I want to give that to you."

I heard every word that he said. I run my fingers over the branches of the tree as the song "What a Wonderful World" plays. He even knows my favorite song. How is this possible? Before I can process what is going on, Jacob reaches for my hand and embraces me as we slowly dance to the music. As we stare into each other's eyes, I can feel my heart pounding, and that old familiar feeling creeps up. Jacob leans into me, and as our foreheads touch, I feel panic. Before I can pull away, Jacob lightly kisses me.

At that moment, I felt something I had never felt before. This man has opened my heart, and the armor I had worn for so long was lifted. I didn't come to Riverville for love. I didn't ask for this. I can feel my throat swelling. "Jacob, I can't do this. This is more than I can handle."

I pull away from him and ask him to leave. "I'm sorry, Jacob, I'm not ready for this."

Jacob hangs his head. "Destiny, I'm sorry if I'm moving too fast. I don't want to hurt you. I know you're scared, but if you keep running, you'll never know what it's like to be loved fully. Your heart hurts from a man who failed to love you, and your heart broke when your momma left this world. Life is so much more if you allow yourself to heal and to be loved. Can you let me do that?"

"Jacob, I'm not ready for this. I didn't come here for love. Maybe Riverville isn't for me. I wanted to start over, just to be me."

"Alright, Destiny, I will leave. I will leave you with your thoughts. I meant no harm, but remember, when you are ready, I will be here waiting."

I can see the hurt in his eyes. He leans down, kisses my forehead, and then leaves me standing alone on the balcony. I throw myself on the chair, sobbing. I wish my mom was here to tell me what to do. I go into the apartment, but as I close the balcony door, I open the curtain so I can see the lights on the tree as I drift off to sleep.

Morning comes too soon. I crawl out of bed and remember the events of the evening. I feel panic set in again. How did I get here? I know how this will end up. He's too good to be true. I grab my bags from under the bed and start packing. I fight back the tears and tell myself to toughen up. As I enter the shop, I see Jacob standing before the Christmas tree. His stance is strong. "Jacob, I just wanted to say goodbye before I go."

Jacob turns slowly toward me. "Miss Destiny, it's been a pleasure to have met you. I will never forget you. I had hoped that I could be enough to keep you from running." He leans into me and hugs me. "You know, it's Christmas Eve. Can I convince you to stay for supper? I am preparing a feast and going to make smores by the fire."

I can see his genuine kindness. His smile is soft but has a sadness to it. "Jacob, I wish that I could stay, but I'm not ready for any of this. I just need some time to find myself." He nods his head and opens the door for me.

I shall miss his softness and his bouncing Tigger happiness. "Thank you for everything Jacob…" As I walk away, I can feel his eyes on me.

I hurriedly walked to my car. It's beginning to snow. As I drive down the street, the townspeople wave goodbye. I look in my rearview mirror and can see the tree on the apartment balcony. It's all lit up, and the lights are twinkling. It's so beautiful. I can see more decorated trees lighting up downtown Main Street. The lights twinkle as I drive by, and then my favorite song, *"What a Wonderful World,"* starts playing on the radio.

I can feel an overwhelming feeling in my heart, and the tears flow down my cheek. Why am I running? I find myself turning the car around. The snow is heavier now, and it's hard to see. The Christmas trees light the way for me. As I pull up to the shop, I can see Jacob in the doorway.

As I get out of the car, he opens the door. "Jacob, I wanted to run, but I found myself running to you. I was afraid of being loved. Since I arrived here in Riverville, I have never felt lonely and have felt like myself. I have been afraid of being hurt, and I didn't ever want to feel the pain of a broken heart again. I lost the Christmas spirit until I came here. When I was lost, you led me to light. Jacob, you have gifted me with love. I could never forgive myself if I ran from you, so instead, I am running to you. I have been so sad and grieving the loss of my mother that I forgot to celebrate the memories of her. You allowed me to grieve, and you also showed me the beauty of Christmas Joy. I haven't felt that until you."

As Jacob embraces me, he says, "Merry Christmas, Miss Destiny. I am thankful you decided to accept love and celebrate the Christmas spirit. Mostly, I am thankful that you decided to run to me instead of running from me."

Jacob brushes the tears away from my face and kisses my cheek. "No more tears Des, only love and joy. Are you ready for some smores?"

As Jacob closes the door he starts singing *"What a Wonderful World."*

The End.

About Paula Eberling

Paula Eberling is Girl on Fire Magazine's exclusive "Dear Paula" column editor; she takes your problem to heart, then answers with empathy and expertise. Paula is a small business owner/entrepreneur, social justice advocate, speaker, trainer, survivor, and leader in the movement to end modern-day slavery and human trafficking. She worked as a victim witness specialist in the criminal justice system for over 26 years. She is a best-selling author in the She is Magic Series and has co-authored several self-help books.

Wings of Love: From India to Iceland

By Pallavee Yovana Periapayen

In the vast realm of social media, where borders dissolve, cultures converge, and connections span across continents, a unique bond began to form between two individuals: Kyara, a spirited young woman from India, and Valdimar, a laid-back soul hailing from the captivating landscapes of Iceland. Their virtual journey started when Valdimar stumbled upon one of Kyara's travel photos and reels on Instagram. As expected, Valdimar was so intrigued by the vibrant colors of India and the stories behind the snapshots that he left a long and detailed comment expressing his fascination. This small interaction sparked a conversation that gradually unfolded like a story waiting to be written. Kyara was so amazed that she started without any second thoughts to share glimpses of her life in India — the bustling markets, the colorful festivals, and the rich tapestry of traditions. From the kaleidoscopic festivals of Holi to the bustling markets of Delhi, she painted a vivid picture of the colors, traditions, and warmth that defined her world — Valdimar reciprocated by offering virtual tours of his Icelandic oasis. His posts featured the ethereal beauty of the Northern Lights, the dramatic waterfalls cascading down Icelandic cliffs, and the cozy charm of Icelandic homes adorned with traditional artifacts. The stark contrast between the vibrant warmth of India and the cool, serene landscapes of Iceland became a fascinating backdrop to their unfolding connection. Their communication transcended the usual pleasantries, delving into shared interests, dreams, and the intricacies of their respective cultures. The exchange of words flowed effortlessly, bridging the geographical gap as well as creating a bridge of understanding between the two worlds.

As days turned into weeks and weeks into months, Kyara and Valdimar found themselves sharing not only the highlights but also the ordinary moments of their lives — the everyday joys, the challenges, and the laughter that echoed through the virtual corridors of their conversations. The curiosity about each other's worlds led to language lessons — Kyara attempting to grasp the nuances of Icelandic, while Valdimar marveled at the melodic cadence of Hindi; it was all fun. Their interaction became a delightful cultural exchange, a dynamic conversation that flowed through comments, direct messages, and even video calls. Their shared linguistic endeavors became a testament to the lengths they were willing to go to understand and appreciate each other's backgrounds. Despite the long distance, they found solace in the sanctuary of their words. Kyara eagerly described the significance of festivals like Diwali, the Festival of Lights, where homes are adorned with lamps and fireworks light up the night sky. Valdimar, in turn, explained the enchanting tales behind Icelandic folklore, where mystical creatures roamed the landscapes, and ancient sagas were woven into the fabric of everyday life. Their cultural sharing extended beyond traditions to culinary delights. Kyara posted recipes for mouth-watering Indian dishes like biryani and butter chicken. At the same time, Valdimar showcased the unique flavors of Icelandic cuisine, featuring dishes like fermented shark and hearty lamb stews.

In between the digital dialogue, plans began to take shape. Kyara dreamt of the Northern Lights, while Valdimar yearned to experience the vibrancy of an Indian festival. The prospect of a real-life meeting lingered on the horizon, a possibility that fueled the excitement of their evolving connection. Time zones posed a challenge, but the anticipation of receiving a message became a beacon of light in the darkness of the night or the busyness of the day. The connection evolved beyond the curated posts and carefully chosen words. They began to discuss dreams, fears, and the intricacies of their respective cultures. The distance became a backdrop to their story, adding a layer of complexity but also a sense of adventure. With time, their connection had blossomed into a deep and meaningful friendship. The idea of meeting in person had become more than just a whimsical dream — it had evolved into a shared plan, a promise to transform their digital connection into a reality. As the holiday season approached, with the air filled with the magic of Christmas, Kyara and Valdimar decided to take the plunge and turn their shared dream into a festive reality. Christmas, a time when the world sparkled with lights and goodwill, seemed like the perfect backdrop for their long-awaited meeting. Kyara, with her vibrant Indian spirit, looked forward to experiencing the enchantment of an Icelandic Christmas. She envisioned snow-covered landscapes, cozy evenings by the fireplace, and perhaps even glimpses of the elusive Northern Lights dancing across the wintry sky. The excitement in their virtual conversations reached a crescendo as the day of their meeting drew near. Flights were booked, travel plans were made, and the anticipation of finally standing face to face sparked a joyful energy that transcended the digital realm. The meeting was more than a convergence of cultures; it was a celebration of friendship, love, curiosity, and the magic that happens when two souls decide to bridge the distance that separates them in this world.

There was an issue that was not being discussed in those amazing conversations. Kyara had a fear of traveling by plane, known as aviophobia or aerophobia, which is a complex emotional experience that can manifest in various ways. Kyara's situation consisted of a combination of psychological and physiological reactions. The anticipation of the journey, the unfamiliar environment, and the lack of control which undoubtedly contributed to a sense of apprehension. She started to engage in catastrophic thinking, imagining worst-case scenarios such as plane crashes or emergencies. Her psychological stress, in fact, manifested in physical symptoms, including increased heart rate, sweating, trembling, and a sense of dread. The day finally arrived. It was unbelievable how the symptoms intensified as the flight departure approached. Kyara's palms were damp as she settled into her seat, her heart racing in tandem with the distant hum of the airplane engines. Her lifelong dream of visiting a faraway land was about to come true, but an unsettling sense of fear gripped her. As the plane taxied down the runway, her mind played tricks on her, conjuring vivid images of catastrophic scenarios. She squeezed her eyes shut, attempting to drown out the ominous thoughts and circumstances that would not happen at the end of it all. The captain's calm voice over the intercom reassured the passengers, but Kyara's anxiety remained to a large extent.

Midway through the flight, turbulence rattled the aircraft. The sudden jolt sent shivers down her spine, and her knuckles turned white as she clutched the armrests. She stole glances at her fellow passengers; their calm completely contrasted with her internal turmoil. At that precise moment, she was so desperate for distraction that without the least hesitation, she struck up a conversation with the person seated next to her, a seasoned traveler, a Mauritian named Coco, who could sense her unease. They shared stories of successful journeys, the beauty of travel, and the statistical rarity of plane accidents. Gradually, the fear that had taken root in Kyara's mind began to loosen its grip. The passenger beside her offered tips on managing anxiety during flights—deep breaths, focusing on positive thoughts, and finding solace in the vastness of the sky.

There were two besties on the plane named Justine N. and Pallavee P.. Their friendship was admirable, built on a foundation of trust and good wishes for each other. They connected on a regular basis and most importantly, they knew that they could always turn to each other in times of need and had a safety net for their deepest secrets. They were like sisters to be honest, sharing a bond that could never be replaced. It was a treasured bond that went beyond bloodline or family ties. Their conversations were filled with laughter, they lifted the spirits of everyone around them. Undoubtedly, they were seen as optimistic, confident, charismatic and career-oriented girls. This kind of genuine friendship is actually rare but these two girls instilled faith that it does exist.

Kyara was having a nap when, all of a sudden, she heard someone crying for help. She jolted awake, disoriented by the sudden cry for help piercing through the humming background noise of the plane's engines. The cabin lights were dim, and most passengers seemed unaware of the distressing sound. It was beyond explanation how her heart raced as she tried to pinpoint the source of the plea. With sleepy eyes, Kyara scanned the rows of seats. In the dim light, she noticed a few other passengers looking around, their expressions shifting from confusion to concern. The cry for help echoed again; this time, she recognized it coming from a few rows behind her. Without hesitation, she unfastened her seatbelt and rushed toward the source of the sound. As she approached, she saw a flight attendant crouched beside a passenger, a middle-aged woman who appeared to be in distress. Other passengers were beginning to gather, their murmurs blending with the low hum of the airplane. The woman whispered: "The plane has been hijacked.

The sudden realization that the plane had been hijacked sent a chill down her spine. The cry for help she initially heard took on a new, ominous meaning. The hijackers' demands for the release of their friend imprisoned in the capital of Iceland became known, a somber mood enveloped the plane. Passengers exchanged worried glances, realizing the severity of the situation. Maintaining a steady voice over the intercom, the captain assured everyone that negotiations were underway with the relevant authorities. It was such a mess. Flight attendants continued to move through the cabin, offering reassurance and trying to keep everyone as calm as possible, given the circumstances. The atmosphere on board remained tense as the passengers grappled with the uncertainty of the situation. Some individuals, hidden among the passengers, were now in control, their motives and potential actions unknown. As the plane descended toward the Icelandic capital, the city lights from Kyara's window could be spotted. The authorities on the ground were undoubtedly aware of the situation, and the captain informed the passengers about ongoing deals. The outcome of the hijacking remained uncertain, and the passengers were left with a mix of emotions—fear, frustration, and a shared hope for a peaceful resolution.

As the plane landed in the capital of Iceland, the authorities, along with the captain, continued to employ a strategy of deception to ensure the safety of the passengers and address the hijackers' demands. The passengers could only observe the unfolding events from their seats. Under the guise of complying with the hijackers' demands, the authorities and the captain provided false information about the release of their friend. As the authorities executed their carefully coordinated plan, law enforcement personnel swiftly and discreetly approached the hijacked plane. Unbeknownst to the hijackers, the element of surprise was on the side of the authorities. Law enforcement successfully apprehended the hijackers without incident, ensuring the safety of everyone on board. Initially tense and anxious, the passengers were relieved as the situation de-escalated. The captain came over the intercom, announcing that the threat had been neutralized and everyone was safe. The passengers erupted in a mix of emotions—relief, gratitude, and applause. The flight attendants moved through the cabin, offering reassurance and ensuring everyone was okay.

The authorities efficiently and professionally conducted their post-operation procedures, securing the hijackers and clearing the plane for the passengers to disembark. As the passengers exited the aircraft, they were greeted by a strong security presence and airport personnel ensuring their safety. The captain thanked the passengers for their cooperation during the challenging situation, expressing gratitude for their patience and understanding. What a terrifying ordeal the passengers on this flight had to go through! The incident, while initially frightening, ended with a positive outcome. The collaborative efforts of the flight crew, authorities on the ground, and the passengers themselves contributed to a successful resolution. Though shaken by the unexpected events, the passengers could now continue their journey with a renewed sense of security and a shared sense of overcoming adversity. Kyara's anxiety transformed into awe. The fear of the unknown had given way to the realization that, statistically, flying was one of the safest modes of transportation. Kyara stepped onto solid ground with a newfound appreciation for conquering her fear. The journey became not just a physical one but a triumph over the intangible barriers within herself. The rhythmic thud of suitcases echoed the heartbeat of the journey's end, each rotation bringing passengers closer to the familiar sight of their belongings.

Outside the terminal, the sunlight bathed the surroundings in a golden glow, casting long shadows as passengers navigated their way to the next chapter of their adventure. Once a maze of terminals and gates, the airport now stood as a gateway to possibilities. As travelers dispersed into the world beyond the airport, a residual feeling of relief lingered—a testament to the human spirit's ability to conquer fears, embrace the unknown, and, above all, find solace in the simple joy of reaching a destination safely. It was a powerful emotion, marking the end of a physical and emotional journey through the skies. Kyara decided to not share what happened on the plane with Valdimar so as not to ruin the spirit of Christmas, but she promised to narrate everything on the 26th of December.

Valdimar chose the *Sweet Serenade Cafe* as the meeting spot. The world around her buzzed with anticipation as Kyara waited for him. They had navigated the challenges of a long-distance relationship for what felt like an eternity, and finally, the day had come for them to bridge the miles that had kept them apart. Kyara's heart raced as she scanned the crowd, searching for that familiar face that had lived in her dreams for so long. The cafe door chimed as she stepped inside, and there he was.. Time slowed as they locked eyes, the recognition sparking a cascade of emotions that words could barely capture. A serendipitous smile lit up her face, mirroring the surprise and delight that danced in her own eyes. But there, in the cozy corner of that bustling cafe, it felt like the Universe had conspired to orchestrate their meeting. The air hummed with the sounds of laughter, clinking cups, and the low murmur of conversation — a perfect backdrop to the reunion unfolding. The warmth of familiarity enveloped them as they hugged, and words spilled effortlessly, filling the gaps of the years that had passed. It wasn't just a chance encounter; it felt like a cosmic nudge, a subtle but undeniable sign that their meeting was long overdue. The synchronicity extended beyond their initial embrace. The stories they shared, the common interests that emerged, and the way their laughter seamlessly intertwined created a tapestry of connection that seemed to defy the randomness of the everyday. The bustling coffee shop was alive with the clatter of cups, the hum of conversation, and the warm aroma of freshly brewed coffee.

It was on the 25th of December 2020. Their first meeting on Christmas Day was a moment frozen in time — a meeting of hearts that had become pure lovers across continents. Whether it was the exchange of cultural gifts, the laughter shared over festive meals, or the simple joy of experiencing the holiday season together, every moment felt like a cherished page in the story they had been writing through pixels and messages. As the holiday lights twinkled overhead and Christmas carols echoed through the air, Kyara and Valdimar discovered that the magic of Christmas wasn't just about decorations or festive traditions. It was about the warmth that radiated from genuine connections and the realization that the bonds formed in the digital realm could indeed transcend into a shared physical reality.

Valdimar explained that in Iceland, the beloved Christmas figure is not exactly Santa Claus, but rather a unique and enchanting character known as "Jólasveinar," or the Yule Lads. These mischievous but ultimately good-hearted beings are part of Icelandic folklore and play a central role in the country's Christmas traditions. The Yule Lads are thirteen brothers who are said to come down from the mountains one by one during the thirteen nights leading up to Christmas Eve. Each Yule Lad has a distinct personality and brings a small gift or a prank to children, depending on their behavior throughout the year. The Yule Lads' names translate to English in various playful ways, such as "Spoon-Licker," "Door-Slammer," and "Skyr-Gobbler." They are often depicted as mischievous characters who either reward or play tricks on children, leaving small gifts or potatoes in shoes left on windowsills. Children in Iceland place their shoes by the window each night, and if they have been good, a small gift will be left by the Yule Lad who visits that night. However, if they have misbehaved, they might find a potato instead. The Yule Lads are believed to be the sons of Gryla, a mythical ogress who is said to come down from the mountains in search of naughty children. In addition to the Yule Lads, there is also Gryla's cat, also known as the "Christmas Cat" or "Jólakötturinn." As per the Icelandic folklore, this giant cat is said to roam the countryside during Christmas time and eat anyone who has not received new clothes before Christmas Eve. Historically, this tradition has motivated people to finish their work and ensure everyone has new holiday clothes. The Icelandic Christmas traditions, including the Yule Lads and the Christmas Cat, add a unique and magical touch to the holiday season, making it a special time for families and children in the country. Kyara was absolutely keen on knowing more!

The magic of Christmas is a spell woven into the air, a transformation that takes place when the world dons a coat of twinkling lights and festive decorations. It was not just a date on the calendar; it was a feeling that permeated the very essence of the season. The first signs of magic appeared with the arrival of winter's chill, as the air became crisp and the scent of pine and cinnamon wafted through homes. Streets were adorned with glistening lights that dance like stars, casting a warm glow that defied the darkness of the night.

Families gathered to trim the tree in their homes, unwrapping memories with each cherished ornament. The carols floated through the air, creating a melodic backdrop to the laughter and joy that reverberated through the walls.

The two souls, bound in love, could not deny the fact that celebrating Christmas was, at that time, a moment to pause, express gratitude, and cherish the connections that make life extraordinary. The air was alive with the festive hum of twinkling lights and the sweet melody of Christmas carols. Snowflakes, delicate as whispered secrets, adorned the world outside, transforming the landscape into a winter wonderland. Inside, the glow of a crackling fireplace cast a warm embrace upon the room, and the scent of pine mingled with the fragrance of cinnamon and vanilla. As the clock approached midnight, soft laughter echoed through the cozy living room adorned with garlands and mistletoe. Kyara and Valdimar, wrapped in blankets, sat close together on a plush sofa, their hearts synchronized with the rhythm of the carols playing in the background. In the soft glow of Christmas lights, they exchanged thoughtful gifts, each one a testament to the careful attention paid to the desires of the other's heart. The exchange of glances spoke volumes, carrying the weight of shared dreams and beautiful promises. The room flickered with the warm ambiance of candlelight as they enjoyed a home-cooked Christmas dinner. This feast transcended the delicious flavors and became a celebration of their togetherness. The clinking of glasses echoed the joyous symphony of love.

Later, they ventured into the winter night, bundled up in coats and scarves, the world outside cloaked in a serene hush. Snowflakes gently kissed their faces as they strolled through the quiet streets, hand in hand, leaving a trail of footprints in the fresh snow. Underneath the celestial glow of stars, they found themselves beneath a mistletoe-laden arch, a moment pregnant with the promise of a tender kiss. Time seemed to stand still as they shared a stolen, magical moment—a kiss that tasted of Christmas, filled with warmth and the sweet anticipation of shared tomorrows. Back inside, the flickering lights and the crackling fireplace created a cozy cocoon. They settled into their own world, sipping hot cocoa and exchanging stories by the fire. The flicker of candles danced in their eyes, reflecting the deep connection that had blossomed through the seasons. As the night unfolded, the echoes of laughter, the warmth of shared embraces, and the flicker of candlelight painted a portrait of a romantic Christmas—one etched in the heart's album of cherished memories. In that moment, the magic of the season wasn't just in the decorations or the snow outside; it was in the love shared between two souls, making it a Christmas to remember.

Kyara decided to stay back in Iceland after Christmas, and they spent one year there before moving to Canada, their dream country. Their journey wasn't a fairy tale devoid of challenges but rather a narrative infused with resilience, where difficulties were navigated with a shared strength that stemmed from their deep connection. Their souls danced in harmony, twirling through the highs and lows of life's intricate melody. He knew the intricacies of her heart, the unspoken desires, and the silent fears, which were admirable. In his embrace, she found not just a haven but a mirror that reflected the essence of her true being. Together, they transformed obstacles into stepping stones, turning the pages of adversity into chapters of growth and shared triumphs.

And so, in the twilight of their years, they looked back on a life well-lived. The final pages of their story were not an end but a continuation of the legacy they had woven together. As they held hands, gazing into the sunset of their shared existence, the echo of their love whispered, "They lived happily ever after, not because every moment was near to perfection, but because they chose to make every moment worth it, side by side, hand in hand." Their story became a testament to the magic of connection, the transformative power of shared dreams, and the unexpected beauty that unfolds when two lives, seemingly worlds apart, converge in the dance of destiny.

The End.

About Pallavee Yovana Periapayen

Pallavee works in the Accounting and Administrative field, in an IT Management Company known as the Leader in the field of IT, office automation, software and cloud services in France. She is also a qualified English language Educator and an international Bestselling Book Author. She recently became a founding member of the Writer's Society, under the Elite Publishing House in USA.

Pallavee attended the University of Mauritius in 2012 where she obtained her Bachelor Degree in English, specialized in language and linguistics, literary analysis, and critical thinking. She also studied at the MCCI Business School in 2017, which enhanced her knowledge about Business Management and Law (Business sphere - ins). She is currently pursuing her LLM - Masters in International Business Law.

In October 2021, she became a contributing author for the #1 Bestselling book Letters of Love in the second series, which she presented in both English and French language. Transformation & Being Human is her second International Book Project. The Magical

Miracles is her 3rd book anthology. She collaborated with several international authors who are mainly from USA, UK, Australia, and Spain. Her 4th book project is She is Magic, Unforgettable. Wish Upon A Star, a holiday book romance collection, is her 5th international book collaboration.

She has a strong interest in subject matters related to: Leadership, Feminism – Women Empowerment, and Education. She is also an experienced Speaker in professional networking events that brings together entrepreneurs, decision-makers, and solution providers globally. As a social work volunteer, she taught English and French languages to vulnerable children of an NGO committed to helping children without parental care.

Whispers of Sakura

By Mayuko Fukino

Chapter 1: A Tale of Love and Discovery

In the picturesque city of Kyoto, Japan, where history and beauty intertwined, an unexpected encounter unfolded amidst the enchanting holiday season. The air was crisp, and delicate snowflakes fluttered from the sky, creating a magical ambiance that heightened the anticipation in Sakura's heart. She walked with purpose, her steps echoing on the cobblestone path, as she approached a quaint tea house nestled amidst the wintry scenery.

The tea house, adorned with festive decorations, stood out like a hidden gem amidst the snowy landscape. Sakura couldn't help but be drawn to its charm. The exterior was a delightful blend of traditional and holiday whimsy. Lanterns with intricate designs swayed gently, casting a warm glow upon the snow-covered ground, while twinkling lights adorned the eaves, creating a captivating display. The sight was mesmerizing, a testament to Kyoto's ability to infuse the holiday spirit into its ancient allure.

With a sense of anticipation, Sakura pushed open the door, and the cozy embrace of the tea house encased her. The air was infused with the aroma of freshly brewed tea, mingling with the sweet scent of cinnamon and pine, creating a sensory symphony that transported her to a world of holiday joy. Inside, the decor was elegantly adorned with garlands, ornaments, and wreaths, reflecting the magical beauty of the season. The soft lighting and flickering candles added a touch of warmth, casting dancing shadows on the wooden walls.

With her ebony tresses cascading around her like a midnight veil, Sakura exuded an air of grace and curiosity. Her eyes, alive with holiday excitement, scanned the room, taking in the sight of patrons cozily wrapped in warm blankets, engaged in hushed conversations, or lost in the magic of the season. The gentle clinking of teacups provided a soothing melody, harmonizing with the enchanting atmosphere of the tea house.

As Sakura found her seat at a small table, she couldn't help but notice a familiar face across the room. It was the traveler she had crossed paths with just days before. A smile tugged at the corners of her lips as their eyes met, the unspoken connection from their previous encounter still lingering in the air.

Sakura (whispering to herself), "It can't be...him again? What are the odds of crossing paths twice in such a short time?"

Ethan smiled knowingly, "I can't help but feel that we've met before. There's something about your presence? That feels familiar...have we met?"

Sakura nodded, "Yes, I feel the same way. We did cross paths just a few days ago, didn't we? It's incredible to meet again in this magical tea house!"

Ethan chuckled, "It seems fate has a way of bringing people together, especially during this enchanted holiday season and in the beautiful ancient Kyoto. By the way, I am Ethan."

Conversation flowed effortlessly as they reminisced about their chance encounter and marveled at the serendipity of their reunion. They spoke of their shared love for embracing the magic of the holiday season and their admiration for the timeless allure of Kyoto. As they sipped their tea and exchanged stories, Sakura and Ethan couldn't help but feel that their paths were meant to intersect once again, igniting a curiosity and connection that held the promise of something extraordinary.

Unbeknownst to them, their destinies were intertwined, and the winter season would play witness to their journey of love and self-discovery. As they stood in that tea house, surrounded by the enchantment of the holiday season, Sakura and Ethan were poised to embark on an adventure that would redefine their lives, revealing the transformative power of love and the wonders that awaited the in the heart of the ancient cities.

Amidst the captivating beauty of Kyoto and the enchantment of the holiday season, Sakura and Ethan's lives were about to collide, weaving a tale of love, destiny, and the infinite possibilities ahead in the embrace of Kyoto's ancient charm.

Chapter 2: Whispers of Love in Kyoto's Splendor

As Sakura and Ethan continued their delightful conversation in the cozy tea house, their connection grew stronger with each passing moment. They exchanged stories of their travels, their shared love for adventure, and their mutual fascination with the rich history of Kyoto.

Ethan, eager to explore more of Kyto's wonders, suggested they venture out and embrace the city's serene beauty. Ethan's memory was sparked by the stories Sakura had shared about her middle school field trip to Kinkaku-ji. Intrigued by her accounts of the shimmering golden pavilion, he suggested they embark on an adventure to visit the temple together.

Sakura's face lit up with excitement at the prospect of revisiting Kinkaku-ji and experiencing it anew with Ethan by her side. She eagerly agreed, eager to discover something different from what she had seen during her previous visit. With the sun shining brightly overhead, they set off on a journey towards the enchanting beauty of Kinkaku-ji, ready to create new memories together.

They soon found themselves wandering through the peaceful gardens of Kinkaku-ji, the Golden Pavilion shimmering in the afternoon sunlight. The reflection of the pavilion on the tranquil pond created a mirror-like effect, amplifying its majestic splendor.

Sakura, gazed at the Golden Pavilion, "Ethan, there's something magical about this place. The golden hues and the serene atmosphere make me feel like we're in a fairytale."

Ethan smiled at her words, "I couldn't agree more, Sakura. This place has a way of captivating your senses and igniting your imagination. It's as if time stands still, allowing us to appreciate the beauty that surrounds us."

Their exploration of Kyoto's hidden gems led them to the Nijo Castle, an UNESCO World Heritage Site known for its breathtaking architecture and exquisite gardens. As they walked through the corridors adorned with intricate paintings and delicate sliding doors, Sakura couldn't help but be in awe of the castle's grandeur.

Sakura was whispering, "Ethan, can you imagine the stories that these walls hold? The castle seems to whisper tales of emperors and samurais, secrets and moments frozen in time."

Ethan was nodding in agreement, "Absolutely, Sakura. It's a testament to the rich history and culture of Kyoto. This place reminds us that beauty can transcend generations, leaving an indelible mark on the world."

The allure of Kyoto's culinary scene also beckoned Sakura and Ethan to indulge in its flavors. They found themselves at a charming traditional restaurant, where the aroma of freshly prepared dishes filled the air. The delicate presentation and exquisite taste of each course delighted their palates.

Sakura was savoring each bite, "Ethan, the attention to detail in every dish is remarkable. It's like a work of art, where each ingredient is carefully selected to create a harmonious symphony of flavors."

Ethan smiled, "I couldn't agree more, Sakura. Kyoto's cuisine is a celebration of craftsmanship and mindfulness. It's a reminder that beauty can be found in the sights we see and the flavors we savor."

As their time in Kyoto drew to a close, Sakura and Ethan found themselves at the breathtaking Kiyomizu-dera Temple once again, under the soft glow of a full moon. The view of the city illuminated by the moonlight was nothing short of magical, casting a romantic ambiance that set their hearts aflutter.

Sakura reached to take Ethan's hand, "Ethan, being here with you, surrounded by the beauty of Kyoto, feels like a dream come true. I'm grateful for every moment we've shared."

"Sakura, Kyoto has a way of bringing people together, of kindling connections that transcend time and distance. I'm grateful for the memories we've created and excited for the journey that lies ahead." Ethan smiled in response.

As the moonlight bathed them in its gentle glow, Sakura and Ethan found solace in each other's presence, cherishing the bond that had blossomed amidst the captivating beauty of Kyoto. Their hearts were now intertwined, and their journey together would continue, guided by the whispers of love and the everlasting charm of the ancient city.

Chapter 3: Whispers of Misunderstanding in Arashiyama

The morning sun shone golden on the enchanting Arashiyama bamboo grove in Kyoto, where Sakura and Ethan stood amidst towering bamboo stalks. The air was laced with a sense of tranquility and mystery, yet unknown to them, this peaceful haven would soon become the backdrop for a clash of cultures and personal struggles.

As they wandered deeper into the grove, Sakura couldn't help but marvel at the ethereal beauty surrounding them. The slender bamboo shoots swayed gently in the breeze, creating a symphony of rustling whispers that echoed through the grove. It felt as if nature was trying to tell them something, but the language barrier between them stood as an impenetrable wall.

Captivated by Sakura's radiant smile, Ethan reached out to hold her hand. But as their fingers touched, Sakura's eyes flickered with a hint of fear. She had always been an independent spirit, afraid of being tied down by the expectations of a traditional relationship. This fear, deeply rooted within her, clouded her judgment and made it difficult for her to fully embrace her connection with Ethan.

Sensing Sakura's hesitation, Ethan withdrew his hand and gazed into her eyes, searching for answers. He, too, had his own struggles. Commitment had always been a daunting prospect for him, driven by past experiences and a fear of vulnerability. He yearned for a deep connection with Sakura, but his insecurities held him back.

As they continued their stroll through the grove, Sakura and Ethan found themselves engaged in a conversation that revealed the chasm between their worlds. With her limited grasp of English, Sakura struggled to express her deepest thoughts and fears.

Sakura started, "Ethan, I... I fear being tied down and losing my freedom. It's been a part of who I am for so long."

Ethan, taking a moment to process her words, responded with a gentle smile. "Sakura, I understand. But being in a relationship doesn't mean losing your freedom. It's about finding balance and supporting each other's dreams."

Sakura nodded, her eyes filled with a mix of understanding and uncertainty. The language barrier added a layer of complexity to their conversation, making it difficult for them to fully convey their emotions.

Sakura asked, "And what about you, Ethan? What are your fears?"

Ethan, hesitating for a moment, chose his words carefully.

"I've always had a fear of commitment, Sakura. Past experiences have made me cautious. But being with you, it feels different. I want to explore this connection, but it's hard to ignore the lingering doubts." Ethan admitted.

Sakura, her voice laced with empathy, tried to reassure him. "Ethan, let's take it one step at a time. We can navigate this together, understanding each other's fears and supporting one another."

Their words became entangled in a web of misunderstanding, misinterpretation, and frustrated attempts at connection. Each sentence is lost in translation, leaving both Sakura and Ethan feeling unheard and frustrated. The beauty of the grove, once a symbol of harmony, now seemed to reflect the complexities and barriers they faced.

With every step they took, the grove whispered their shared struggle. The strong and resilient bamboo reminded them that overcoming these barriers required patience, understanding, and a willingness to embrace vulnerability. And so, amidst the whispers of the bamboo, Sakura and Ethan vowed to continue on this journey of discovery, determined to bridge the gap between their cultures and find a way to communicate their deepest desires and fears.

As the sun set, casting a warm orange glow over the grove, Sakura and Ethan realized that their journey was just beginning. In this land of enchantment and challenges, they would learn to navigate the cultural and personal obstacles that stood in their way, and in doing so, they would uncover the true strength of their love amidst the whispers of misunderstanding.

Chapter 4: A Winter's Embrace

Sakura and Ethan were transported to a magical world of imagination after a series of heartwarming and adventurous moments together in the bamboo grove. Walking hand in hand through the winter landscape, they closed their eyes and envisioned the enchantment of Kyoto's cherry blossom season.

In their minds, they could see the vibrant pink petals painting a picturesque scene around them, and they could almost smell the delicate scent of blossoms in the air. They imagined themselves strolling through a cherry blossom grove, with the soft whispers of the wind carrying the promise of spring.

As they continued their walk, Sakura and Ethan stumbled upon a wall adorned with a realistic art depiction of blooming cherry blossoms. The art captured the season's essence, mirroring the blossoming love they felt within their hearts. It was as if their imaginations had brought the cherry blossoms to life, creating a moment of pure magic.

Unbeknownst to them, a mistletoe hung above their heads, a symbol of love and affection. The universe seemed to smile upon them, offering them an opportunity to express their feelings in this winter wonderland.

Ethan, feeling a surge of courage, gently turned Sakura towards him. With a shy smile, he cupped her face in his hands and looked deeply into her eyes. The soft melody of his favorite holiday music played in the background, adding an extra touch of serendipity to the moment.

Although it was the winter season, devoid of cherry blossom scent, Sakura and Ethan felt an enchanting aroma engulfing them, as if their love was being celebrated. As Sakura experienced the gentle touch of Ethan and looked into his eyes, a sense of magic filled the air. In that fleeting moment, everything else faded away, and they could hear nothing but the rhythmic beats of their own hearts, as if nature was rejoicing in their connection.

Ethan's voice, filled with tenderness, whispered, *"Sakura, there's something I've been wanting to do, to show you how much you mean to me."*

Sakura's eyes sparkled with anticipation; her whole being yearning for the connection they were about to share.

Ethan leaned in, their lips drawing closer, their breaths mingling. And in that perfect moment, beneath the mistletoe and surrounded by the imagined beauty of cherry blossoms, their lips met in a gentle and passionate kiss.

Time seemed to freeze as their hearts danced harmoniously, their souls intertwining amidst the winter landscape. It was a kiss filled with hope, promise, and the blossoming of their love.

As they broke apart, their eyes met, and a sense of warmth and belonging washed over them. No words were needed to express what they felt at that moment. Their kiss spoke volumes, affirming the depth of their connection and the beginning of a beautiful journey together.

Hand in hand, they continued their walk through the winter wonderland, their hearts filled with a newfound joy and a sense of shared destiny. The whispers of the grove seemed to echo their happiness, as if nature itself celebrated their love and embraced their union.

In that magical moment, Sakura and Ethan knew that their love story was just beginning. Together, they would navigate the adventures and challenges ahead, their hearts forever intertwined under the mistletoe that marked their first kiss.

Chapter 5: Enchanted Pathways

The air was crisp, carrying the faint scent of the sea mixed with the fragrance of cherry trees that stood proudly along the streets. The branches of these trees were adorned with twinkling Christmas lights, creating a whimsical sight that illuminated the surroundings. It was as if the cherry trees had transformed into enchanting beacons, casting a warm and festive glow on the path ahead.

As Sakura and Ethan strolled through the town, their steps synchronized with the soft melodies of holiday music that filled the air. The town was alive with the season's spirit, with vibrant decorations adorning every corner. The joyful ambiance created a sense of wonder, as if they had entered a magical world where dreams and wishes come true.

"Look at how the cherry trees have been transformed, Ethan! They look like they're celebrating the holiday season with us. It's as if they're whispering tales of joy and hope." says Sakura.

Ethan agreed, "You're right, Sakura. The way the lights twinkle amidst the branches brings these trees a new beauty. They tell us that even in the darkest times, there is always a glimmer of light and happiness."

As they continued exploring, Sakura and Ethan immersed themselves in the festive atmosphere, exchanging stories and laughter. The sight of children building snowmen nearby and the aroma of freshly baked gingerbread cookies added to the charm of their surroundings.

Sakura takes in the beauty, "This town feels so alive, Ethan. It's as if the holiday spirit has breathed new life into every corner. I can't help but be filled with a symphony of optimism and bliss."

Ethan nodded, "I feel the same way, Sakura. It's amazing how the season's magic can transform the surroundings and our hearts. At this moment, I can't help but believe that anything is possible."

United by the enchantment of the holiday season, Sakura and Ethan's conversations took on a renewed sense of possibility and optimism. They spoke of their dreams, desires, and the future they hoped to build together. The shimmering lights of the cherry trees seemed to reflect their growing connection, reminding them that love, like the holiday season, was a time for warmth, togetherness, and shared dreams.

Sakura noted "Ethan, these trees have shown us that love can light up our lives even amid uncertainty, Let's embrace this season's magic and face the challenges ahead with open hearts."

Ethan agreed, "You're right, Sakura. Love is like these cherry trees adorned with lights, illuminating our path and guiding us forward. Together, we can create something beautiful, like the enchanting scene before us."

As the holiday season continued to work its magic, Sakura and Ethan made a silent promise to cherish the joy and hope it brought into their lives, ready to embark on a journey filled with love, laughter, and the unwavering belief that their dreams could come true.

Chapter 6: Bridges of Resilience

As Sakura and Ethan embarked on their journey of self-discovery and personal growth, they found themselves drawn to the coastal side of Tottori. The crashing waves, accompanied by a gentle breeze, provided a soothing backdrop to their conversations. Overlooking the majestic Mount Daisen, which stood tall and proud, covered in a pristine blanket of snow, they marveled at the beauty surrounding them.

Sakura broke the silence, "Ethan, standing here, gazing at the snow-capped Mount Daisen, I can't help but be reminded of the resilience and strength that nature possesses. It's a reminder that we, too, can overcome any obstacles in our path."

Ethan looked over the scenery and then her with the same loving eyes, "Yes, Sakura. The way the sunlight reflects off the snow, creating a dazzling spectacle, reminds me of the beauty that lies within our differences. Just like the unique facets of this landscape, our individual strengths can complement each other and help us grow."

In this breathtaking scenery, Sakura and Ethan found solace in each other's arms. They shared their dreams, fears, and vulnerabilities, creating a safe space where they could be their authentic selves.

"Ethan, I've always dreamt of starting my own art studio, but I've been hesitant, fearing that my creations won't be appreciated. But being here with you, I feel a newfound confidence to pursue my passion," she said softly.

"Sakura, your talent is undeniable, and your art has the power to touch people's hearts. I believe in you and your dreams. Together, we can find the courage to face any challenges that come our way," his voice encouraging.

As they opened up to one another, their conversations delved deeper, exploring the intricacies of their thoughts and emotions. They discovered that their differences enriched their connection and gave them a broader perspective on life.

"Ethan, growing up in a bustling city, I've always been drawn to the energy and vibrancy it offers. But being here, surrounded by the tranquility of nature, I've come to appreciate the beauty in stillness and silence."

"And I, Sakura, have always found solace in the quietude of nature. But your love for the city has taught me to embrace its excitement and possibilities. Together, we can create a harmonious balance between our worlds."

As they explored the coastal side of Tottori; Sakura and Ethan encountered obstacles along the way. They faced moments of uncertainty and doubt, but their shared determination and unwavering support for one another carried them through.

"Ethan, I'm afraid of failing, of not living up to the expectations I've set for myself. But with you by my side, I feel stronger, ready to face any challenges that may arise," Sakura admitted.

Ethan smiled, "Sakura, remember that failure is not the end but a stepping stone towards growth. We will face obstacles together, learn from them, and emerge stronger than before."

As the holiday season continued to weave its magic, Sakura and Ethan discovered that their differences were not obstacles but bridges that connected them on a deeper level. They learned to celebrate each other's strengths, embracing the unique qualities they brought to their relationship.

"I used to think that love meant finding someone like me, but now I understand that love is about accepting and embracing our differences. It's about growing together and supporting one another's dreams."

"Sakura, you've taught me that love is not about finding someone who completes us but someone who complements us. Our differences make us stronger, and together, we can create a resilient and enduring bond."

While overlooking the snowy Mount Daisen, Sakura and Ethan felt a renewed sense of purpose and connection. The beauty of their surroundings mirrored the beauty they found within each other. With hearts full of hope and a shared vision for their future, they took a step forward, ready to face whatever challenges lay ahead, knowing they could conquer anything together.

Chapter 7: The Brink of Separation

As Sakura and Ethan continued their journey of discovery, they found themselves in the historically significant city of Hiroshima. Despite the weight of the past, they believed this visit would deepen their understanding of the world and strengthen their bond. However, little did they know that their time in Hiroshima would become pivotal, testing the foundation of their love.

As they walked hand in hand, exploring the Hiroshima Peace Memorial Museum, the weight of the past settled heavily upon Sakura and Ethan's hearts. The images and stories of the devastating impact of the atomic bomb left them speechless, feeling the immense pain and suffering endured by countless lives.

"Ethan, this museum reminds us of the fragility of life and the importance of cherishing every moment. It's a stark reminder that love and empathy should guide our actions."

"You're right, Sakura. It's essential to remember the past and strive for a better future. Let's promise each other we'll always choose love and understanding, even in adversity."

Their words carried a profound meaning, but soon, miscommunication and external pressures began to creep into their relationship, pushing them to the brink of separation.

A series of misunderstandings led to heated arguments, causing their once harmonious connection to falter. The weight of their individual fears and insecurities clouded their judgment, making it difficult for them to see the love that still burned within their hearts.

"Ethan, I never thought we would reach this point. The miscommunication and emotional distance between us have grown too great. I don't know if we can find our way back together."

"Sakura, I never wanted it to come to this. But the pressures from the outside world, coupled with our own doubts, have pushed us apart. It breaks my heart to face the possibility of losing you forever."

Emotions ran high as they faced the stark reality of their situation. The fear of losing one another forever loomed over them, casting a shadow on the once bright future they had envisioned together.

In this turmoil, they found themselves standing in front of a memorial, a symbol of the resilience and hope that emerged from the ashes of Hiroshima. The deep-rooted pain and sorrow etched into the city's history served as a reminder that even in the darkest moments, love could prevail.

"Ethan, standing here, surrounded by the echoes of the past, I realize that the love we share is worth fighting for. We cannot let our doubts and miscommunications tear us apart."

"We've come so far, Sakura, and owe it to ourselves and the love we once shared to find a way back to each other. Let's break down the walls that separate us and rebuild the trust that once bound us."

At that moment, Sakura and Ethan made a pact to confront their fears and insecurities head-on. They vowed to communicate openly and honestly, to listen with empathy, and to prioritize their love above all external pressures.

As they left the Hiroshima Peace Memorial Museum, their hearts heavy but determined, Sakura and Ethan knew that the path ahead would not be easy. But they were ready to face the challenges, believing their love was worth fighting for. Together, they took a step forward toward healing and reconciliation, hoping to emerge stronger and more united than ever before.

Chapter 8: Love's Resilience

The story unfolds a few days before Christmas Eve, as the holiday season blankets the air with joy and anticipation. Sakura and Ethan are standing on a picturesque snow-covered bridge, surrounded by the enchanting beauty of twinkling lights and festive decorations.

"Ethan, as we stand here, I can't help but feel that this holiday season reflects our journey. Just like the lights that illuminate the darkness, our love has the power to guide us through the toughest times."

"You're right, Sakura. Our connection is stronger than any cultural boundary or societal expectation. We must confront our fears and fight for our love."

Beneath the winter sky, they take a deep breath, ready to face the challenges. Their determination remains unwavering, and their love for each other burns brighter than ever before.

As they walk through the bustling streets, hot cocoa and freshly baked gingerbread fill the air. The joyous laughter of families and friends echoes around them, creating a warm atmosphere of togetherness.

Amidst this holiday cheer, Sakura and Ethan encounter the people and places that have played significant roles in their journey. They meet the wise old man who taught them the importance of embracing different cultures and traditions and the kind-hearted café owner who provided a safe haven during their darkest moments.

"Ethan, as we revisit these places and meet these people, I realize how far we've come. We've learned to embrace our differences and find strength in our love."

"Yes, Sakura. Our journey has taught us that love knows no boundaries. It transcends cultural differences and societal expectations. We have the power to create our own happily ever after."

Their determination leads them to a grand ballroom, where the holiday celebration is in full swing. The room is adorned with sparkling lights and shimmering decorations, creating an atmosphere of magic and enchantment.

As they take to the dance floor, Sakura and Ethan's graceful movements mirror the harmony they have found within themselves. With each step, they let go of their fears and insecurities, allowing their love to guide them towards a resolution.

Leaning her head on his chest, Sakura whispers, "Ethan, I believe in us. Let's leave behind the doubts that have held us back and embrace the love we share. Together, we can create a future that defies all expectations."

Ethan whispered back into her hair, "Sakura, you've always been my guiding light. I choose to fight for our love, no matter the challenges that lie ahead. Let's build a life together, filled with love, understanding, and acceptance."

In that magical moment, Sakura and Ethan's determination and love collide, creating a resolution that brings them closer to their happily ever after. The crowd around them fades into the background as they seal their commitment with a passionate kiss, surrounded by the joyous melodies of the holiday season.

With their hearts alight with love and their doubts extinguished, Sakura and Ethan step into their future, ready to embrace the unknown together. Their journey has taught them that love can conquer all, and as they embark on this new chapter of their lives, they are filled with hope, anticipation, and the unwavering belief that their love is worth fighting for.

Chapter 9: Love's Gift

Christmas Day had arrived, and Sakura and Ethan found themselves back in Kyoto, the city that had witnessed their journey of love and self-discovery. As they stood in the serene surroundings of Kiyomizu temple, the beauty of their love and the magic of the holiday season intertwined.

"Ethan, it's hard to believe how far we've come. This journey has taught us much about ourselves and the power of love."

"Yes, Sakura. This holiday season has been a turning point for us. We've learned to embrace our unique bond and celebrate the love we share."

The temple grounds were adorned with delicate snowflakes sparkling in the winter sunlight. The atmosphere was filled with tranquility and hope, reflecting the peace they had found within themselves.

Sakura and Ethan sat on a bench overlooking the breathtaking view of the city below. They shared their dreams and aspirations, planning for a future that would honor their love and the lessons they had learned during this holiday.

Let's continue to cherish our connection, Ethan, and never forget the lessons we've learned. Our love is a gift, and we must nurture it daily."

"You're right, Sakura. We must always be open to new experiences and embrace the beauty of our differences. We can create a life filled with love, understanding, and adventure."

As they spoke, their hands intertwined, symbolizing the unbreakable bond they had forged. The wind gently whispered through the temple, carrying their hopes and dreams to the universe.

At that moment, Sakura and Ethan understood their love was a rare and precious gift. It had the power to transcend time, cultural boundaries, and societal expectations. They were determined to honor their unique bond and never take it for granted.

As the sun began to set, casting a warm golden glow over the temple, Sakura and Ethan exchanged a knowing glance. They felt a deep gratitude for the love they had found and the journey they had embarked upon.

In the distance, joyful laughter echoed through the temple grounds, reminding them of the spirit of the holiday season. They stood up, hand in hand, ready to embrace the magic of the festivities.

As they walked away from Kiyomizu temple, Sakura and Ethan knew that their love story would continue to unfold, filled with joy, adventure, and the unwavering belief in the power of love. Their journey had taught them that love was worth fighting for, and as they celebrated their unique bond on this special Christmas Day, they were filled with hope, happiness, and the promise of a happily ever after.

And so, Sakura and Ethan embraced their love, cherishing the lessons they had learned and the love they had found during this holiday. Their story had come to a beautiful point and moment, capturing the essence of their love and the magic of the holiday season. As they walked hand in hand, their hearts filled with gratitude and love, they knew their journey had only begun.

The End.

About Mayuko Fukino

Mayuko is a mindful life coach, yoga teacher, ancient wisdom keeper, and Japanese language teacher. With a deep connection to nature, she finds solace in the serenade of the sky and cherishes the harmonious melodies sung by all beings on Earth. Her journey towards self-discovery and inner peace has led her to embrace ancient wisdom and share its teachings with others. As a coach, she guides individuals on a path of mindfulness, helping them cultivate self-awareness and find balance in their lives. Combining movement and breath, she creates a sacred space in her yoga classes for students to explore their bodies and minds. Infused with the wisdom of ancient traditions, her classes allow students to connect with their inner selves and find tranquility. In addition to teaching the Japanese language, Mayuko imparts the wisdom of Japanese ancient traditions, inviting students to delve into the rich cultural heritage and profound wisdom of Japan. With a compassionate heart and gentle spirit, she is dedicated to supporting others on their journey towards a mindful and fulfilling life, enriched by the teachings of ancient wisdom and the Japanese language.

Happy Holiday Vibes

By M. LaRae, M.Sc.

Flight 117 from New York to Sweet Creek, Alabama, is arriving on time, so please return to your seats and buckle your seatbelts as we prepare for landing.

It's been 12 years since Riley Donavon has been home. As he stepped outside the small airport to hail a cab, the fresh southern air took his breath. That's nice, he thought as he removed his jacket and scarf. The temperatures in middle earth Alabama, were a bit warmer than those in New York. As a cab rolls to a stop before him, he closes his eyes and takes a few more deep breaths. A burly man with a scruffy red beard and a side jaw full of dip (chewing tobacco) rolls down the cab window and says, "If you're ready to go, then I'm ready to roll?"

The cab ride to the hospital offered the scent of coffee and beef jerky with a pleasant side of conversation from Earl, the cabbie, who Riley quickly learned has been driving for the same company for the last 35 years. More information than he felt was needed but it was the week before Christmas, and hospitality seemed in order. Riley chuckled quietly and listened to Earl's time-seasoned stories as they took the long route to Sweet Creek General Hospital.

Riley wasn't looking forward to returning to his quaint little hometown, but Walter Donavon's health had rapidly declined, and

Riley knew he needed to be here now as hospice care was in the works. Riley and his dad, Walt, were close but in a distanced way. After Riley's mom passed away when Riley was young, Walt became more withdrawn and reserved than usual. Riley had taken after his dad in many ways, including his tall, lanky stature and sandy blonde hair. Both were intelligent, shy, and typically quiet. He kept in touch with his dad through the years but hadn't seen him since Riley left town after high school.

The small town offered little promise for the aspiring architect, and soon after graduation, Riley moved to the larger city to find bigger opportunities. He had done well since landing a prestigious position with a successful architectural firm. They had just finished a large project, so he could easily take the necessary time off to care for his dad.

As Earl slowly but safely delivered Riley to the hospital's front door, Riley thanked him with a generous holiday tip for the long but enjoyable trip. Taking note of his cab number to give a favorable review, he noted Earl Cab #17.

Walking through the hospital hallways, suitcase wheeling behind him, Riley anxiously scrolls through his notes for his dad's room number. Ah, there it is, and as he quickens his pace toward the room, his phone rings. It's Sarah. Riley had recently canceled his engagement to Sarah, but she was not exactly accepting of the fact. With a slightly annoyed and tired sigh, he tells Sarah that he has just arrived at the hospital and now was not a good time to talk. He proceeded to tell Sarah that they were different people now on different pathways, and realizing he had reached room 177, he pushed open the door with a loud *ka-thud*. The collision with someone on the other side of the door jolted him backward a bit and sent books falling to the floor. His wire-rimmed glasses bent sideways and hung off his ear from one side.

A woman on the other side of the door gasped from the surprise of the collision. Riley started picking up the books while repeatedly saying, "Ohhh, I'm so sorry, ma'am." He noticed one of the books was "*Ask and It Is Given*" by Jerry and Ester Hicks. Interesting, he thought. He was looking to order that book just a couple weeks ago. Returning to an upright position, he noticed her colorful bohemian-style skirt and long, wavy brown hair. As he handed her the books, his face lit up. Surprisingly, but happily, he asked, "Lydia? Lydia Jenkins?" Her large brown eyes widen as she recognized him.

She replies, "Riley? Riley Donavon?"

In perfect sync, their voices say, "Oh my goodness! How are you?" and then, "How long has it been?" Their in-sync words lead to a united giggle and blushing smiles.

Riley's phone was now blaring. "Who is Lydia Jenkins? Riley, Rilllleeeey?" Sarah only knows a little about Riley's hometown. Since they met two years ago, their life has been centered around her and their life in New York. Her voice finally overrides Riley's surprise. He puts the phone back to his ear and tells her he has to go, promising they can talk later; he ends the call.

Lydia asks if that's the wife, to which he quickly replies, "No, no, no, she's my ex-fiancé." Lydia offers a soft I'm sorry, and Riley promptly tells her not to apologize as he quickly changes the subject.

He asks Lydia if she also has family in the hospital?

"No," she replied with a chuckle of relief and explained that she visits every Wednesday to read to some patients. She enjoys spending time with them, and the patients look forward to her visits. They think she is a golden ray of sunshine that floats in and out of spaces, lighting them up with happiness and joy.

Lydia says she is happy Riley could return to spend time with his dad. He says he is glad too, but admits it feels a little weird being back in town after all these years. She gently smirked, telling him she wouldn't know since she had stayed there in town all these years. She says she won't complain as she laughs and states how much she loves this little town and the people too.

"Staying put here does grow on you after a while, and you know life is what you make of it," she says. He turned his head sideways with an inquisitive nod, remembering someone else had recently mentioned that same 'life is what you make it' statement.

Realizing the time, Lydia tells him that another patient is awaiting a story, and she must be going. He says it was so good to see her and that they should meet for coffee and catch up soon. Lydia replies that she would like that and tells him that she has a coffee shop at the bookstore now, so he should drop by when he gets the chance. "Seriously," he asks? "Your own coffee shop? That's great. Oh, wait, are you talking about your mom's bookstore? Oh yes, I remember your mom had the little shop downtown on Main Street, and so you have that place now?"

"Yes," Lydia replies, "I have had that place since Mom passed away earlier this summer. A lot of learning and a few challenges, but I'm enjoying the whole process. Just living in the moment," she says. Riley gently shakes his head at her remark, realizing he has also been hearing that sentiment lately. He seems to fade into deep thought about it before nodding in agreement.

As Riley worked to adjust his twisted glasses, he couldn't help but notice the adorable little sashay of her bohemian skirt and the free-flowing bounce of her long hair as she turned and walked out the door and proceeded down the hallway. A sheepish grin blushed his cheeks as he turned to settle into the room for his long-awaited reunion with his dad.

The next morning, as Lydia shook a little cinnamon in her freshly brewed cup of coffee and straightened the napkins and creamer packs, the front doorbell chimed at Serene's Bookstore and More, and in walked Riley Donavon for that proposed cup of coffee.

Serene was Lydia's mom and a long-time fixture of downtown Sweet Creek. She was odd, but everyone in town loved her despite her unusual qualities or because of them. Although Serene was accepting of almost everyone, she was undeterred by being in a town that wasn't quite ready for her. She was an open-minded, free-flowing spirit, and along with the so-called typical books she kept readily available for the 'normal' customers, she also had a supply of candles, crystals, cards, and metaphysical books for the so called 'woo woo folks.' That's the 'more' part of the eclectic and charming store. These items weren't acceptable to some town folks, so she always kept them in the back and available only to the few woo woo's. After Serene's passing, Lydia never hesitated about keeping the store open. She wasn't as versed in the 'more' stuff, but she was interested now and learning as she goes.

"Regular, Decaf, or Chai Tea? What would you prefer, Mr. Donavon?" Lydia asks in a cutesy, professional tone. "Why, thank you, Ms. Jenkins; I will take a regular with a creamer and stevia." They both chuckle as they begin to sip their cups of deliciousness, letting their eyes close momentarily as they enjoy the warmth that radiates throughout their bodies and seemingly fills their souls with joy. Riley inquires since it's the week of Christmas, where's the hot cocoa? Lydia raises her eyebrows and says that they can do that later in the evening, but for this morning, she needs her coffee fix. They laugh in agreement.

They walk around the shop, reminiscing and fluffing around the tinsel and holly she has decorating the shelves. They seem to feel like two kids exploring a new toy store. Noticing a section of books labeled New Age, he points to them with an inquisitive look. She asks if he has read the Abraham Hicks books? Surprised and excited, his eyes opened wider than he thought possible, and his bottom jaw fell to the middle of his chest. He tells her that he had just started following their teachings and that he was taken aback when one of their books fell out of her arms when they collided at the hospital. He said he noticed that what he was thinking about just keeps showing up like they teach about in their books. She affirms that she, too, had noticed how things continue to fall into place and that it's sometimes really cool and sometimes a little freaky.

Lydia tells him that she didn't pay much attention to her mom's ideas when she was younger, but she did listen to bits and pieces. Her mom had talked about manifesting and creating our own experiences. Since her mom's passing, Lydia had decided to read some of her mom's favorite books. Those included exploring and learning about our energy field and how we manifest. Lydia was beginning to understand what her mom was talking about with the creating and manifesting stuff. They both agree that it is all kinda odd sometimes, but they are enjoying learning.

Riley suddenly notices the vinyl albums sitting inside an old wooden crate. "Oh wow," he says as he starts thumbing through the selection. Like a child discovering new toys under the Christmas tree, he looks at Lydia with wonder in his eyes as he rhetorically asks, "Vinyls? You have vinyls?" He lifts out the Journey album, shaking off the tinsel surrounding the crate.

He says, "This takes me back to the 80's flashback homecoming dance. Lydia? Do you remember that dance? What a blast from the past" as memories flow into his mind.

He says, "Do you remember the spandex and the leather pants?" They both laugh until their insides are hurting.

She says, "And how everyone's hair was so long and sky high thanks to all of the hairspray, and don't forget the sunglasses and penny loafers?" These memories have them both laughing so hard they can barely breathe.

"That was a fun night for sure," Riley says.

"Totally," she agrees, as they roll with more laughter.

As the humor simmers down, Riley admits with a sheepish grin how he remembers the beautiful girl working the snack table at the dance and how her long, wavy brown hair and big brown eyes captivated his attention, leaving him unable to look away. She blushes with a grin. He remembers when things were winding down and it was time for the night's last song. *Open Arms* by Journey started playing, and he wished he had enough courage to ask her to dance. What felt like two seconds became the song's ending, and his last chance to muster up the courage had passed. He looked at the dance floor as the people left, and when he turned back around, she was walking out the back exit as the night finished.

Lydia blinks her eyes as she catches her breath. "Why Riley Donavon! You wanted to dance with me? Seriously? I never knew."

He says "Oh, absolutely, but you know how shy I was in school and still am a little now, but I'm working on that."

When he reached to put the album back in place, she reached to move back the other albums, and his hand landed right on top of hers. A gush of warmth and excitement rushes through them both as they turn their eyes toward each other. Time seems to stop, and they stand practically frozen with hands unmoved and eyes locked in a heartfelt and wondrous gaze.

The spell is broken by a brisk, cool wind that blows in through the open shop door, knocking over the candy cane jar Lydia has out for customers. The open door welcomes in fresh air as much as the weather will allow. "Where did that come from?" they both exclaim with a slight shiver.

"Yesterday, it was warm and toasty," he firmly states.

She laughs, "Have you forgotten that in middle earth Alabama, you can sweat and freeze within the same twenty-four hours or less?"

Riley says he guesses so, as he isn't used to any warmth in winter now, only an overabundance of holiday snow. She thinks that must be fun, to which he quickly dispels. It was fun the first couple of years, but it wouldn't hurt his feelings if it moved somewhere else or passed him by one year. They share a mutual grimace as Riley walks toward the door to halt the stout breeze.

A cab screeches to a stop in front of the shop as Riley closes the front door and walks back toward Lydia. The door suddenly swung open, and a petite, stylish woman barged in. She vigorously brushes the blonde, wind-blown hair back from her face. She proclaims in a loud, stern voice, "Riley Donavon, you will not ignore me!" Riley's face freezes in shock and fear as he turns to see Sarah, who continues her rant without stopping for a breath.

"Riley, who do you think you are not answering my calls? You can't just brush me off like this. You cannot just break up with me. I can't tell my family, friends, and the ladies at the club that YOU broke up with me. This isn't how an engagement works, Riley Donavon. I am not someone you just let go. Do you understand me? Do you hear me? What is wrong with you? And who is this? Omg, is this the woman from the hospital? You must be kidding me? Is this a thing? Riley, this is unacceptable, and you better get this straightened out right now! Do you hear me? Riley? Riley? Do you hear me?"

Riley's face, still frozen, glances toward Lydia as she states that she thought he said ex-fiancé. He assures her that he did indeed say ex.

Sarah pipes in quickly, "No, I am NOT an ex," with a firm emphasis on not.

Riley quickly responds with matched firmness, "Yes, you are. Sarah!"

Lydia chimes in that she thinks he should go handle this situation, to which he agrees and apologizes for the unexpected drama.

Riley motioned Sarah to the front door, and they walked out, still arguing back and forth. The doorbell chimed as the door closed behind them. Lydia shook her head in amazement and surprise and then returned to her cup of coffee and the store duties.

Later that evening, a strong cold front brought out the heavy jackets, gloves, and hats. Tonight, the volunteers were decorating the hospital courtyard for a retro Christmas party for the hospital patients. Some patients weren't able to return home for the holidays, so the nurses and volunteers wanted to share a little holiday cheer with them.

Lydia was wrapping a red garland around a lamppost when Riley's voice asks, "Can I help?" She responds,

"Did you get your ex-situation handled?" He tells her he surely hopes so.

She admits that Sarah seems like a sure handful of spirit, to which Riley shook his head, looking downward as he mumbled, "Spirited? Well, that's one way to describe her. Can we please change the subject?"

Riley questions Lydia about celebrating Christmas. He says that he doesn't remember her being involved in the holidays when they were in school. She explains that growing up, her mom had taught her that all faiths and spiritual paths had a right to their own celebrations and observances and that she tried to respect them all. She had told Lydia that many people of different theologies celebrate holidays during December, so she preferred Happy Holidays to include everyone. Lydia admitted that this gave her a teenage rebellious excuse to not celebrate anything as she gently rolled her eyes at herself and shrugged. She tells him that she rather enjoys the festivities now as she understands more about the spirit of the holidays.

With the garland now secure, she stepped down from the small ladder and continued her story. "You know, Riley, over the past few years, I've come to understand my mom's ideas about Christmas, and I feel that it's about the spirit of Christmas. It's about sharing and the warmth and compassion people show each other during this time. It's about coming together as a community and making sure everyone feels loved. It's also about having fun and enjoying each other's company. That's what Christmas is to me, Riley. It's about the spirit of loving each other."

Lydia says, "Well, it looks like we are done here, so how bout we head back to the shop for that hot cocoa?"

He happily nods in agreement. As they head toward the front doors, he motioned her to stop, "Please wait here for just a minute." He walks into the gift shop just before it is time to close to get the plush snowman he noticed in the window. The cashier said that the card machine was not working and asked if he has the correct change since she had already put away the cash bag. He said "Sure, how much is it?"

She replied it was seventeen dollars and seventy-one cents. He handed her a fifty-dollar bill and requested that she keep the change. "Happy Holidays," he said with a smile as he left. He presented the snowman to Lydia. Since there aren't many native snowmen around, he said. She thanks him and blushes as they grin like teenagers on a first date.

Lydia had already called for a cab, and they walked outside just as it pulled into the circle drive of the hospital entrance. As they climb into the back seat, Mr. Earl says, "Good evening, Miss Lydia. How are you tonight?"

She answers, *"Perfect, Mr. Earl. How are you?"*

Earl smiled, "I'm fine, thank you. Where would you and your friend like to go tonight?"

"Just to Serene's Mr. Earl," she tells him.

Riley chirps in, "How good to see you again, Mr. Earl."

"You know Miss Lydia," Earl says, "you remind me so much of your mother. She was such a strong, sweet, and beautiful soul. Always thought she was just the most beautiful woman I had ever seen. Sure do miss her round here" Earl says with a little sniffle.

"Why didn't you tell her that Mr. Earl?" Lydia says, "She really would've loved to hear that."

Earl replied that he had a terrible shy streak back then and couldn't tell her. Sadly, he regrets it now but can't go back in time. Riley's eyebrows are raised at thoughts of his own shyness. As they approach the bookstore Lydia reaffirms to Earl that her mother would've loved that. "Thank you Mr. Earl," Riley and Lydia say in unison.

Mr. Earl says, "Have a great evening, you two, and good night."

Riley looks up at the sky full of stars as he climbed out of the cab, and his eyes caught the address at the top of Lydia's shop.

Dumbfounded, he said out loud, "Are you kidding me? What is happening?"

With uncertainty, Lydia asked, "What's wrong?"

Riley asked if her address was seriously 1717 Main Street.

Slightly puzzled, she answered, "Yes. Is that a problem?"

Riley explained that he thinks he is experiencing one of those freaky kinds of energy things with a little flustered tone in his voice. "Okay, let me think," he pauses as his mind searches through the last couple of days, "flight #117, cab #17, room #177, snowman $17.71, and now your address is 1717. SERIOUSLY?! What does this mean, Lydia?"

She responded, "The way I understand it, Riley, is when you see repeating numbers, it means you are in alignment with your true self or maybe on a path that aligns with your true nature. Perhaps you are finding the true you, Mr. Donavon," she says with a cute little shrug. "Come on, the cocoa is waiting, sir."

The next evening, the nurses and volunteers began bringing patients into the courtyard for the retro Christmas party. When Riley wheels his dad into the courtyard, Walt's eyes sparkle like it's his first-time seeing Christmas lights. "This is so nice," he tells Riley and thanks him for being there. Riley says that he is glad to be there too. They head toward the table full of homemade goodies and treats as Lydia walks through the entrance into the party.

Once again, Riley was completely captivated by this beautiful woman with the long, wavy brown hair and big brown eyes. In his eyes, she seemed to float above the ground, and he couldn't help but stare. When she noticed his gaze, she raised her eyebrows and gave him a wink. Trying not to feel embarrassed, he quickly looked down toward the ground. She laughed as she continued walking toward the table to deliver the gifts she had brought.

Wildman Dan, a first-year med student turned DJ for the night, is hyping up the crowd. "All right, folks, are you ready to jingle bell rock, and rock around the clock?" He had a random playlist of Christmas music mixed with some golden oldies from the 70s, 80s, and 90s. "Time for a rock and roll retro Christmas party, ya'll," he says as he cranks up the music.

After a wonderful evening of singing, dancing, and feasting on goodies, the night is winding down to a close. Suddenly, they hear a loud drunken voice shouting Wiley, Willleeyyy, no no, Riley, yeah RILEY, that's it, "RILEEEEEEEEYYYYYYY! You're mine, Riley!" They all turn to see Sarah stumbling into the courtyard after a few too many spiked eggnogs. As the guests take a communal gasp, Sarah spots Lydia and staggers toward her while swinging wildly like she wants to fight.

Riley yells, "Sarah, stop it," as Earl intercepts and scoops up the stumbling Sarah. Earl says he will take her back to her room at the inn and make sure she is okay for the night. Turns out Earl is also a security guard, bodyguard, and whatever else people in town need, so she is in good hands.

"All right, all right, ladies and gents," Wildman Dan says, "Let's calm down and close it out. It's time for the last song of the night. Playlist, playlist, give us one last song."

Lydia and Riley had already begun cleaning up, and the last song started playing. Riley's head rises slowly from the floor as his eyes open wide in disbelief. "This can't possibly be," he says. "This is too freaky!" He flung his arms into the open air as if questioning the Universe, "Are you serious?"

His eyes rotate to where Lydia is clearing a table. She realizes the song is *Open Arms* by Journey and she turns toward Riley. They both had a complete look of shock and surprise on their faces. In unison, they shook their heads and threw their hands in the air with a big

"WHAT?" He thinks this is beyond his comprehension, but he will not let this opportunity pass him by again.

With a steady gaze between them, Riley walked across the small dance floor to Lydia. He extended his hand in a silent request for hers. She softly accepted as she extended her hand toward his. As their hands met, Riley raised them together and gently kissed the back of her hand. "Lydia Jenkins, you are the most beautiful woman I believe I have ever seen, and I would be honored if you would have this dance with me." Lydia happily accepted, and they began gracefully dancing, finally wrapped in each other's arms.

As the cold night air started gently dropping snowflakes on them, they both gaze up at the sky.

"Really Riley? You must've brought the snow with you?" Lydia says softly.

He replies, "Yes, I guess so, and you know, this town is really beginning to grow on me."

"Happy Holidays, Miss Lydia Jenkins." He whispered in her ear.

"Happy Holidays, Mr. Riley Donavon." Lydia echoed the whisper back.

The End.

About M. LaRae, M.Sc.

M. LaRae, M.Sc. is an Intuitive Metaphysician, Reiki master and best-selling author.

From the lens of her own experiences through domestic violence and childhood trauma, she found a passion for helping others rise out of the trauma frequency. Her bestselling book Vibrational Badassery is a simple and down to earth guide for living intentionally while manifesting life on purpose through awareness of the vibrational flow of frequency.

She is also a co-author in multiple bestselling collaboration books with Elite Publishing and a columnist for Garden Spices Magazine. M. LaRae loves to listen to music, cook, travel and spend time with friends. She is the founder of The Positive Power of You and The Bliss Life Academy where she offers courses, her book, singing bowl meditations and oracle card readings.

You can connect with M. LaRae at:
https://www.facebook.com/thepositivepowerofyou
www.linktr.ee/thepositivepowerofyou

Jingle Bali

By Kim Pierre

The letter box was full of so many bills, so much junk, thought Malika as she walked through the front door of her London apartment. Malika felt the cold of the November chill and suddenly began to feel sad and lonely. Tears slowly began to fall down her cheeks.

Malika sat on her sofa, mail in hand, as she sobbed, wondering what life had become for her.

She had been blissfully in love the day she had married Phil, a handsome colleague of the law firm they both worked for as criminal lawyers. They married within 12 months, and life was perfect.

They worked long hours; they were both very focused on becoming senior partners in the firm.

They also loved their life and loved renovating their idyllic Victorian 5-5-bedroomed home. They enjoyed the three holidays they took every year around the globe with family and friends, as well as small weekends away when they could afford them time-wise.

Children had not been on the agenda as they decided they were simply way too focused on their careers, enjoying life, and each other to want children.

Christmas was always very special for them, and they always spent Christmas Day alone, as the anniversary of the day Phil had plucked up the courage to ask her out for a Boxing Day date all those years ago.

They got married on Christmas Day the following year; it was so intimate. Christmas lights, red roses, and a feel of magic in the air. A love forever, or so Malika had thought.

Christmas Day was always spent cozy. Breakfast in bed opening gifts they had lovingly bought each other, making love in the shower with a glass of champagne, preparing their Christmas lunch, eating way too much, snuggled up watching Christmas films, open fire glistening whilst they lay wrapped in each other's love.

This day to them was always their absolute date of the year, a special celebration of their love and marriage. It was always perfect.

After ten years, Malika had started to think about having a family, Phil reminded her of the pact they had always made. One that consisted of their amazing life, and one that simply didn't have room for sleepless nights, nappies, or baby vomit.

Malika was startled by her mobile ringing out, and it was Phil.

Malika put on her best false cheery voice, "Hi" Phil made small talk about how cold the day had been. He sounded distant, "Did you open your post?"

Malika knew what Phil meant, he meant, did you receive the decree absolute? A final closed door to her divorce.

Malika's hands holding the mail shook, dropping the envelopes to the floor. As the mail scattered at her feet, Malika was thinking loudly in her mind: "I am divorced and single. In as much of a focused, steady voice that she could manage, Malika responded, "Oh no, I've not had any mail today, why do you ask?"

Phil remained silent for a few seconds too long, which told her everything, and her heart sank, in a low voice, Phil said, "I've received the decree absolute."

Malika simply answered, "I will no doubt receive mine tomorrow; I must go as my bath is running."

Phil replied, "Yes let me know if you do. We need to have closure."

Malika, as bravely as she could possibly muster, replied, "Yes, sure, speak soon."

Hanging up and sinking to the floor like a baby sobbing. Malika was in so much pain. This pain was different than ever before. It was something she had never experienced in her whole life. It ran through her whole body like a sword piercing every part of her being.

At that moment her mobile rang out again, through Malika's bleary eyes she saw it was Kay, her best friend who was more like a sister than a best friend. Malika thought about ignoring the call, but she knew she needed her best friend now more than ever.

Kay and Malika were best friends, they had started nursery school together, too many years ago to remember.

Kay was a very spiritual person who believed in the universe and that we all become what we think, say, and feel. Malika, despite always feeling a sense of peace and love, real love around Kay, her beliefs were different. A much more logical person, as they often say, opposites attract, and both Kay and Malika agreed they were like chalk and cheese, who got on like a pair of thieves.

Kay asked Malika how she was doing; Malika could not hide her pain and sobbed, "Badly"

Kay went into her usual pep talk of "We are energy, and we send our energy out, and this energy returns to its source, negative and positive."

Malika was in such pain, too much pain to be in the mood for this positive mumbo-jumbo talk. Malika didn't hide this annoyance.

"Kay, please, my world has fallen apart. I'm really not in the mood to listen to this nonsense."

Kay was used to Malika's skepticism, and she understood Malika needed her to use a very different tactic.

"Ok, I understand, but I was going to ask you if you would like to escape the Christmas hype and come away with me to Bali for the Christmas holiday. Just us, cocktails, great food, and sunshine."

Malika's mind went into the misery of thinking about the office chit-chat of the Christmas holiday. Of spending time snuggled in the sprint of Christmas trees, presents, arrangements, Christmas shopping, what they were hoping their lovers may surprise them with, and what they excitedly were buying to make their day special. The Christmas hustle. The Christmas madness. Being all wrapped up in wanting to spend the perfect day with their loved ones regardless of what was wrapped under the tree.

Malika finally resurfaced to the present conversation and sighed with a definite, "Yes I'd love that, Kay, I simply can't face this Christmas here."

Kay was a very wealthy lady who was quite famous on social media for her ability to heal, help, and supporting people who wanted to heal in her coaching business program. Money was no objective to her as a multi-hippy, happy millionaire offered to pay for the trip as a Christmas gift to Malika.

Malika cried, this time with joy, love, and appreciation for her friend. "I love you Kay, let's do this."

Kay got busy with booking the trip, and Malika got busy blocking out of her mind life's reality and occupied her spare time online shopping for summer wear…closing her eyes and ears to the Christmas holiday. Instead, focusing on her out-of-office day on the 20th of December and their flight day to Bali on the 22nd. The new focus helped Malika to cope.

Kay and Malika had arranged to meet in the VIP lounge at Heathrow Airport at 9:00 a.m. to share a few glasses of champagne prior to their flight departure at 10:30 a.m..

The airport for Malika was like a huge escape from her pain and misery of recent months, the love and gratitude she had for Kay took over, and Malika was actually relaxing for the first time in a very long time.

They took off on time, and the ladies laughed and enjoyed the VIP first-class flight treatment of leather wide recliner seats, sipping champagne, reminiscing of their first girly holiday in a budget girl's holiday to Spain many moons ago, thinking they had made it, both giggling with the memories.

Both Kay and Malika had been so excited the night before the flight, they did not sleep well, and only a few hours into the flight after a few glasses of champagne and a lovely chicken salad they were sleeping reclined like a pair of babies.

Two hours prior to landing the aircrew woke them with the offer and the smell of breakfast. Kay and Malika were well-rested and very hungry. They had poached eggs, smoked salmon, coffee, and of course a celebration glass of champagne just as they were ready to land in the amazing Bali.

Once at the amazing 5-star hotel the both of them began to unpack. Both eager to check out their environment. Kay explained to Malika that there was a bit more to this holiday than she had disclosed.

Malika rolled her eyes; she knew this meant Yoga classes, meditation sessions, discussions about the universe, and Kay trying to make her think about her life and what she wanted to see in her life.

Malika relaxed and thought, you know what, I'm going to simply allow and enjoy whatever happens to happen. Since landing in Bali, she had a new feeling of "letting go.

Since landing in Bali, she had felt a feeling of peace. Since landing in Bali, she had been able to forget it was the Christmas holiday and that had she been back at home, she would have felt sad and lonely.

Kay and Malika had woken up on a very hot, sunny Christmas Eve and had decided to spend the morning walking to the beach to start the holiday with a yoga class booked in for the afternoon, and there was a dinner dance in the evening.

The beach was serene, with sparking blue water, blue sky, and white sands. A relaxing slight breeze that was so welcome and blissful, thought Malika.

Malika suddenly thought about Phil and his new lady, with the thought, she felt a sudden pang of emotion and began to cry, Kay suddenly woke from her sunbathing and hugged Malika.

Kay didn't say a word. She knew that this day and the holiday would not be easy. It was Malika's first Christmas without Phil, and this time of the year for anyone, especially the first Christmas apart would be hard. However, for Malika, this time of year was so special for her and Phil. They had married on Christmas Day all those years ago and spent every year after that in a love bubble over the Christmas holiday.

Malika wiped her eyes and apologised to Kay. Kay told Malika to allow her emotions as it was part of healing. Malika loved her best friend for the love and care she always had given her.

Kay and Malika got back to the hotel, showered, and got ready for the yoga class. Malika had strangely started to look forward to the class, the class was full, and people were introducing themselves with small talk.

Malika noticed a man she thought she recognised, she thought she was imagining it but no, it was him, it was Joel she had met at law school many moons ago.

They say life has a strange way of working out, and Joel had been her first ever love.

Malika suddenly became nervous as it was clear he had recognised her and he started to walk towards her. He had not changed if anything, he looked more handsome than ever with age.

"Malika, well, well, well, how are you? I can't believe it's you after all these years. How are you?"

"It's really you, Joel," was all Malika could muster to say. They suddenly hugged as if all the years had suddenly melted away.

"Hey, listen, let's catch up over a drink later," Malika agreed and Kay suddenly walked over from chatting with others in the group.

"Kay, this is Joel, you remember him, don't you?" Malika asked her friend.

Kay did, "Of course, oh wow, I can't believe this, it's great to see you!"

The yoga teacher called out, "Can you all sit on your mats to start?" The yoga class went by in a blur as Malika thought about how it ended with her and Joel all those years ago and how she had never set eyes on him again until now.

After the yoga class, Joel came over and asked Malika to meet him for a drink; they agreed to meet at the hotel bar at 5:00 p.m.

Once back at the hotel room, Malika sat on the bed and said to Kay, "Life is so weird sometimes, and what a massive coincidence this had been." Kay reminded Malika there is no such thing, and life's path is already pathed the way it's pathed; Malika thought maybe Kay was right about some of this.

Malika had a shower and wondered what Joel's life had been like and why he was here. Was he, too, healing from a broken heart? Malika told Kay she would be back by 7:00 p.m. for their dinner, and Kay was happy for some alone time, as she was going to do her meditation.

Joel was sitting at the bar, looking so handsome, relaxed, and happy; Malika decided he didn't look like he was healing from a broken heart, "Hey Malika, you look amazing." Joel said, as he stood up and kissed Malika on the cheek.

"You too," replied Malika, thinking how gorgeous Joel smelt when he leaned in for the kiss on her cheek

Joel ordered a drink for them, and once the drinks arrived, Joel asked Malika what had happened between her and Phil.

Malika felt her cheeks blush, reminded that she had left Joel for Phil and had broken his heart "I'm so sorry." Malika said, Joel told her it was okay, he had forgiven her many, many years ago.

Malika explained what had gone wrong. How she had wanted children, and Phil really didn't, how this had driven them apart eventually, and here she was. Joel reached out his hand to comfort Malika. He too had married, Lou, a doctor who was all about her career, a future that did not include children, and this had also driven a wedge between them.

Malika looked at Joel, and she could see that she had made a huge mistake all those years ago, though she at the time could not see it. They both hugged.

Malika asked Joel if he would like to join her and Kay for dinner later.

To her surprise, he said "Look, Malika, I'm going to be honest. I don't want lies between us. Kay won't be there at dinner tonight; it will be just you and I. Kay and I met a few months ago, and she had told me about you and Phil splitting up. I told her about Lou and I, and she then had the idea of us meeting here in Bali for the Christmas holiday."

Joel was worried that Malika might be angry with Kay as Malika sat silent for a while; instead of anger, Malika started to laugh.

"Kay had always said I'd made a mistake leaving you. It seems she knows me better than I know me." Malika said in between bursts of laughter.

Malika and Joel both started to laugh, "Cheers to Kay," both said, clinking their wine glasses together. It seems the Christmas magic was just about to start in a very different way than Malika had ever known and had always wished for. Isn't that the beauty of magic?

The End.

About Kim Pierre

Kim Pierre has previously worked with Blair Hayse on two chapters in the books: *She is Magic* and *She is Magic, Too*. Those chapters were real stories of her life. Kim enjoyed writing this chapter that is fictional and hope you enjoy it too! She named her main character after her friend Malika Gandhi a very creative writer and artist. Kim is a life mentor helping people to "get out of their own way to understand what their purpose is here on this planet." She can be reached on Facebook at Kim Pierre.

Note from Kim: I hope you enjoyed my Christmas romance story. Merry Christmas and Happy New Year to you and yours. Remember you are enough, with love.

Père Noël

By Kathryn Denhof

"Crap!" My feet slid on the ice that had taken over the streets of New York City. I felt my body collide with something unremarkably hard, not stiff like concrete but hard like someone who had just come from the gym after working on their upper body. I couldn't have been more wrong or right.

My eyes glanced up, and there he was, a man with a lean body; some would call it a sleeper build these days. He was clad in a cozy-looking beige sweater; it made his eyes look bluer than ever. His hair was dark, a raven color under the sun shining between buildings on us.

"I am *so so* sorry!" He says quickly, trying to help me up off the pavement that I had crashed into at some point without my knowing.

I swat his hands away, "Maybe you should watch where you're going next time." Standing back to my full height, I brush off the pieces of ice that stuck to the bottom of my dress pants. Getting out of work for the holidays was a blessing and a curse. Most people would be happy, but I was not. Work was my haven; it's where I went to get away from all the Christmas cheer. Christmas just wasn't my cup of tea, I guess you could say.

"Oh well, still, I'm sorry." He gives me a sweet smile, and just now realizing how close I am, I move back a few steps. I hum in response, and he gives a slow nod. His smile never left his face as he drove past me to continue on his way, but not before giving me a "Merry Christmas!" in an overly excited voice.

I almost groaned, but I held it in for his sake. With a shake of my head to rid myself of the memory he brought back by saying those simple words, I continued on my way.

A sharp knock on my office door, "Come in."

I instantly regret saying those two words when the door opens, and in walks his tall, lean body, the man I met a couple of days ago. What are the odds that he's who I think he is?

"Oh, hi!" His enthusiastic voice meets my ears, and I suddenly want to bang my head against my desk.

"Are you the new intern?" I ask him in my most monotone voice, hoping to bring down his enthusiasm.

"Yes, I sure am! Are you going to be my boss?" He has a specific tone mixed with sarcasm that makes me feel as if he knows who I am. It gives me the chills.

Without giving him the answer he wants, I gather up some of the papers on my desk, hand them to him, and he takes them without a hassle. Most workers need to ask if those papers are for them even though they are being handed to them. Of course, who else would I be giving them to?

"My name is Elliana Harrington. Call Kimberly if you need me for any reason."

"The lady at the desk?"

"Yes, she's my secretary; she'll be the person you go to before you come to me."

"Okay! Have a Merry Christmas!" There those words are again. There is a reason we don't have Christmas trees or any holiday cheer in this building. Has no one told him why?

Once he leaves, I get up and walk across my office; the view of the Brooklyn skyline is shown in the floor-to-roof windows covering two entire walls. Black curtains draped on either side of the windows, waiting to be closed at the end of the day, and sheer curtains covered the windows, hiding some of the bright light that would shine in if I didn't have some kind of block. My bare feet sink into the rug that covers the wooden floors in the middle of the room. People don't come in here very often, and I refuse to wear my black heels all day when I'm going to be in this giant office with no one to impress.

Opening the filing cabinet in the corner of the room closest to the door, I pick out the file named *'Père Noël'* The new intern has the same name as Father Christmas. What is the Universe trying to tell me here?

I'm gathering my stuff and putting it into my purse when another knock hits my door. Kimberly knows not to let people in here when it is time for me to leave, so who in the hell would be knocking on my door?

The person, Noel, doesn't even wait for my answer as he waltzes into the room. He sits in the chair before my desk and folds his hands across his lap.

"Do you need something?" I ask with a raised eyebrow.

"Yes, I need to take you out." He responds with zero hesitation. "Tonight."

My eyebrows shoot straight up in surprise. I don't realize how long I've been staring at him until he clears his throat.

"You do realize most people ask the person on a date before saying they are taking them out?" He gives me a shrug as a response and stands up, his hand extended in my direction. My lips almost, almost being the keyword, curl into a smile, but I catch myself before I can.

Picking up my bag, I grab his hand, fingers grasping around my entire hand, and before I can say a single word, he pulls me out my office doors and past the empty desk where Kimberly typically sits. No wonder he got up here so easily. She must have gone to the bathroom or left early. He presses the down button on the elevator, and knowing it will take a while, he decides to start a conversation.

"Why are you working so late when Christmas is just around the corner?" He asks. Turning my head, my eyebrows narrow, most likely portraying my annoyance with his topic.

"I don't see how it's any of your business," I reply, my voice sharp and cut off. He was caught off guard, but he composed himself and turned his head to look at the numbers above the elevator slowly ascending.

"I suppose you're right. I'm sorry." He apologizes after a long silence.

I had nothing to say back to him, so I kept quiet. The air surrounding us is cold and silent. Tension fills the bubble of space that the two of us are in. Noticing my hand was still attached to his, I quickly pulled it away and crossed my arms over my chest, my bag moving up my arm and sitting on my shoulder.

Catching his face in the corner of my eye, I can see his head is turned towards me, and a slight frown crosses his lips, bringing a small sadness into his crystal blue eyes. Sadness shouldn't be in those eyes.

Eventually, the door to the elevators opened with a small ding, indicating that we could step on. He gestures with his hand for me to enter first, and I do. I step over the small crack and lean against the wall closest to where all the buttons are. I reached out and pressed the 'L' label at the bottom of all 65 numbers. He walks in and rests both hands on the railing behind him, the mirror wall showing off a cool logo on the back of his beige sweatshirt. This angle gives me a good look at how his butt looks in the light-washed jeans he has on. And it looks absolutely delicious.

The journey all the way down in the pregnant silence was making me regret ever accepting his invitation to go out. At the same time, I was happy I wasn't going home to the house that didn't feel like home, the darkness and silence and me. It's not a good combination at all, and the insomnia that it brings doesn't stop me from sitting on my couch and working myself to death.

When we reach the 50th floor, I break the small beeps from the elevator, "So what do I call you, Père Noël?" Because you're crazy if you think I will call you Santa Claus in another language."

"Don't tell me my parents put that on my application." He lets out a small groan, but there is a small, knowing smile on his face for reasons I don't know.

"Parents?"

"Yes, this was their idea, and while I'm not completely against it, I did tell them to put the name I go by." He slightly shakes his head, "Please, call me Nicholas."

"Why did your parents want you to come here?" I ask

He takes a minute before he replies, seemingly thinking over what to answer with. "I'm here on another business of work, which, fortunately, involves you."

I raise an eyebrow in question, but he has nothing else to say as he looks away and stares at the mirror behind me, signaling that it is the end of our conversation. I move my eyes to look at the floor and wait for us to arrive on the ground floor.

He leads the way out of the elevator, looking over his shoulder every moment to ensure I'm still following him. He doesn't have to worry about me going my own way because, honestly, getting kidnapped sounds better than going home right now, especially with two days before Christmas. The crowd in New York is extensive, and our office building is a couple blocks from Rockefeller Center, so leaving at night is a nightmare. It's a little after 11:15 pm, and people are everywhere.

People push left and right of me. Noise is carried by people who are far ahead. I'm almost scared I will lose him in this mess, but his hand tightens around mine as he pushes past people, creating a way for me. Some people give us odd looks and shout at us, while others choose to ignore us and continue where they are trying to go. Most tourists come to spend the holiday in the Big Apple and have to see the famous tree every night they're here. The Christmas crowd is insane.

People come from all around the world to see all the "amazing" sights we have, but they never see what New York City has to offer. There is more than Times Square, the Empire State Building, the Statue of Liberty, and the Christmas tree that comes around during the Christmas holidays and leaves until next time. You can find cafes hidden with some of the most delicious scones and sausage balls. They have amazing cappuccinos and hot chocolates that will have you drink them at the slowest speed possible so you can savor every taste. You can find gardens with some of the most beautiful flowers in the spring, places you will never want to leave.

After thirty minutes when it should've been only eight minutes on a typical day, we arrive at Central Park; snow covers the grass while the cobblestone on the walkway is cleared, only small patches of snow littered around from where snow has dropped that hasn't been pushed away.

This crazy person that I decided to follow willingly is leading me toward the snow-covered grass while it is below freezing, and he doesn't even have on a coat. He has got to be mental. No sane person would be outside with it this cold, only wearing jeans and his sweatshirt.

"Follow my lead." He says, kicking me from my thoughts. He releases my hand to put his uncovered fingers into the freezing snow, rolling it into a small ball.

"You better not throw that at me." A warning is evident in my voice. He looks at me from the corner of his eyes before a slow grin appears. I cross my arms over my chest, giving him a look I give my employees when they know I'm about to fire them. The countenance doesn't do what I hoped as he launches the snowball into my shoulder. He crumbles over in laughter as my jaw falls slack. I look at him in disbelief as he almost falls to the ground.

While he's still laughing, I take the chance to make a snowball, my hands clad in thick black gloves. He doesn't stop his deep chuckles until snow makes an impact right in the middle of his face.

"So that's how you want to play this?" He asks, a mischievous look in his eyes as he begins to grab more snow crumbles into his hands.

I take off, my feet falling into the deep snow, but I don't let it slow me down as I reach the top of a hill. I grab more snow every few moments until I can make a proper snowball. He has hit me at least four times in the back when I'm finally able to throw one back at him, and the sad part is he was expecting it and managed to dodge it thoroughly while still making snowballs. I don't notice that laughter flies out of my mouth until I'm on the ground, and he is also laughing above me.

"You should laugh more often," He says with a smile, "It's beautiful."

My mouth shuts firmly in a tight line once those words leave his mouth. I sit up from the snow, and like clockwork, his hand reaches out to help me, but I don't take it. Standing up on my own, I brush the snow off the back of the trench coat that I have on and turn around to begin walking away from him. I don't hear his footsteps for a while, and my shoulders start to release tension, but then I hear the slight crunching of snow as he begins to run after me.

"Elliana, wait. Please. I'm sorry, just wait a second." He begs. If I didn't know he was following me, I would've assumed he was on his knees begging right now, just based on his tone of voice.

Suddenly, he's in front of me, "What." It's more of a statement when it leaves my mouth than a question.

"What happened? We were having fun."

"Maybe I don't want to have fun. Have you ever thought of that?" My tone is sarcastic, and it makes his face fall into a deep frown. God, why does he have dimples? This isn't helping my situation.

"Why not?"

"I just don't," I reply firmly, closing the argument and stepping around him.

"Let me at least buy you something to eat. It's cold out here, and you need to eat something." He pleads.

Giving a deep sigh, I think things over in my head and promise I won't have fun. It's just free food, and that's it. What harm could free food cause?

"Fine." That single word causes a smile to appear on his face.

Dimples.

Crystal eyes.

Perfection.

"We must go through Rockefeller Center again, so you might want to hold tight." A small smirk lights at one corner of his mouth. Rolling my eyes, I grab his outstretched hand, and he leads the way out of Central Park toward the giant crowd still there.

The bell above us gives a small ding as I'm blasted with warm air in my face. The smell of fresh scones and coffee wafted through the air, catching my curious nose. I follow the scent with my eyes, leading me to a large display case with muffins, scones, and many other pastries, all perfectly decorated. People sat on chairs adorned with bows tied around the wood at the tops, and small pillows were hooked on the seats. The lighting was warm, with only one overhead light and candles and small lamps lighted the rest of the place.

"Wow, this is beautiful," I say, shrugging my coat off and removing my gloves.

"Thank you. I helped Decorate it." His reply wasn't at all what I was expecting. He leads me to a spot in the corner where a small navy-blue couch and a coffee table are placed in front, a 'Merry Christmas' sign hanging above the sofa with small snowy pictures around it.

"I'm sorry?" I sit down with him, sitting beside me on the small loveseat. He folds his feet on each other and turns his body to face me.

"This place belongs to my parents. We opened it when I was a kid, and I helped decorate it as a kid and even when it's gotten remodeled." He says, his head turning to survey the place, a sincere smile on his face causing a warm feeling to spread through my body. "We moved here from France, and my mom makes handmade pastry. They are our secret family recipes."

Speechless, I just stare at him. I only look away once he turns his head to look at me. A small, petite woman with short, curly white hair wearing a red dress and white apron with minor stains of chocolate walks over to us. A bright smile adorned her face as she reached out and hugged Nicholas. She sways him back and forth for a moment, whispering something in his ear, which causes him to push her away with an annoyed look.

"Momma, please stop." He puts his head down, and a slight blush covers his cheeks.

She laughs and gives a swat on the shoulder as she turns to me, "Hello darling, what can I get a beautiful lady who is friends with my son?"

"Oh," I hum, "I'll take a Pain Au Chocolat."

She pushes her small round glasses down her nose as she stares at me, shock evident on her features. "Your French is gorgeous!" She says excitedly. "Oh, Nicholas, she's perfect!"

A small smile makes its way onto my face. She gives such incredible motherly vibes. My smile fell after that thought, and my lips turned downwards as I thought about my own mother. The mother that isn't here anymore. The mother who would do my hair for me even if I was a grown adult, and the mother who would bring my coffee in the morning to help wake me up. The mother that would climb into bed with me and get mad when I started to fall asleep while she was ranting to me. The same mother walked me down the aisle the day I was getting married.

I can feel the tears burn in my eyes as I begin to remember the past, the things I would sell my soul to have again.

FLASHBACK

"Oh, come on! Let's get some coffee and go look for more Christmas Decorations!" Mama says with excitement, her voice getting high-pitched because she was trying to get me to match her enthusiasm.

"Sorry, Mama, but I promised Rachel I would go out with her today. We are going to get dinner and then maybe swing by the mall because I saw a charming watch I wanted." I tell her, a secret smile sitting on my face as I put my lipstick and lip gloss into my purse in case I need touchups on the lips. "Hey! Maybe you could ask Leo to go with you."

"He asked me the other day what he should get you for Christmas. Maybe I can help him pick out some things at the vintage shopping center you like so much."

"It's a day before Christmas Eve, and he still hasn't gotten me anything?"

"Well, he has. But more gifts never hurt anyone!" A thoughtful look is in her eyes as she turns at the sound of a soft knock on my door.

Leo walks in, dressed in his standard attire, an all-black suit with some fancy dress shoes that cost more than anything I have ever owned. His Blonde hair is swept over to the side, and his deep brown eyes look me up and down. The butterflies go crazy just by that simple look.

"Hey, Darling." His deep British accent is very noticeable to anyone who hears him talk. He gives me a small peck on the lips as he wraps an arm around me. I can feel his wedding band digging into the thin dress I have on as he pulls me into him.

"Hi.." I say, "So, Mama is taking you out while I go Christmas shopping with Rachel. Behave yourself." I give him a small poke on the chest as I say the last words, followed by another kiss, before I pull away and pick up the Miss Dior purse Leo bought me for our second anniversary.

He smiles cheekily, "You got it."

FLASHBACK OVER.

I tilt my head down as the memory surfaces in my mind. The thoughts that consume me after are all I can think of. *What if I stayed? What if I went with Mama? What if I never let her and Leo go to the market? What if I told them we could've just gone to look for Christmas decorations together?*

A hand lands on my shoulder, jerking from my memories and thoughts. "Hey, Elliana, Are you okay?" Nicholas asks. I notice both pairs of eyes are on me and that a couple of tears have dropped onto the hands I have crossed on my lap.

"Yes." Weak. "Yes, I'm fine." My voice comes out more confident than I feel. Using the pads of my fingers, I run them under my eyes to dry them.

"If you're sure."

I nod, and he removes his hand from my shoulder. "I think I should get home now. Thank you for bringing me here. I swear I'll come back, and I never got to try that Pain Au Chocolat.

Giving Nicholas a small wave, I enter my brownstone, shutting the door with an everyday wreath hanging on the giant window that shines light from outside onto the entryway floor. I drop my purse onto the table to my right, almost knocking over a vase with beautiful blue hydrangeas—my mama's favorites.

FLASHBACK

"Mama? Leo? I'm home!" I call out. An echo is the only answer I get. They should be back. It's way past the time that the market closes.

Setting my stuff down on the entryway table, I kick off my winter boots and walk through the living room. I checked all the rooms downstairs and then moved upstairs to check the other rooms but found nothing. There wasn't a single trace of Mama or Leo. I walk back downstairs to grab my phone from my purse. I ring Leo first. No answer. I ring Mama next. No answer.

What the hell?

I throw my phone in my purse, fix my coat, and slip on my house shoes, not bothering with my winter boots, and I'm out the door in record time with almost everything I had entered the house with two minutes ago. Walking out into the middle of the street, I flag down a taxi. It comes to a slow stop beside me, but I don't give it time to stop completely. I throw the door open and sling myself inside, rattling off the address for the vintage mall and telling him to step on the gas.

The ride took entirely too long for my liking, but when we pulled up to the mall, I didn't have time to think about anything other than the fire and many sirens. I'm out of the car with the taxi driver yelling at me for almost damaging the door because of how hard I slam it, but I pay no mind. Running towards the tape that is blocking the way into the mall, many people are gathered around, with police officers keeping everyone held back. I reach the beginning of the crowd, and I pull on a police officer's uniform, "What happened here? Is everyone okay?"

"Sorry, ma'am, but I need you to let go." He tells me. That wasn't what I asked.

"What the fuck happened here?" I ask him again.

"Please remain calm and stay behind the line." Still not answering my question.

"My husband and mother was in there, tell me what the fuck happened."

He ignores me this time, not even paying attention to me.

FLASHBACK OVER.

The newspaper lies on the table by my purse. It's dated a day off from two days ago to the date. The headliner is plain as day and a reminder for me never to forget.

"Tragic bombing kills 2,000 people in the vintage shopping mall on–"

I don't need to read anything else to know what it is. A day I'll never forget. A day that will always haunt me while I'm awake and asleep. I throw today's newspaper on top to cover it up and continue the journey into the house. The place is cold and empty without the life of my mother and Leo here. No silver and blue Christmas tree like she would've liked. There are no snowmen decorations on the fireplace mantle. No candles are lighting up the place. No Christmas was here. It was just me and the house.

I didn't want to leave my bed. It wasn't one of those mornings where your bed was so comfortable and warm that you didn't want to leave. It was the kind that made you feel like you didn't have a reason to be awake, much less leave your bed. I just wanted to curl up in a ball and cry, cry an ugly cry that had your face red and snot going everywhere—the kind you never want anyone to see or hear.

I didn't have work today, so if I wanted to, I could stay here. I could ugly cry. I could never leave my bed. But the joy of being CEO is making your work days. Leaving the comfort of my bed was probably one of the hardest things for me to do, knowing that two years ago, I woke up with him lying in the bed beside me, and now he isn't anywhere to be found. My engagement ring and wedding band are lying inside their box, stuffed inside my sock drawer, out of sight, out of mind. But it wasn't ever entirely out of my mind.

I pad softly down the wooden stairs, the floorboards creek under my feet. Soon enough, I'm sitting on the couch that feels similar to what I would think a cloud would feel like, with my feet curled up under me as my laptop sits on my lap. The screen is one of the default images. New York City, how convenient. I don't even have time to pull up the page to *"Harrington Empires,"* and there is a knock on my door. It's loud and echoes in the house. As if the reverse wasn't loud enough, the doorbell ring follows.

"Coming!" I shout, getting up from the couch and going to the door. I open it to find a familiar face at the door. I almost want to smile, "What do you want?"

"Get dressed." Is all he tells me, his blue eyes staring at me with a smile gracing his lips.

"Why?" I ask.

"Because I said so. Go on now."

Slowly opening the door wider, I allow him to come inside, and he lays his long coat on the back of the couch as he makes himself at home on my furniture. He doesn't say anything else to me. He just sits there, waiting for me to "get ready."

"Okay..." I whisper to myself as I go back upstairs and into my closet to get dressed. It's a walk-in closet, and the entire space is filled with my stuff. One side used to hold all of Leo's clothes, but all that is left of his is the cologne he used to wear all the time. A Tom Ford cologne. It fit him. It's what made him *him*.

I go downstairs after changing into something warm and throwing my hair into a ponytail to distract people from the insanely oily hair. Nicholas is still sitting on the couch, but now he has my laptop in his lap and looks exceptionally comfortable. He stole some cookies from my kitchen and made hot chocolate based on the candy cane sticking out of the mug.

"I see you made yourself at home," I say, and the sad part is that I could see this being his home, too. But I don't think I can replace Leo, ever. I loved him, and I will always love him. I could never give my entire heart to someone else when Leo still has some of it.

"Yes, your hot chocolate is delicious. Where did you get it?" He asks, without looking up. His fingers are still scrolling on something that is on my laptop.

"It's a special blend," I say blandly.

He nods, and I'm thankful he doesn't ask any more questions about it. Sitting beside him, I look at what he's looking at, and he's looking at my photos. He's so far up that there are pictures of my mom, Leo, and me. I quickly take the laptop from him and shut it, tossing it to the side.

"So why am I ready?" I ask, getting my mind off the fact that he saw photos that weren't meant for his eyes.

"I'm taking you somewhere."

Wow, thank you, Captain Obvious. I roll my eyes at him as he stands up, grabbing my hand without my permission, not that I mind, causing me to stand too. He puts on his coat before leading the way to the door and allows me time to grab my purse, but he doesn't wait for me to put on my winter boots. I sat on the bench by the front door, across from the table, and he kneeled on one knee in front of me, propping my foot on top of his knee. He ties the strings of my shoes. He does it the odd way. Not the two rabbit ears and loop them through. He does it differently, and it's cute. He looks so concentrated as he does the other shoe, too. Butterflies that I haven't felt in years make my stomach their home. Rent free.

"Thank you," I tell him as he sets my feet back on the floor and helps me off the bench. Even going as far as to open the door for me and then helping me down the stairs of my brownstone.

I tilt my head down, hoping to hide the blush, but he puts his finger under my chin and lifts my face, "Don't." Is all he says, a smile kissing his lips the way I want to.

He flags down a taxi, and we both get inside after one stops beside us. He gives an address, which I think is the address for the cafe we were at yesterday. I was right when we pulled up at the restaurant where I met his mother.

"Why are we here?" I ask him, "Not that I'm complaining." I quickly put in when he turned to look at me.

"We have a Christmas 'Party' here every year, and you're my plus one this year." He tells me, the smile never leaving his face as he walks me to the door. He had put 'party' in hand quotes, which makes me curious about what that means.

"Why does it start so early? Wait, I'm not wearing anything formal enough for a party. Also, it isn't Christmas yet."

"Today is Christmas Eve…" He says slowly.

"No, it's not," I argue.

"Yes, it is." He took his phone from his pocket and showed me the date.

'December 24th'

Oh my God. It's Christmas Eve. How did I not realize this? Today can't be Christmas Eve. I didn't visit Mama and Leo's graves yesterday.

"It's okay. Come on, let's go inside." He takes me from my thoughts as he says that. He doesn't give me much more time to think as he leads me inside.

I was wrong if I thought the place was prominent before yesterday because it looks tiny with how many people are here. Many chairs are put together with tables, creating one large seating area with many different types of food placed on top. Garland hangs from each arch and doorway, candles are lit everywhere, and the table is decorated with beautiful ribbons. There are people his mother's age (50s-60s), and some look a little older. There are also some younger people, some the age of children, while some are Nicholas's age. The place is beautiful, and looks like Christmas puked everywhere.

"Come on, you need to meet my father." He drags me in the direction of two people, one of whom I notice is his mother.

She's dressed in a beautiful red dress with white detailing, her hair pulled back in two white clips, her curls falling out. Her glasses sit on her nose as she smiles at me, wrinkles curling around her eyes.

I'm assuming the other guy is his father. He has a white beard that reaches the middle of his chest. He's wearing a red coat with white fluff along the edges. It's buttoned at the front, so I don't know what he's wearing underneath it. He's got on some black boots and has matching glasses that sit on his nose. He has a kind and friendly smile as he turns to me after Nicholas's mother pulls on his sleeve for him to look at me. He seems highly familiar as he stares me down.

"Let me have your coats!" Is the first thing out of her mouth, followed by a deep chuckle that almost shocks me. Imagine Santa Claus and Mrs. Claus because this is precisely how I imagined them to look.

"Hang on, Mom," Nicholas says. He helps me out of my coat before handing it to his mother and then taking off his own to give her. She walks away from us with our coats, and I want to run after her because what if I want to leave and don't have my jacket right next to me?

"I have heard so much about you." Nicholas's father says, "My name is Nick. Nice to meet you, dear." He extends a white-gloved hand. I shake it politely and smile at him back because his smile is too contagious not to.

"Hi, I'm Elliana, as you seem to know already." He laughs and nods. He looks at his son, and after getting a weird confirming nod from him, he steals my hand from Nicholas and leads me towards a couch in front of a window. The snow falling outside hypnotizes me for a second.

"How are you?" He asks me as he takes a seat after me.

"I'm good," I say like on autopilot. "How are you?"

"Don't lie to me," He says, the smile never leaving, which is kind of creepy, "I'm always watching." And that made it even weirder.

"That's creepy," I tell him, moving my body away from him so I'm pushing myself into the side cushion.

"I didn't think that through, sorry, Elli."

Elli.

Elli.

Elli. That's what Mama called me.

"That's what your mother called you, isn't it?" I swear he just read my mind.

"How did you know?" I tilt my head in question.

"Because, as creepy and weird as this may seem, I know everything about you." He tells me, "I know what happened to Amelia and Leo. I know you forget that yesterday was their day. And I hate to say it, but I was the reason you forgot about yesterday."

I stayed quiet. I don't know if it was because of fear or shock. Maybe both.

"How does someone say this to a random person without seeming crazy?" He whispers to himself, but I hear it.

"What?" I ask.

"I am Santa Claus." And just like that, I'm up and away from the couch.

"You're crazy," I tell him. "Crazy. Insane actually. Santa doesn't exist."

I'm out the door before anyone can stop me. I can hear the faint calling of Nicholas yelling my name, but I don't heed it any attention. I don't stop running, taking taxis, more running, walking for a bit, and sitting on a bench as I think until I'm at the graveyard where Leo and Mama are buried. I have to walk for ages until I find their graves, their headstones being small crosses poking out of the ground with their headstones sitting in the dirt.

I sit on the ground between them, with multiple small white crosses surrounding us.

"*Leo Harrington.*"

"*Amelia St. Louis.*"

Staring at Mama's grave, I almost want to pray for her advice, the type of advice I'd like right now. Despite not believing in a higher power, I pray to multiple things. God, Buddha, Universe, I try it all. *I just wish for some of her guidance.*

Sadly, even though "Santa Claus" is real, those higher powers aren't because my prayers aren't answered. Looks like I have to figure this one out on my own. And that's when it hit me. I thought "Santa" looked familiar because he was at my work. A day before Nicholas was hired. He was dressed in beige slacks and a black button-up shirt. He examined the same but without his glasses. He came in to discuss some topics about stores on my radar. I was going to invest in stores, and he was trying to get me to buy into a coffee shop. Kimberly had fixed us tea when I went to the bathroom, and when I returned, my coffee looked more like tea. When I was sitting down, I noticed a small amount of gold dust on the carpet and on top of his shoes. He even kept sneezing.

Did he seriously erase my memory or something? What the hell? Why am I even thinking about this? This stuff doesn't exist.

I feel a small hand land on my shoulder and just about jump out of my skin. I hear a small laugh, "Sorry darling, I thought you might be here, and I came to talk to you. Figured you might be having trouble processing things since he just decided to drop this on you."

Nicholas's mother, or Mrs. Claus, sits beside me in the grass, her hand moving down my shoulder to give my hand a pat before moving to where her whole body is facing me.

"So, Santa.." I start, "Does that make you Mrs. Claus?"

"Yes, but please call me Carol." She tells me with a soft smile, "The original Mrs. Claus was Jessica; every 2000 years, there is a new Santa. Nick was born into the family, and he had just brought me into it. Much like you, I had lost my brother to suicide and my mom and father to old age. I was adopted after my biological parents died in a fire, so when my adopted parents died, I was only 31. They were old, but I loved them like no other; to me, they were my parents. My brother died long before them; I was 19. I had lost all spirit in Christmas and thought there was no reason to celebrate Christmas. That's when I met Nick. He was young then, 768 years old. Sounds old, but in their years, that's young." She laughs.

"He had been assigned to help bring the spirit of Christmas back to life inside me, and it took him four days to do that. It turns out that all I needed was someone to show me that Christmas is still alive and that I can always find more people who love me, and I love them. And he would not let me go. No matter how much I tried after he broke his secret to me. I tried leaving the country, and he followed me to Brazil. Let me tell you that he isn't one to give up." She has a faraway look in her eyes, like she's recalling a memory. "My point is, don't give up. Nicholas is assigned to many people, but you are the first person he has come home with nothing else on his mind except for you. He talks, and talks," She sighs, "and talks. About you. Just you. He has so much to say about you."

"Like what?" I ask her, interrupting her following sentence.

"Maybe you should ask him because I haven't seen him since you left." She says, a slight frown adorning her face. She lays a coat on my lap, which I never grabbed after running out of the cafe. "I'm sure you'll know where he is."

Picking up my coat, I stand up and quickly thank her before I take off through the graveyard, avoiding dead people and trying to wave down a taxi from afar. I don't get one until I'm half a mile down the street, and one finally decides to stop. I gave the directions to the only place he had taken me other than the cafe, which we knew he wasn't there, Central Park.

It feels like centuries before I got there. That's comical because Nicholas is probably centuries years old. I roll my eyes at my joke and grab my purse, climbing out of the taxi. Traffic was horrendous because of its benign Christmas Eve. I had stayed for a while at the graveyard, so it was already 9:00 pm. Imagine New York City on Christmas Eve, lots of people, and when I say lots, I mean LOTS. I searched so many spots in Central Park, people everywhere, before finally finding the area where we attacked each other with snowballs.

There he is.

He's lying in the snow; a shadow of a snow angel is embedded beneath him, but now his hands are crossed over his chest as he stares at the sky through the tree canopy. Light is coming from a nearby lamp post; it casts a shadow on him, and I can see the outline of his jaw and hair that looks like it's had a hand run through it a million times. He's beautiful.

I lay down beside him in the snow silently. He doesn't move his head, "I can't believe you're here." He says.

"I thought about everything and realized that every time I was with you, I forgot about my past. I forgot about everything wrong because you made everything in my head quiet. You made everything seem perfect, okay even." I tell him, my voice soft as I turn to stare at his sharp jaw. His eyes narrow at the trees above, seemingly thinking over things.

"I just want you to know that I wanted to tell you so many times, but my father always said no, and my mother always said I should. She said you deserved the truth, but then I had Dad in my ear saying, 'No, you'll ruin everything and scare her away,' blah blah blah. I should've never listened to him." He says, a smile making its way onto his face as he turns his head towards me.

"It's okay, I understand," I whisper.

"I'm still sorry. I should've told you because after your past, it's the least you de-." He's interrupted by my lips on his. The sound of people talking disappears, and the sounds of crunching snow with our slightest movements are gone. Everything Is quiet, it's just me and him. Us. Together. On the snow. In a perfect moment. My wish came true.

My Santa Claus is real. But this one goes by Nicholas. Or, as I first met him, Père Noël.

The End.

About Kathryn Denhof

Kathryn Denhof has been an aspiring writer most of her life, with a few published pieces in the She is Magic series and some fanfiction. This is her first truly published piece of fiction in print and hopefully, the first of many more to come. Kathryn is an Instagram Fashion Influencer and graphic designer for Elite Publishing House/Girl on Fire Magazine. When she is not working on her projects, Kathryn enjoys, spoiling her baby sister, shopping with her mom, traveling (or dreaming of traveling), and annoying her brothers.

Dear Universe

By Heidi Plumberg

There I was, a 26-year-old hustler, studying in the university business faculty and keeping two jobs that pay well and even give one the possibility to manage people. Also, that November, I felt like I had everything figured out. Looking back now, 20 years ahead, I would just love this girl and say - learn to love yourself - you have no hobbies, and where are your dance lessons?

What made a perfect relationship for a girl who is 26 years old, working in two high-paying corporate jobs, and leading a sales team? Well, I started dating a man I met on the Internet, and after five months of letters, we finally met. No photos were sent, and it was as if I were going on a blind date. I had several boyfriends before this relationship and had been dumped by one boyfriend before finding this guy online. He felt so safe.

He was not a guy I would have chosen by his appearance, but I had an instant crush on him because of the poems he had sent me. Yes, they were love poems full of sexy remarks on my beauty and shine. Enough to make a girl happy and blissful. My heart melted. I printed all the emails out and saved them in my secret binder. No one had ever sent me poems before. I was so happy.

As our relationship moved forward, I found the guy was helpful in cleaning, cooking, and pleasing me. I had nothing to do at home; it was all done for me by him. I lost attraction in him as he got better at housework. I was building a career in the corporate world, and he was not interested in any new challenges. However, it felt safe. I had someone I did belong to, which was a sweet thought.

One day, I was surfing the Internet and found the poems he had sent me as his own. My heart was crushed, but I did keep silent. More things were happening.

But let's get on into the holiday mood!

Just travelling back in time, it was a cold November, and I had just found out that my boyfriend for five years had a hidden relationship with another girl who was five years younger than me. They had amazing sex; suddenly, I was 26 and felt old. All the dreams of him proposing to me and asking me to marry him were useless and dead. I felt so lonely, old, and not sexy at all. Why was he cheating on me? All those emotions started flushing over my body and through my mind. The fear of being alone. Having to spend Christmas with my mom again alone. It all felt like a terrible nightmare.

I cried and begged him to come back to me. And he did. Then, I proposed to him. I had so much fear that no one would want me and that I was not good enough for anyone. I had a well-paid job and started showering my boyfriend with expensive gifts. A new bike. I even took him to a jewelry store and bought our engagement rings. We picked out a really nice and expensive one, and I bought it. I bought a ring for myself, too.

It was two weeks before Christmas, and we were finally engaged. White snow and Christmas carols made everything look better. I was a perfect pride. I cleaned the house and cooked the dinner for Christmas. My fiancée disappeared and did not answer any of my calls. He was meeting another girl and still had another relationship with the girl in November. More women. More talks. More messages. I felt so ashamed of my actions.

How could I stoop so low as to ask him to marry me? I felt sick to my stomach and lost my voice. I spent Christmas in bed feeling so sorry for myself and nervous about the outcome of my life.

You know that feeling you get when you think you have lost everything? Too busy pleasing others and end up putting yourself down? That was me during that Christmas. Feeling shame and pity for myself. I felt embarrassed that I had gone shopping to buy rings and presents for my boyfriend. How low can a lady go?

I was just sitting and eating. Of course, I gained weight. At the moment, I did not care about gaining weight or my good looks. Some days, it was hard to make myself to take a shower. I felt a deep sadness, which was holding me back from joy. I had to fully let myself experience all the feelings, and the breakthroughs started to happen.

I started to feel my body and tune into my feelings more. It was like a huge onion. Peeling each layer off after the other. I did not know that was the method I would help people learn 10 to 20 years later so they could find their joy and happiness. I just knew I needed to find mine.

In a few weeks, we ended our relationship, and I wrote a letter to the Universe. My second deepest fear was to spend Valentine's Day alone. I started going out with my friends from the university and bought a ticket to a concert for Valentine's Day.

My older sister married at 19 and had a baby some months after her marriage. I was several years older than her, yet had no marriage or kids to show. I felt like I was letting others and myself down.

You know those letters you write on New Year's Eve?

Finding a man felt impossible at this point. I had a deep belief that all good men were already taken. Well, I did not get out alone during my relationship. My boyfriend and I were always together. Plus, I had no eyes for other guys while I was dating, and no one ever asked me out. How can I change impossible to possible? One thing I knew was that I did not want to change myself anymore. I wanted my old me back from high school. I had lost her on the way to hustling, pleasing my employer and boyfriend. And I definitely had tried to please my mom. So, I wrote a letter of deep feelings about it! *'Do something about it,'* was the voice in my head. And yes, I did write. Four full pages of writing with messy handwriting, old me and my future, living in my house with my husband and kids. Cooking, cleaning, and smiling. I wrote it all. Even writing this now clears my mind. It happened. I was a stay-at-home mom for 14 years, longing to go to work, but here is the root - I did not because of this letter. A letter I have never told anyone about until now.

The feeling I got from this exercise was freedom. The uncomfortable feelings had gone away. The not feeling good enough was gone. All good men being taken thinking had shifted.

Instead, in the place of those feelings, there was me. I am a deserving girl. I deserve enough of everything, girl.

Some days after that, I started to connect again with my old girlfriends. Some had disappeared, and the connection was gone after six long years. I joined a university women's corporation and forced myself to attend the meetings. I had a deep sense of needing to belong. The corporation had stringent rules for freshmen participants. You had to show up daily, or you would not be accepted. That is what I needed - the rules!

I needed the rules to make me stick to things that I knew were good for me. Within weeks, I felt happier. It was easier to say no to evening shifts at work because I had to meet with the university girls in the corporation. We cooked, cleaned, danced, and even took dancing lessons with boys. They were much younger than me, but this was suddenly unimportant. Feeling old was gone! It has disappeared like last year. You know, you cannot go back to last Christmas really!

I now had a safety net. Everything that got discussed there - stayed there. Those new friends really saved me from the old me. The one who was always comparing herself with others and not feeling good enough, smart enough, or doing enough - even when reality proved the opposite.

Suddenly, I stepped out of the box of being the secret person at home. I felt the dream existed outside my box. Even if my weight had not dropped, I felt good in my body and shopped for new expensive clothes. My friend Mirjam took a photoshoot of me. Those pictures were stunning.

How do you feel about your work? I asked myself. How can I reveal how I am more to the people around me? A true change in words and body language occurred. I was so passionate about connecting with even strangers. The feeling of connection I had lost over the last five years has disappeared. I started to see into people, and people started to see into me. I was vulnerable and funny.

Suddenly, I felt the choice - it was safety or success. I took the leap and chose success. I was acting as if I had it all figured out. Feeling sick to my stomach. Feeling the joy and sometimes allowing the fear.

Will people like me because my boyfriend said I am disgusting? It made no sense that he said so many things at different times or places. Like I was good in sex but slow in bed. An amazing cook but awful when I made pasta. Sexy in a nightgown but not sexy in my jeans. It did not make sense to me. I was deeply confused by his words and actions. Just like he loved me and still disliked me?

It never made sense, and I never asked.

Maybe it would have looked as simple as saying, "Hi, can you please explain why I am such a burden? What do you mean that I tell you to do things?"

I later learned most of the things when his new girlfriend told me! Yes! I was so miserable that I called his new girlfriend and confronted her. She said that my ex-boyfriend had confessed he was a victim of mine. That was mind blowing to me! He had told her he needed sex because I was so awful at sex. Wow! I had burst into tears. How could he?

That conversation helped me to heal. A lot. Because tears started flowing like a river, and it took hours to stop them. Then I grabbed my breath and built myself up.

As I started to see growth in myself, I could also see growth in all other areas of my life. My job turned out only to simply manage and balance the exchange of energy I gave up.

And then...*it* happened. I met a guy there who had dumped me six years ago, just before meeting my boyfriend, as described in my sad love story. At first, I tried to hide myself from him, but he was very confident. He stepped by my side and asked me to come out for dinner with him just after the concert.

I blushed and said yes! I had experienced such a deep sadness during Christmas that I had no bad feelings towards this guy. He was so happy to see me that I felt deeply happy in my heart. How could I say no? I was dressed extremely casually and I had no intention that night of finding someone. I can recall wearing a blue woolen jumper and old jeans. I felt totally unsexy in those clothes.

We went to a nice restaurant, and what happened there was mind blowing. The guy said he had been looking for me for some time and knew I was in a relationship, so he did not contact me. But now he feels he has won the jackpot because he wants to start a fresh relationship with me and marry me.

I had lost my voice, and I could only smile. I was so angry with this guy when he had dumped me six years ago, but now there was no anger left. I looked into his grey eyes and melted. He talked the whole time about me and how he had understood later what a fool he had been. I felt as if I was in someone's own story, and listening to him made me feel relaxed. That was a feeling I had not ever felt before. The feeling of not needing to prove myself. The feeling that I was already good enough. The feeling that love is available to me.

Those grey eyes loved me so completely and trusted me. Could this be true? That working through those deep feelings during Christmas was finally bringing me joy?

That was a lesson I now teach to my kids. All you have to do is ask. The ask is your offer. And my husband was the first man in my life to ask the question.

I felt total safety. As if all of it came back together. All my needs were met. I had pulled the vision.

Counting my blessings has brought me to a very different day. Seeking connection had brought me *the* connection. That seemed to have been a secret weapon of mine.

'What would I love to happen next?' That was the lingering question in my head.

I tried to feel my stomach and suddenly felt hot in the woolen jumper.

'Be me!' The voice helped me to cool down and relax. I did not even feel the sweating and wool on my body.

And it was a full body, yes! I leaped into the love and let the love bathe me with all those stories, kisses, and smiles! We ended up starting our life together, and some months later, he proposed to me. Our wedding took place on Valentine's Day the following year. Now we have been together for 21 years.

And the boyfriend who cheated on me - he dated that second girl, the one from that November, but they are not married yet. He is still wearing my engagement ring, which I had bought him. For 22 years! Isn't that weird? In April, after Valentine's Day, he messaged me to celebrate his birthday together, and it felt so easy to say no to him.

Saying no to him felt like saying yes to myself and my own new relationship. I was no longer haunted by feelings and the need to be loved by him. I was free of that hurtful relationship, self-pity, and shame.

My confidence had grown in a way I had never dreamed of before. I had 10 times the confidence I had the year prior. I had found my purpose to connect people. I was the connector. Life was so easy now. I still needed to push myself as an introvert outside of my home (it was really cozy to be home alone). But your purpose is supposed to force you to come out from being a best-kept secret. And yes, it needs you to step out every day, even if you feel uncomfortable doing this. So, that is what I did.

If you don't learn to transform your pain into purpose, you will be a survivor but not a warrior. I had become a warrior within a few months. Letting my hand write what I wanted and sobbing all the tears had made a difference.

The Universe is here for me! To reverse everything in a matter of seconds. Feeling your purpose, facing challenges, seeing progress, and creating a community and connection - all were my deep-buried needs. When my ex stopped loving me, I had lost myself. Even without knowing that, I had lost something.

If you had all the time, money, and network, what would you be doing? What would you be doing if it was impossible to disappoint someone? What is worth doing or trying - even if you fail?

Wouldn't it be cool if....

I started to do the things that I loved instead of the things that made me think people still loved me. Giving myself permission to disappoint others started to grow the flower of joy in my heart in a way I never knew possible.

Head first is the quickest way through. Say more yes to the feeling in your stomach. Wow, this felt powerful. I did not know that it was called Intuition (well, I know it now), but I just started to observe my body and how it reacted brough me chills. Things started to shift really fast.

I started to face my problems and started to see that other people have it worse. I found myself before Christmas in a charity bus bringing Christmas gifts to Ukrainian Estonians. People had brought hundreds of gifts, and it turned out it was much cheaper to take the gifts there by bus and share them in person. Focusing my attention on those kids and families made a shift inside me. Suddenly, I had no time to cry and self-pity myself anymore. Seeing how well I was in my reality pushed me out of drama.

It was messy! But the messy worked for me. Driving to the Ukraine by bus took three days, and I started to knit socks. That was my first time doing it. As a schoolgirl, my granny helped me with the socks. She was so good at knitting and even created her own brand of socks with snowflakes in them. But yes, 40 years ago, the word brand did not really exist. The main story here was by pushing me, she did it for me and I never learned the magic of knitting a sock or two. Here I was, sitting on the bus, printed paper with instructions ahead of me and I did knit my first pair of socks.

This is the reason now, 22 years later, I am not doing things that many moms do for their kids. I let them learn it the hard way so they can thrive.

We have four kids now. Two of them are already entrepreneurs. And the funny thing is, they are successful without any conscious mentoring from me. It is the mindset that is inherited from me and my husband. Sometimes, I wish they would ask me for guidance! But that is just the way it is.

The stories are so powerful! And to see the beauty in your experiences is the love God gives us. The beautiful breakthrough of the year. Realizing that these are only experiences, we can choose the perspective of the things happening to us. Or for us.

And did my husband in this story turn out perfect? No way! And nor am I. I love to call myself a work-in-process, and so I let him be a work-in-process as well. And I just do me every single moment. Not to please him has also been a story of its own. No dinner? Yes, we have to order food or eat a meal available. No feeling to connect? Let it be. We all need a moment in our cave.

My perspective about life had shifted, and the self-love journey that one Christmas had paid off. Like a fast track to love. From manifesting as if something was happening to me to it actually being me. Much like going from school to university, skipping college.

Pain is powerful. There is another story of pain for my next book! But the insights it brings are nothing more than powerful.

All the worst-case scenarios happened not to be true. There were lots of smart and handsome men out there I dated before Valentine's Day. But none of them asked.

How can it be better than this? And it could be better as I gave birth to our beautiful daughter 16 months after that Valentine's Day.

I was so sure that I could not become pregnant that I even signed up for surgery to find out why with my last boyfriend. We never tried consciously, but I had a belief that there was much wrong with me because my life proved it. I started to investigate everything about my body and myself, but I could not see the real reason I felt unhappy in my own body.

It was never about him or my mom; it was me who always wanted to be more. There is no more. So, my new quote in life is to be less. To do less. To relax more. To sleep more. To love more. And yes, as my purpose is connection, I also connect more people with each other. That is why I created an online community that gives skills with connection with yourself and others. And that deep connection with God, Source, Universe - whatever way you call the ultimate power source that is here to support you. The question is, "Can you accept the love and support first?" Because that became the lighted way in my story and it may also be a way for you too.

The old me was like, I am so happy that they feel happy. The new me is like I am happy, and also people around me are happy and I am happy with them.

It felt as if I had suddenly provided the healing. The law matches the feeling. You can be the right person, doing wrong things, and it turns out right. Or the opposite. The wrong person doing all the right things, and nothing happens at all.

Your vibration matters and we as humans can cause a lot of self-sabotage if we lack self-love and appreciation. Those two are so important. Love the preciousness of yourself. On the mental, physical, and emotional level. I was happy I let my ex-boyfriend go so he could find his amazing sex and pretty women elsewhere to marry and live forever with. But then, why did he not let go of the ring I bought him? It would be nice to send it back to me? I might love that action step if you ever read the story.

There are some details that I did not put into this holiday love story because they are not important for you to see the point. I am sure some more stories will point out some other learning points of this true romantic story of finding your true love. Is it ever there? I can assure you that the right love story is happening with you and God (or Universe, Source, whatever you want to name it).

And this has always been there to catch you with the safety net. Is this aligned with who you are, and what is your vision?

What is your success rate in your life? Let me know how this story inspires you and if you are ready to take a leap and write your own letter to the Universe! You can even write it today!

Leave all doubt, worry, and fear! Or whatever objections you have, and start creating your life in a new spiritual way.

Love yourself! It is not that scary. And this is not that woo-woo at all. My fear, I never knew was brought to me through love and abandonment. But no one can abandon you if you do not abandon yourself. Are you?

Isn't that extraordinary what a brief letter to the Universe can create?

Is that story true or not? Who knows! Are the stories in our lives always the way they are? The storyteller has the power. Like a kid wanting a new fairytale or listening to the Cinderella story, looking for romance. It is there if you want to find it.

The End.

Story Inspiration:

The above story is a true story of Christmas. A Christmas of not needing to hide away and feel sorry for yourself. This unique and amazing story will hopefully give you back your belief in romance. It is based on my own story of forgiving myself and others. The beauty of change that happened many Christmases ago.

About Heidi Plumberg

Heidi Plumberg is a transformative figure in the realm of business coaching, seamlessly blending the principles of entrepreneurship with spirituality. As a self-made entrepreneur, dedicated spiritual coach, loving wife, and devoted mother of four, Heidi embodies the essence of multi-dimensional success.

Her journey from humble beginnings to the pinnacle of success is a testament to her resilience, self-belief, and the transformative power of a positive money mindset. Heidi has turned challenges into stepping stones, proving that with determination and the right mindset, there are no limits to success.

As a spiritual coach, Heidi offers a holistic approach to financial success, integrating elements of spirituality into her coaching practice. Her work has empowered countless individuals to break free from limiting beliefs about money, unlocking their full potential, and guiding them towards financial success.

Heidi's accomplishments extend beyond her coaching practice.

As a celebrated author, Heidi has added another feather to her cap with three Amazon bestsellers to her name. Her profound insights and innovative approaches have not only gained her a wide readership but also recognition from reputable platforms such as Forbes. This recognition further cements her authority in the field, reaching an audience beyond her immediate circle of influence.

In today's dynamic world, Heidi continues to strive for excellence, pushing boundaries, and setting new standards in the realm of spiritual business coaching. Her story is a testament to the fact that success is not a destination, but a journey of continuous growth and learning. As she continues to inspire and empower others through her work, Heidi Plumberg is a name that resonates with transformation, success, and the power of a positive mindset.

Last Christmas Wish

By Blair Hayse

I tighten my scarf around my neck as the wind blows bitterly at my petite frame, causing it to be almost impossible to walk. I wrinkle my nose, looking at the sky; *where the heck did this weather come from anyway?* It never is this cold in the South...and if it has to be this cold, please let it snow. I will myself to shut my eyes and try to wish snowfall from the sky, but even I, Brianna Davis, the ever-optimist, know the percentage of that happening is zero. Finally, I open my eyes and decide to plow through the wind to get to my car, with the assurance that warmth will be there once I turn it on. I didn't have to close the car door behind me because once I got in, the wind slammed it shut for me, barely missing catching my scarf in the act. Pushing the start button in my car, I hear it crank, and the warmth starts to blow. I cannot hold it in any longer.

Tears fall down my frozen red cheeks, and I do nothing to brush them away. Instead, I put my head down on the steering wheel and cried the ugliest cry I've had in years. The sobbing, snot everywhere, pretty sure people walking by can hear me, sort of cries.

It is back.

The cancer is back.

Reality starts to feel as chilling as my breath in this un-cranked car.

I had my annual appointment with the oncologist a few days ago; they finally called me today to tell me that the results were in, and the verdict was my cancer was back. I guess I had always known it could happen, but now that it is here, it made me sick to think I might not fight it this time. As a matter of fact, I wasn't even sure I wanted to fight it.

I am tired, so tired.

Maybe succumbing to the illness was better than willing it off.

Angrily, I brushed the tears lingering on my cheeks and drew in an icy breath. Pulling my phone from my pocket, I hesitate, contemplating as my finger hovered over Levi's name to decide if I wanted to call him next.

Levi had been my best friend for years and was one of the only people I allowed myself to talk about the C word with. I always wondered why. *Maybe because I felt safe with him, safe to be myself without judgment, or perhaps it was just because...*

I notice some families walking across the shopping center, happy despite the bitter cold. I set my phone down. *I miss happiness. Gosh, I need to get home.*

Driving out of the parking lot, I kept feeling as if I was forgetting something, but lately, I felt like I was *always* forgetting something, so I merely tossed it aside as I drove home.

The sun shone through my windows, and I moaned as I rolled over in bed, grasping my hand towards the nightstand to find my phone without fully waking up.

He had texted in my dream.

I had seen his name on the screen of my phone, so real, but besides wanting to know if it was just a dream, I was actually worried about the time.

What time is it? Please don't have overslept, Brianna.

Rarely did I worry about oversleeping; being my own boss as an aspiring writer came with its perks, and no alarm clock was one of those. But today was different. I am supposed to catch a flight to New York City for my long-awaited writer's conference, and the closest airport is three hours away. My hand finally connected to my phone, and I squinted at the time before letting out an even louder moan. *Levi Arrington*, across the screen, glared back at me.

He had texted.

I almost fear sliding the button and unlocking my phone to see his text. I have been avoiding texting him for months now. To put it lightly, being best friends with complications was the theme of our relationship. He had been dating Carrie, and I had a complicated relationship; avoiding him and the truth seemed easier.

"Hey, B, What's up?"

One simple text. Four simple words. And yet, it stirred in me emotions that I didn't want to feel because it meant things I could not explain or that would even be reciprocated. I sat up, dazed, glaring at the screen as if the words would somehow change or make sense.

How can he just text like we have been talking like old times?

There is no explanation for not texting for months.

No, I miss you.

Nothing.

It was a simple text as if the world was playing out another day.

Ugh, it is evident he does not care the same way I do. If he did, he would have replayed songs to settle his heart the last months and drove by my house to see if I was still alive without any indication of stopping.

Am I the only one who feels all the feelings in this complicated friendship?

Yes, I am.

Clicking the phone screen off, I tumbled out of bed and started to make coffee. Levi can wait. It will be at least a couple hours until I have coffee in my system.

Standing in the kitchen, I let coffee spill everywhere because I forgot to turn off the coffee maker to get my cup.

Brianna, what the hell is wrong with you? Why do you literally act like you cannot think straight these days? Am I really old enough to be losing moments of memory? Is it stress? I have to slow down.

Sipping my coffee, I knew I had to text him back. I wanted us to talk again. I missed him more than life itself. Everything is off when we are not talking. Especially my creativity. My writing tends to go to nothing because he has always been my inspiration. I needed him, much like someone needs oxygen, and no one will ever understand that about me, especially him.

I sip my coffee and weigh my options. I can text him, be as conveniently available as always, and be distracted the one time I need to be on my game in New York City when pitching my book idea to the big publishers. Or, I cannot text him back and be super focused during my trip. Wait, would I?

I click back on my phone and hesitantly text back. The whole time, I secretly hoped I was not making the biggest mistake I would regret when he disappeared the next time.

"Hey, mister. I am good. I'm busy as always. How have you been?"

I look it over. *Safe. Lying, but safe.* I click send, and almost immediately, he texts back.

"Good B, been thinking I need to write my own book, but I need your help."

Hmmm. Safe enough, I guess. He needed something. Without thinking, I pull out my more professional tone and type back.

"Well, I am off to New York City for a writer's conference, but when I get back, I will circle back, and we can talk about it then."

Clicking my phone off, I knew I had to try to put him out of my mind. At some point, I had to tell him about the cancer, but I would wait until tests were run and I knew more. There is no need to tell him when I don't know what I am dealing with yet.

I grab my keys and already packed luggage.

If I hurry, I can catch my flight on time, and for once, this is important.

"It has moved to your brain." I watched the doctor's mouth move, hearing the words, but it all felt surreal. I had beat the cancer twice before, and I expected some speech about the odds being in my favor, not exactly the odds being against me. He was rambling on about a care plan they had drawn up for me and how it was an aggressive cancer that we needed to be on top of it all.

I am pretty sure I had questions, but when he asked me if I had any questions, I oddly shook my head no. I felt like it was a dream. One I was sure to wake up from tomorrow morning. I wasn't young, but I was young enough, and dying was not on my radar at the moment. I still had a lot of life I wanted to live. I want to fulfill being a fiction writer, with my name being known in most households as they cozy up with my latest suspense novel I had just pitched in New York. Which, by the way, was received really well. I had three literary agents' cards tucked in my small Kate Spade purse beside me, wanting to see the manuscript when I finished it. It was my first time pitching, and I didn't know if that was good, but according to the masses of people there, and only 11 of us got literary agent cards, it seemed like three of them meant a lot about my writing.

"Ms. Davis?" I hear the doctor calling my name and snap back. I shook my head, agreeing to whatever he must have been speaking about because my mind was clearly not here.

"Can I have a copy of the care paper, in case I need it?" I asked timidly. I still hated to admit I had cancer to anyone, most often myself. I tended to avoid the hard stuff and just try to plow through it, but this time, I might need to at least acknowledge just how hard this fight for life would be.

The doctor warmly smiled, too warmly, like he felt really sorry for me at that moment. I grabbed the papers from his hand and then forced myself to look at the prognosis in black and white. My hands were shaking, and my voice was trembling on the verge of tears. "Is there something more we can do to increase the odds in my favor?" I hear myself asking, afraid of the answer I would get back.

"No. I am sorry. This is one of the most aggressive cancers, and to beat it, well, it would take a miracle, but they can happen."

I sat there, knowing he was being honest with me because he always had. It was why I traveled over state lines to the oncologist instead of trusting anyone in my small town.

I stood up and shook his hand. "You got this, Brianna; see the receptionist at the front on your way out to set up your radiation times and to get your prescription for chemo. The bright side is that these chemo pills do not make your hair fall out, and you have always worried about that aspect."

I was thankful for a doctor who understood me and knew my fears already, but this was a big-league cancer, not the small-league ones I was used to dealing with. I was unsure if I had the fight to beat this before I walked through the doors today, and now I was even less sure.

Pulling my car over halfway home, I pulled out my cell phone and texted Levi.

I have to tell him.

If there was ever someone who knew the right thing to say that might even remotely make me want to fight this, it would be him. Despite our odds and the excessive amounts of time we stopped talking to each other, I almost always could count on him to be there in the really tough times. Well, mostly. Sadly, in the past couple of years, I had seen him not there for me during some tough times, and I realized that I needed to accept this friendship as unhealthy so I could move on.

You tried to move on, Bri. I remind myself silently. It is the whole reason I am stuck in a relationship that is toxic and that I do not even love him. I had hoped it would make me happy enough to not think about him, but all it did was put me in an awful relationship I couldn't find my way out of and invoke more tension between Levi and me. Great job, I sigh.

I knew better than to let myself linger on the fact that he continually chooses toxic circles to hang in and considers people his friends that I hear talking about him behind his back in town. I will never understand; if I try to tell him what they are saying, it somehow gets turned on me. I finally had just stopped telling him. Clearly, he believed they were friends, and I needed to stay out of it as much as it hurt me to hear people talking badly of him. If I stayed lingering in these thoughts, I would talk myself out of calling him.

I took a deep breath and texted instead. Safer. I won't have to hear his voice.

"My cancer is back."

Might as well be straight and honest.

"What? When did you find out?" His text seemed honestly concerning.

"Just a few weeks ago, but I just got the prognosis and care plan. It is in my brain, and the odds look bad."

"You got this, B. You have beat it twice before; it was crazy to come back for more." I felt myself smile. Yeah, the cancer is crazy to think I won't beat it.

"Thanks, mister. I needed that. I am scared."

I took a picture of the care plan and prognosis and sent it to him. Maybe he would understand why scared was the best word I could find, but terrified seemed more adequate. Actually, I don't even have a word for how I feel.

I knew his answer would be he was going to pray for me, which I am a lot of things, but religious isn't one of them. I clicked the screen of my phone off and put my car into drive. It was time to get home.

Maybe I would look up some research tonight on alternative options. I had to cling to hope. Even if it took all I had.

I checked and triple-checked the recipe to ensure it had all the correct ingredients. Lately, my memory seemed to be a lot worse. I couldn't remember the smallest of things. The last thing I need to do is screw up his Christmas gift, rum cake. I tasted the batter with a spoon and nodded my head in approval. It tasted right, though honestly, he was the only person I ever made rum cake for, and it had been a few years since I had made it. I was sure the taste was on point. *At least my taste buds don't fail me*, I thought.

I dump it into the Bundt pan and slide it into the already pre-heated oven. I shut the door and took off my apron. While it cooked, I could get some research done. I pulled out my laptop and punched the timer on my phone so I wouldn't forget the cake. I reviewed my calendar notes to ensure I hadn't missed any appointments today and hoped I hadn't forgotten anything. Since the doctor told me memory loss was a side effect of the Cancer, I had recently started making a lot of notes on my computer and phone to try to remember things. Even small things, like my birthday, social, phone number, and address. I kept notes on each person I talked to, what they liked or disliked, and memories I had flashes of to help me seem more competent when speaking to them. It had been challenging and exhausting. It made me doubt myself and everything I thought I knew.

The other day, I had pulled up something with the name of Eric on it, and I had no idea or recollection of who that was. I finally texted Levi to ask him. I felt like an outsider living in my body. Re-learning everything again. I didn't talk to anyone but my doctor about how bad the memory loss had gotten because I knew people would think I was crazy. As a matter of fact, they had already threatened to take my keys away, thinking it was unsafe for me to drive. My own freedom was in jeopardy. Sometimes, I wasn't even totally honest with my doctor because I was afraid of the outcome that might happen if he knew the truth.

I pull up Google and try to find the words to put into the search bar. That might be the most annoying part of memory loss. Knowing what I want to say, I can feel it right there, but it won't come to the surface enough to get it out. I am a words person. I rely on them to make a living, and I can't even get simple words to surface enough for me to talk coherently.

Gosh, Bri, you are really winning at this thing called Cancer.

Finally grasping the words I needed for 'alternative cancer treatments,' I pulled up the Google search history and skimmed through it. There has to be options. It cannot just end with no hope. I have to find something. Every week, the prognosis gets worse, and the amount of time I am given seems to dwindle too fast. My eyes land on a cancer clinic in Houston, Texas. I hate Texas, but if they have answers, I will start to like them a little. I clicked on the link and read about clinical trials. Risky, but what do I have to lose right now? I jot down the number and vow to call them on Monday when I have time next week.

The timer goes off, and I snap my laptop shut. It's time to get this cake out and put the rum mixture into the holes I put on top. A secret of mine to keep the cake super moist and well, more rum is never a bad idea, right? The cake looks perfect, and I take it in for a minute. I might be losing bits of my reality, but I can still cook a pretty darn good cake.

He better love this.

Traffic is backed up for miles on Glesson, the main strip through town. The mall is there, and people are trying to get a head start on their Christmas shopping. I squint, and as far as I can see, there are cars. It will take me forever to get to the sporting goods store where I was supposed to meet Levi to give him his cake.

"Traffic is horrible, but I am on my way." I texted him to alert him that even pacing ahead of schedule, I was pretty sure I would be late looking at the traffic ahead.

"Just drop it off at my apartment, B."

I stare at the text.

Bad idea. Do not do it, Bri.

"Okay, I will be there once I get through traffic."

I did it.

"I am jumping in the shower; just let yourself in."

And he did it too.

The root of our complicated friendship is right here. Proof with the exchange of texts and an underlying hint of more, but never allowing that to happen.

Pulling into his apartment, I walk up the stairs, carefully balancing the cake because lately, I have been falling a lot. Another stupid side effect of the cancer. Losing my balance while just walking or getting out of a car. Falling and getting hurt because my bones are not strong and my Vitamin D is bottomed out. I open the door, carefully calling his name since he might still be in the shower.

Sitting the cake down on the counter, I glance around the apartment. Neat enough for a bachelor and pretty well-decorated, someone had definitely helped him. And by someone, I was sure it was a female. That was not a surprise; he was known for getting around the town, another reason I could never see things being honest between us. He had too much to give up to settle down, and I didn't want someone unwilling to. I had lived the wild stage and was over it now.

"Hey B," I turn to see him with his pants on and no shirt, drying his hair with a towel. His eyes were crystal blue, as always.

"Hey, mister," I wave my hand to the cake. "I just wanted to drop this off early. My December usually gets crazy busy, and I wanted to make sure you got it."

He walks over and gives me a hug. His eyes are super sincere with gratefulness.

"Thanks, B. You know I love your rum cake. How have you been feeling?" His eyes were now clouded with concern. I bit my lip, wondering how much to tell him because I hated to be a worry or burden with my health.

"It is all good. My memory is bad, and I keep losing my balance, but otherwise, I am okay. I put in my application for a clinical trial at a cancer clinic in Texas. Maybe they can help." I try to sound as positive as I can for him.

"You got this, B. I don't believe the doctors at all. They are wrong. You will be fine and live to be an old lady, retired on the beach, just like we planned."

I chuckled softly.

"Thanks, Levi. I am trying hard to believe and have faith, but some days it is hard."

Levi pulled his shirt over his head, and my hand reached for a piece of lint on his chest. Our hands met at the same time, and my eyes darted up to his. I can feel my heart pounding.

Don't do it, Bri.

Don't fall for him again.

Keep the distance.

It is safer.

He doesn't love you back.

You will only get hurt.

Thousands of warning thoughts go off in my head. His hand grabs mine, and he tilts his head down to me. I can feel his breath hit my face and his heart racing as much as mine. He leans down, and I start to close my eyes.

Suddenly, he jerks away.

"I forgot I have to meet one of my buddies to pick up something and do some Christmas shopping today. I better get going."

Pain shot through my heart. There was the Levi I knew. He was too afraid to admit his feelings, and we would both die with something unsaid between us. Only dying for me had become a reality I was slowly starting to accept. Maybe I must begin accepting that I will never have him as mine. The fantasies I have in my head. The things I wish he would admit to stop this in between torture. I have to let it go. I have held onto it for over a decade, and here we still are.

"Sure, I best get going anyway." I nervously laugh.

"Thanks for the cake, B. Take care of yourself."

I clutch my keys and turn on my heels, willing myself to not look back and to try to erase the almost kiss that just about happened. It was just like our love.

Almost.

The email stared back at me on my phone screen. "Status of your clinical trials application" in the subject line. I had been waiting for this. Hoping for it. I was scared of rejection when it was the only thread of hope I had left, and even that thread was held over a fire of uncertainty in trials. Nothing promised.

Clicking on the email, I braced myself for the bad news.

> *"Thank you for your recent application to our clinical trial program. We are pleased to notify you that you have been accepted for clinical trials with our facility. Please contact Susan Russell to set up your appointment and travel arrangements."*

Hope. One word that summed up everything I felt, and yet, I had no one I could share it with because I don't tell anyone about my cancer except for Levi.

I screenshot the email and press send to him.

"They accepted me," I added to the text.

"I told you, B. The doctors are wrong. You are going to be fine." His text came back rapidly.

Maybe, just maybe, there was hope in more ways than just my health. Perhaps I needed to cling to the hope that he would love me the same way I loved him one day. Just like my cancer, that took a lot of hope.

I stare at the doctor in front of me, digesting the news. Clinical trials were an unknown world to me. I should have brought someone with me to understand this better.

Yeah, right, Bri. Who would you have brought? Levi? He refuses to do anything with you, which puts him in a too-close range of facing the emotions he has closed off so well.

The last thing I want to discuss is that hope seems to be running out. I need a vacation. I could ask Levi to go with me on vacation. I can't ask anyone else because they would see me behind closed doors. The sickness. The frail nerves I have. The crying. The falling. And worst yet, the memory loss. I could put on a decent front in front of people for a few minutes, but on vacation, I knew I could not, and it probably wasn't safe for me to travel alone.

Levi had been distant since the almost kiss at his apartment a few days ago. Typical short texts and barely answering, sometimes not answering.

I unlock my phone screen and text him before I lose the nerve.

"Beach vacation with me? You down for it?"

Safe enough, I thought. I hit send.

"Can't B, I have too much work."

I shut the phone off angrily. It doesn't matter how hard I fight. Fighting a brick wall is never going to change with him.

I turn my attention back to the doctor, who is clicking away on the screen. We will get you in this week and start the clinical trials, he was saying. I nodded my head. Fighting my health needed all of me. I would have to sort out Levi at a different time. Maybe never.

"Schedule me in, doc. I am ready. Let's get started!" I muster up the best peppy voice I could manage.

Rolling over in my bed, I reached for my phone. What time is it anyway? I have to go do some errands today in town.

Levi Arrington

A text from Levi so early this morning? I clicked on it, and it immediately had pictures of the blue sky, a video of the beach waves in California, and a picture of him. A smile crept over my face. There was the Levi I needed.

"Jelly," I respond back. And I was jealous of the blue sky, Cali, the beach waves, and of him.

"How are you feeling?" He responded back. My heart stopped beating for a minute. He cared.

"Tired and sick, but okay," I respond back. Watered down the truth because lying to him was something I had never been able to do.

"You need to rest, B. You need to focus on yourself and stop worrying about everyone else."

The reason he knew me so well.

"I am trying; that is hard for me to do."

"I know."

The whole conversation made my hope soar, and I felt better about life. Just talking to him picked me up. Sparked my creativity. Made me smile. Laugh more. He held all of the power, and it was not fair. Because when he disappears, my world goes dark and cold.

Sipping my coffee, I adjust my earrings to new Christmas ones I bought and throw on my wrap. I had to get some things done today. I had a list on my phone, so I was sure to remember where I needed to go and for what.

Levi Arrington

Again? I swipe left to see the text pop up. It is a video of him. I push play.

"Just felt you might need a pep talk. You got this, B. You have so much to live for and have to live because we have to retire to the beach. I just wanted you to know to keep your head up; you are one of the strongest women I know. Love you, B."

Tears fell down on my cheeks.

"I love you too. Thank you. I did need that today." I texted back.

I heard he hadn't dated anyone since Carrie, and I wished I could keep it that way, but I knew I couldn't. He was mine for the small fleeting moments he chose to share himself with me and nothing more.

I saved the video for when I needed a reminder. A reminder to cling to hope for my cancer and hope for him or us.

"Your only option is brain surgery."

"But Christmas is merely weeks away," I argued.

"You don't have time to wait, Brianna. If you want to live, this is the time slot we have to work with. Zero options are left, and this surgery is still being tested in our trial program. It is not a solid guarantee, but the only option we haven't tried. Besides, we can have you in and out; brain surgery is done with a laser now, and you won't be in Texas for more than a few days most."

"Book me in. I will be there." I said with my voice crackling.

My mind raced on who I could have come with me. I had to have someone there, and yet, not a single person came to mind. *Wait, what about my assistant, that booked all of my author stuff? She knows about it.*

I open the phone and text Ashley, "I need to have surgery; it is the only option; if I pay you to work, can you just come to Texas with me for the surgery? They say it will only be a few days."

"Sure, give me the dates."

"December 5th-8th"

My mind goes into high gear. I only had a few days to pull my life together and be ready for surgery, but my mind was blank all of a sudden. I blink my eyes, willing the list I was forming in my head to come back, but nothing.

I needed hope again. And the only person I could find it with was states away traveling with work.

"Brain surgery next week. That is the only option I have. I am scared."

"B, you are going to survive this. What are they saying?"

"I don't think I am going to beat it this time. This surgery is my only chance, and even with it, the chances are slim since it is still a surgery they are researching."

"B, not to sound cheesy, but you are magic. Believe in that." He continued on, "You still have to write my book."

Tears fall down, and I cannot stop crying. When I did not respond, he texted again.

"I love you."

My fingers and hands are trembling so much I can barely type back, "I love you, too."

I glance around the hospital room as I set my bag down. Ashley insisted that she would stay in the visitor's waiting room and work some until it was near time for my surgery.

The room is a soft color of cream and blue, different from how most hospital rooms look. It seemed nice, more spacious, and built with the patient in mind instead of just the staff.

"You can change into this hospital gown and put your things away." The nurse smiled warmly as she placed the hospital gown in my empty hands. "I am going to go snag you some warm blankets. Do you want some Sprite before we get you settled in for an IV?"

Slowly, I nodded my head, "No, thank you. Warm blankets would be nice, though."

She hurried out of the room, and I changed into my gown after putting away the few things I had brought in my small bag. I didn't need much. A good book to read. My laptop so I could work. My phone and charger. A couple pairs of comfortable clothes for when I get ready for discharge. I crawl under the warm blankets, thinking I must text Levi, but sleep sounds much better. I drifted off.

The nurse woke me up in what seemed like seconds, though the time on the clock said differently. I had slept for a whole hour. My eyes were so heavy I felt like I could sleep 5,000 more hours and still not feel rested.

"We are going to start your IV and get some blood work. Your blood platelets must be good enough for surgery, so let's hope they are."

A doctor came through the door I had never met before, but he peered warmly over the top of his glasses. "You must be Brianna Davis?" He asked.

I nodded; the lights in here were just too bright. My head hurts.

"I will be the surgeon for your surgery, and I wanted to go over some things with you if you have a moment.

"Well, it doesn't look like I will be going anywhere anytime soon," I attempted an answer dripped with sarcasm.

He smiled. "Touché, Ms. Davis. Let me get to the facts; I am sure you have questions, too."

I nodded my head, but honestly, I had zero questions. I didn't want to know. Living in the unknown was safer than knowing anything that might make me change my mind.

"We are going to go into your brain right inside your hairline. We try to do this to make the scarring as minimal as possible, and it will only be an inch or two at most for the laser. It is our mission to try to get as much of the cancer out as possible."

He glanced up from his papers to look me in the eye; I could feel him studying my face for a reaction. My face stayed blank.

"Once you come out of surgery, we will keep you sedated for a while so that your brain can take a break and heal. When we start to wake you up, we will keep you in the ICU for at least 24 hours to make sure you are stable. If all goes well, we will move you to a regular room shortly after that, and if all goes well there, you can go home."

Looking at me again, he pauses, waiting for some reaction.

I sigh, "That doesn't sound as bad as I had pictured."

"Brain surgery has come a long way, Ms. Davis. You will just need a long time to recover once home."

The nurse was busy adding an IV to my hand and taking blood while the doctor kept me occupied in conversation.

I nodded my head. "Will my memory get better?" I ask the one question that plagues me every moment of my day now.

"If we do it right, yes. This surgery is still being researched; I am sure your doctor reviewed those details with you, right?"

I nodded, understanding he didn't want to repeat saying that the odds were still not in my favor as much as I didn't want to hear it.

"We will wait for the bloodwork, and if it is all good, I will see you first thing in the morning."

I nod my head again as he exits the room.

Out of nowhere, darkness creeps into all the corners of my mind.

You are not going to make it.

You are grasping at straws, Bri; you will still die.

I want to argue back, but I am too tired. Something else I had seen creep into my life more lately. I didn't fight it either. I closed my eyes.

The nurse coming in to check my vitals jarred me awake. It was dark in my room, which I was thankful for. The lights were too bright lately. I had a headache that would not go away.

She smiled at me sweetly, "You slept for several hours; I tried not to wake you up."

The people here were genuinely lovely. Something I needed at the moment because even her sweet words made me tear up for no reason.

"Thank you," I replied with a smile, "If it isn't a lot of trouble, can I get some ice?"

"Of course, I will get that for you. Also, I wanted to let you know the bloodwork came back good, so you are all set for your surgery tomorrow morning. They scheduled it really early." Her voice still was gentle, but I could feel the empathy she was pushing through when she said the word surgery.

"Do I need to do anything to be ready?" I asked dumbly. Just look at me. Hooked up to monitors and IVs. I can't really do anything but lay here.

"No, we will come in and prep you so you are ready to go. Oh, and before I forget, we do a Christmas Wish Bucket at the hospital. Everyone gets to write their Christmas wish on a piece of paper and fold it up to drop into the bucket. We trust that the Christmas magic will grant the wishes each year." She smiles genuinely, then laughs. "I know that sounds cheesy, but we can all use some Christmas magic, right?" She nodded, suggesting I needed it for my health, but I nodded in agreement.

"I would love to participate. I could use some Christmas magic this year for sure ____." I grasped for her name but realized I didn't know it. I glance at her name tag, Jessica C.. "Jessica," I finish off.

She reached into her pocket and handed me a small piece of blank paper and a pen.

"Here you go, write down your Christmas wish, and I will bring the bucket for you to drop it in when I bring your ice."

She disappeared from the room, leaving me in the rather dark room, alone with my thoughts.

Why did I feel like a dying person, scribbling my last wish onto a small piece of paper, hoping that it was granted to me?

Maybe because you are, Bri. Hello. You are literally having brain surgery tomorrow. No one knows you are here but Ashley, your medical team, and Levi. You will die. It is your last wish, probably your last Christmas, if you even make it till then.

I shake my head, trying to get the awful thoughts to stop. Just the head shaking made my head hurt worse.

My vision blurred, and I blinked, trying to clear it enough to see to write on the paper.

I guess I could wish my cancer be gone.

Or a successful surgery tomorrow.

Living for another day would be a great start.

I scribble my wish on the paper, two simple words, and fold it up.

When the nurse returned, she set my ice on the tray and apologized that I did not have real food to eat due to surgery.

"I am not hungry anyway; ice will be great."

She hands me the bucket with her eyes twinkling, "Do you have your wish?"

"Yes, I do." I smile as I drop the wish into the bucket. I close my eyes and send all the good vibes I can on the wish. I need them.

She smiles and whisks the bucket out of the room.

I pop on my phone and see a text from Levi.

"Did you make it? When is the surgery?"

"Sorry, I had fallen asleep. Surgery is first thing in the morning."

"I will be praying. We got this."

We?

Just the thought that I wasn't alone made tears fall on my cheeks.

"Thank-you. Love you."

"Love you too."

I messaged Ashley to let her know she could go to the hotel and what time my surgery was; I figured they had already told her, but they probably told her I was sleeping, and she was the kind of person who was super thoughtful and would not come back here in fear of disturbing me.

I clicked off my phone again and fell asleep. Tomorrow would be here in just mere hours, and I was anywhere but ready mentally.

Groggily, I opened my eyes.

Where am I?

Ouch, the light, it hurts.

I close my eyes back quickly. I felt Ashley squeeze my hand.

Wait, I made it through surgery!

My head, it hurts.

Everything is hazy. How long was I out?

A nurse tucks warm blankets around me, and I hear the monitor beeping.

Too loud. Make it stop.

The fact that I am alive is enough for me to be thankful for now. I let myself go back to sleep.

"B, can you hear me?" His voice sounds as gentle as always. A side of him I am not sure everyone knows. A switch off from the suave boy toy of town, he turns into a real knight when he is with me. Mainly because I know he is not a knight. He has dark secrets and harmful addictions, just like me. Besides, we share our secret. One that only we know.

I smile in my sleep.

Please don't let me wake up. Let me see him in my dream. I hear him. Where is he?

"B, I love you. I am sorry I never told you that before. I was scared. You made me realize things about myself that I had never realized. Things I thought were safer hidden away. I was terrified of losing you as a friend. I listened to all the wrong people. I knew in my heart what they told me was untrue, but I stupidly listened anyway. Please, please forgive me. I can't, no, I don't want to do life without you."

Tears fall on my cheeks, and I only blink, trying to open my eyes.

Get out of the dream, Bri. It is too real. You know he would never say that to you. His ego is too set on being what others want him to be.

As my blurry vision starts to focus, I see Levi sitting by my bed, holding my hand. His cheeks have fresh tears to match mine.

Wait. Let me close my eyes and wake up again.

This isn't real.

Brianna, wake up. You are dreaming.

No, he was still there.

Nothing makes sense. I searched the room for answers, but the hospital room was the same as the one I left for surgery.

"Levi, how did you get here?" My words sound slurred.

"It is called a plane, B." His crystal blue eyes danced with twinkles, and his mouth curved into a half smile. I fell in love with the same lazy half-smile the first time I saw it.

I chuckle. "Stop; it hurts to laugh, talk, or think."

His smile vanished. "You need to rest. The doctor said the surgery went perfectly. He used that word. Perfect. I knew you would be fine. I tried to tell you I was right. You just need a lot of rest, and I will make sure you get that."

"You are?" I heard the surprise in my own voice when I said it.

"Yes, I am," He replied back with assurance.

I smile and drift back to sleep. This was a dream I needed to continue.

Before I could get back to sleep, the nurse came through the door. "Ms. Davis, some carolers are out at the nurses' station. Do you want to try to walk out there? I would do you good to walk; you must do some of that before we send you home." She said in an urging tone.

Levi nodded in agreement, "Come on, B. I will help you walk down there."

His strong arms lifted me as I slowly rose from the bed. I barely had to find much strength in myself because he was doing it all for me. "We can go slow," he said. I nodded. Squinting my eyes. The lights were still bright, and my head still hurt.

When we finally reached the small marathon to the nurses' station, the carolers were all dressed in holiday attire and singing beautifully. I leaned against the hallway doorway to give Levi's arms a break.

As they started to sing my favorite Christmas song, "Carol of the Bells," I felt Levi lean into me and whisper into my ear. "B, I meant what I said earlier. I love you. Let's stop fighting this. We both know we need each other." I looked up into his blue eyes, my head spinning, but I wasn't sure if it was medicine, my surgery, or the daze of love. Just beyond his head, I saw a sprig of mistletoe in the hallway arch. I smiled and nodded my head up. His eyes shifted to match mine, and his smile grew bigger. His arms wrapped around me tightly, assuring my fragile self I was secure, and kissed me with so much passion I felt my whole body tingle.

I had dreamed of this moment, but it was even more magical than my dreams.

He loved me. Levi loved me.

Jessica passed by and smiled at me with her twinkling eyes, "Ms. Davis, I see Christmas wishes do come true! I am sure glad to see your wish was granted by the Christmas magic."

I went to open my mouth and ask how she knew my wish, but on second thought, I would leave it with the magic.

Happy Ever After did exist, and Christmas magic saw the two words I had written on that paper. I never had to have another wish granted; it could be the last Christmas gift or wish I ever received because it was all I had wanted for over a decade. I had cried for. Prayed for. Wished for. Dreamed for.

"Levi's Love"

The End.

Story Inspiration:

The above is a short portion from Blair's debut trilogy novel series that will be releasing its first novel in the summer of 2024. Please follow Blair Hayse on Facebook, Amazon or Goodreads to read more about Brianna and Levi when the books release.

About Blair Hayse

Blair is the CEO & Founder of the Girl on Fire Media Group and Elite Publishing House. When she is not working the wee hours of the morning with deadlines, she enjoys traveling, shopping, spending time with her children, meeting her best friend for drinks, and pretending like she is not thinking about work while doing all of the above. Blair loves to read and has written ten bestselling books including the magic series that has stayed on the bestseller list for three years straight. She is currently working on her first fictional series that she is brave enough to pitch to literary agents and film based on her own true-life story. Other than that,...her life is a series of late nights and lots of morning coffee.

www.ingramcontent.com/pod-product-compliance
Lightning Source LLC
LaVergne TN
LVHW041744060526
838201LV00046B/907